# THE
# MARLAGANS

BOOK ONE

# THE
# MARLAGANS
## FOR MARS

ALTON BRYANT

LitPrime Solutions
21250 Hawthorne Blvd
Suite 500, Torrance, CA 90503
www.litprime.com
Phone: 1-800-981-9893



Published by LitPrime Solutions    01/20/2023

ISBN: 979-8-88703-138-5(sc)
ISBN: 979-8-88703-139-2(hc)
ISBN: 979-8-88703-140-8(e)

Library of Congress Control Number: 2022923984

# Contents

# Introduction

SINCE HUMANS first traversed the land beyond the Garden of Eden, we have slowly begun taking from planet Earth. In the twentieth century Anno Domini, our taking without replenishment approached critical mass in terms of our erosion of her natural and atmospheric resources and refuge due to the industrial revolution, which propelled us toward the technology age. In light of this information, many of the most powerful chose short-term family fortunes over long-term generational survival. Fortunately, by the twenty-first century, an ample number of new industries emerged to change the landscape of human impact on nature despite the opposition of those powerful giants who were completely opposed to the reality of the needed adaptations to save the planet on which we relied for everything.

Our entire population was miraculously successful in saving itself from the brink of destruction in the year 2142. Against all odds and common belief as well as corporate opposition, humanity has ultimately unified and accepted its share in its own demise and resolved to work as one people to save our only home and the future of humanity. India and the former United States of America, now part of the UAC, two of the biggest polluters, were the final holdouts, but eventually, they would succumb to the intense pressure and scrutiny of their neighboring countries and the rest of the world to protect the future of all humanity, not just a privileged few. Through the efforts of TRM (The Relief Movement), sweeping and extreme pollution elimination initiatives such as zero-emission factories and transportation; forest, safari, farming, gardening, and desert mandates; and atmospheric cleansing services, the Earth and its atmosphere are becoming healthy for humans, flora and fauna again.

Environmental advances such as mandatory household air gardening, hybrid home units for multi-family communities (population control has even been successfully legislated in some countries), hydro-nuclear power, 100 percent radiation-free nuclear recycling, Piloted Air Pollution-Reduction Services, magnetic propulsion drive (MPD) vehicles, crystal self-recharging battery-powered aircraft, Kinetic-Catapult Launch technology, etc., have enabled the increasing populous to leave an ever-smaller pollution footprint than mankind has managed since early in the eighteenth century, even though the world population is nearly a hundred times the population of that time.

A vocal minority protested that some of the penalties for TRM violations were too severe, but those in power elected that making examples of the early few violators were a necessary evil of making this world endeavor successful. As a result, violations only occurred in small pockets and usually in protest. Many of the technological advances which helped create these new regulations along with others, such as magnetically manipulated gravity (MMG) and renewable fresh air circulators, would become paramount in the efforts to further man's exploration beyond our home planet.

In the Earth Year 2199, mankind has begun to desperately outgrow the Earth. Though she has a clean bill of health again, the twelve billion humans populating her along with the growing seas and deserts stretched resources to the limit. In 2221, early volunteers were heavily incentivized to move their families to the first massive Earth Hope Orbital Community. Hope1 was born. When faced with the reality of the first humans having a permanent address that is not on the face of the planet, countries of the United Consortium of Nations (UCoN) collectively determined that all time outside of Earth's atmosphere would follow the unifying Universal Coordinated Time (UCT) or Zulu Time in an effort of easily managing the continuity of time among all humans. They also endorsed the creation of one universal digital currency, the Universal Unit or Unies, as it is more commonly called. More and more individuals, societies, and eventually countries within the confines of the Earth's atmosphere also voted to follow suit in an effort to feel a sense of unity with their growing numbers of family members who are "off terra." Sol Clocks are designed to show current states of sunlight throughout the solar system to keep distant friends, relatives, and business associates from disrupting sleep patterns in other realms of the system.

The Hope1 Space Station with its MMG systems and recirculating fresh air could easily be seen passing overhead with the naked eye. Louis and Annie Zanabe and their four children were the fourth family to enroll in the program. Louis has amassed a fortune in his space junk retrieval business, and while that did not help his petition to purchase two lots on Hope1 for his family, it did help him secure a victory as the first mayor of his orbital community. His participation in the Hope endeavors gives confidence to millions as to the safety of living in orbit since he heads Qleen Sweep, Inc., the world's leading space junk services empire. Life on Hope1 received high marks from its residents. Each of the five hundred families was allotted one and a quarter acres of space. One acre was theirs to configure and design as they desired. Most opted for half an acre of exterior space and half an acre of living space, while some others built full-acre living units. That remaining quarter acre was provided for community support space. The first community of families became a harmonious, caring, and sharing neighborhood. Each family was delegated a responsibility of providing specific goods and services to the community thus establishing the Care to Share System in which no financial currency would ever be necessary among Hope residents. Popular belief is that this lifestyle was the original intention for humanity. Care to Share caught on in many parts of Earth and was eventually instituted as standard practice in the early settlements on Luna and on Mars, but as populations grew, Care to Share became impossible to maintain.

With the success of Hope1, the World Space Exploration (WSX) built and launched several larger orbital communities. Hopes 2, 3, 4, and 5 were launched at progressively higher altitudes. These communities proved to be equally as successful…for a time. As this process became more routine, some of the later orbital residential candidates were not given the same thorough acclimating training and intense screening as those of Hope1. Each community seemed to be given less and less processing and vetting before launch and experienced more human behavioral failures as a result. This would later turn out to be a major issue leading to unforeseen consequences. After learning to adjust for such failures, the WSX thought it wise that we venture further into space. While prioritizing the correction of the experiments in Earth's orbit, WSX boldly leapt further into Luna and Mars occupation initiatives as well as Solar moons exploration in short order.

The sixth Earth orbital station came last and was the farthest from Earth at launch. The "No Hope"—as it is nicknamed—is the 3,000-inmate UCoN Total Security Penitentiary Station. Only serial murderers, recaptured maximum security prison escapees, or maximum security prison rabble rousers are sentenced to spend the rest of their lives at No Hope. On its 5-year anniversary, there were 1,223 inmates confined to this solitary institution. Inmates are allowed no outside communications but are privileged to a video feed controlled by the warden if the warden felt it has been earned. The cells are spacious enough that there is no community exposure allowed aside from meal, medication, and linen delivery, armed technical support units, and armed cleaning service units. Life aboard this station is maddening for inmates and guards alike. Fortunately, the guard teams rotate quarterly. The cells are made of a soundproof ballistic material known as salt84 with an ionized field that electrocutes inmates if they approached a barrier within one inch of the cell door. Conditions are akin to permanent solitary confinement.

Exploration beyond Earth, which is often referred to as Mom, and Luna first began in 2300 with pioneers who explored the potential of Mars beyond the capabilities of the rovers, then engineers and architects, who came equipped to begin the foundational infrastructure required to support human colonies. Four generations have passed since Earthlings first colonized Mars, and the number of native Martians has been slowly growing ever since. The original two hundred Earthlings who ventured to Mars for the purpose of colonization have now become a population of seven hundred fifty-seven native-born Martians and nearly three thousand others from various parts of the system. Earthlings have orbital stations in other places throughout the solar system as well, but aside from Mars, Luna is the only other colonized celestial body thus far.

Technology and space exploration took a giant leap in the year 2289 when Powell Zanabe, a Zambian student at MIT and grandson of Louis and Annie Zanabe, unlocked the powers of a unique African crystal which helped uncover the secrets and properties of dark energy as well as taking technology to limitless potential. The ZiP Crystal, named after its creator's own nickname, increases computing capacities and power management beyond anything humans thought possible. The use of dark energy has advanced space travel to over a thousand times humanity's previous heavy lifting, power, and propulsion capabilities for a hundred times lighter weight than the previous best nuclear powered options.

This story is about Fernando Abernum, who is born on Mars in the Earth Year of 2424 and is a direct descendant of Powell Zanabe. His parents decided to be the first Martians to risk pre-conception gene manipulation so their only child might be born their ideal vision of a person. Somehow, that experimental advance manipulation partially failed, causing Fernando's premature and defective birth. He was born prematurely at just twenty-two weeks with only one fully formed arm and leg. He remained in advanced incubation after delivery until his organs had fully formed. He nonetheless remained blind in his deformed right eye after incubation. Due to his great-grandparents' decision to join the Mars colony, he was privileged enough to receive top-notch medical care, which including an organic bionic leg and arm, to save his life and compensate for his natural deficiencies. Some say they overcompensated. His parents spared no expense in making sure their child would grow up without experiencing any defect. He was even given the ERB Brain implant, which increases brain power to commonly acceptable levels by manipulating neurons and synapses as well as an option to directly link his mind into intelligent computing devices. However, Fernando's implant was enhanced. His organic bionics grew with his natural body and operate using circuitry that integrates with his natural blood flow, nervous system, and enhanced ERB implant.

At this point in the colonization of Mars, the past and current generations of Martians are still only permitted to have one child maximum per couple. Several opt for zero due to the limited resources while even fewer are exempt from this restriction due to extreme contributions toward furthering the health and sustainability of Mars colonization. Fernando's best friend, Khan, is the eldest son of such a family. Fernando, though, is very fortunate as well. At 2m tall, 38Mkg (Martian kilograms) or 100kg (Earth kilograms), and an IQ of 176, gaining rank through the WSX was not very challenging for Fernando, but childhood was not so easy on him emotionally. With his telescoping computer-enhanced eye, bionic limbs, and high IQ, he was often teased and called names like Martian Borg, Android, Mr. Robot, etc. As a result of youthful insecurities, he usually secretes his incredible gifts of genius and strength from the public unless it is absolutely imperative to the current circumstance. He does not keep his genius from benefitting his family, though. Since his childhood, he has been creating forward-thinking programs and apps that have been major revenue streams for his family and for Mars. He has hacked and upgraded his internal computing implants to create an extremely advanced internal artificial intelligence system with full-scale computing and communications abilities.

Fernando, being the only child, has an extremely close relationship with his parents. He joined the WSX because of them, in the hopes of spending more time with them, going on missions with them, but mostly to make them proud of him. Two months ago, Fernando's parents, Brigadier General Alton M. and Major General Esther R. Abernum, endeavored on a secret WSX mission. Their mission has never been officially announced nor disclosed to the public nor anyone inside the WSX without need to know clearance. Fernando had a long conversation with his parents before their departure. For the second time, they left him with no mission information other than it was above top secret. He doesn't even know the mission's end date. As his parents have always taught him, he is respecting the chain of command and the law of the WSX. Fernando has been keeping a secret diary since his parents left to share the details of his life during their absence in case this is another long secret mission akin to the mission three years ago that kept them apart for nine months. At least, he knew the projected end date of that one. He neglected to keep a diary during that nine-month mission as they'd requested, and they were so curious to know every detail of every day. So this time, he is honoring that daily diary promise for them in order to give them what they seem to crave so much when they return home, details of his every day.

Captain Abernum, or Abs, as most call him in adulthood, is now second in command and the Science Officer of a group of misfits who turn out to be the most elite Excursion Team Mars has to offer the universe, the Marlagans. They are a ragtag, purpose-built team of six. Well, they were until the last mission when Lt. Dr. Hassan Banthira, their former Medical Officer, succumbed to a heart attack after the shock of an intense claustrophobic episode when their experimental vehicle malfunctioned while encapsulated in ice underground, and Sgt. Li Ling, the former Navigator, was released from the team due to inability to perform under pressure. The team is now a tight group of four plus a new addition, Lt. Rebecca Williams, a nascent Medical Officer and lifelong friend of Abs. She is only two years out of Officer Medical School, but Captain Abernum has spent the past six years grooming her to join the Marlagans as a favor to her older brother and Abs's best friend since childhood, Khan. With her youthful physique and amazing bone structure, she oozes muliebrity, which originally gave Captain Slight pause for various reasons, but he has come to appreciate her talents quicker than Abs expected.

Jim Slight, creator and leader of the Marlagans, is Abs's good friend of ten years. Jim is more by-the-book than "improvise-to-meet-the-occasion" Abs and a very wise leader who is willing to run the team as a democracy to a point, but beyond that point, he will make the tough calls even if his team disagrees. He is generally a kind man with a commanding presence who tries to be as faultless as he can be, but he is human. His distinguished career with the WSX has given him the privilege of forming his own team six years ago versus having a team forced on him. Abs was his first recruit to the Marlagans.

Zintia B. Romero, the Mech Tech (Mechanical and Technology Officer), is incredibly shy and quiet but possesses an unmatched talent in the field of robotics and mechanics as evidenced by her pet robot and assistant, Elf, who follows her everywhere he's permitted by use of facial, form, and thermal recognition. Zin is adorably small in stature and has incredible team spirit and esprit de corps. Though small, she uses her diminutive nature as an asset to surprise and devastate any opponent in hand to hand combat, most of which she learned from training with her brother, Rhoan. In most circumstances, she is a shy and quiet observer, but when she is comfortable (as in the company of her family, with the Marlagans, or with Elf, with whom she holds deep conversations), she seems to voice herself much more effectively. Most believe she finds more comfort in machinery than humanity. For the most part, they are not wrong. She was Slight's second addition to the Marlagans after Abs.

Her younger half-brother, Rhoan B. Romero, the Sinew (Security and Safety Officer), was the fourth addition to the team after Lt. Dr. Banthira. He was born on Earth after Zintia's father left Mars at the end of his Union term with Zin's mother. Rhoan began his adulthood in the Marine Corps of the UAC (United American Continent) infantry, then was snagged by the UCA (United Continent of Afrika) for three years to train as a member of the ASTF (Afrikan Special Tactical Force), the most elite fighting force in the known universe, before going to Mars to train WSX Mars special forces in universal tactical combat. His combat skills are unparalleled after implementing his own improvements and enhanced techniques, which exert less energy than current combat practices. His specialized focus is efficiency of movement, and he is constantly improving his own techniques.

We catch up with the Marlagans as they are leaving Mars for another tough mission to Io to mine for siolens, one of the universe's most rare and precious resources. Siolens is a weightless and clear firm slime-like substance used to eliminate all temperature and sound effects on any structure or material. Once processed, a two millimeter layer of the unique substance can render a cannon blast silent and a volcano's temperature harmless. WSX Mars is the only supplier of processed siolens, and the Martian economy is heavily dependent upon the steady production of the substance to the rest of the solar system.

With the latest advancements in chemical engineering, the Universal HAS4/LGS7 series space suits are 100 percent temperature resistant. Each suit is filled with .8 centimeters of weightless and nonrestrictive clear gel mixture of siolens and Altonium84, another WSX Mars exclusive substance found on Europa. The siolens/Altonium84 mixture (named salt84) allows explorers to roam freely into volcanoes and areas completely cooled by liquid nitrogen. Salt84 also is impenetrable by all forms of radiation. All WSX space faring vehicles are lined with salt84 as well. There are currently test simulations for future voyages to Sol and beyond Pluto. This mission will be the Marlagans' fourth journey to the home of siolens, Io, the moon of Jupiter.

# Chapter 1

## Railway

"ONE MINUTE and holding, *Nigeria*. Final checklist please."

Captain Jim Slight, leader of the excursion team, replies, "Everything looks good here, Launch. Running final checks."

"Roger. Report completion."

"Wilco, Launch."

All launch indicators are steady green on the sparsely populated titanium instrument console with the exception of the dim ROD light. The metallic surface is so pristine that at first glance, one would expect to hear an onomatopoeia of gleam. The six passenger crew has been unusually professional since seated. It could be that the new fifth crew member and the visiting sixth passenger are causing more caution in conversation than is typical for the crew.

"*Nigeria*, Launch."

"Go ahead, Launch."

"Verify status of R-O-D indication."

"R-O-D is dark."

"Copy. Thanks, *Nigeria*."

As usual, Captain Fernando Abernum is this WSX Exploration Corps excursion's second in command. They are about to redeploy to Io on another siolens mining expedition.

Fernando gives a noticeable sigh while thinking how the last few times the ROD lit green for a crew, things went far less than ideal. So the unlit ROD indicator provides him the tiniest taste of comfort considering the fates of the past few launches. He understands what they were trying to do with it, but cannot fathom why they installed it during live launches without proper vetting of the system in real-life application. He silently takes a moment to remember the good friends he lost in those experimental launches.

The Corps has had its share of issues with launches into orbit lately. That explains why the Marlagans and their engineer passenger, Dr. Shanee Wilson, who is hitching a ride to the orbital station since there was a vacant sixth seat created by the events of their previous mission, seem a little more tense than usual on the *Nigeria* before this trip.

Fernando takes a sip from his helmet's hydration straw and swirls the water around to ease the metallic flavor from the roof of his mouth. The taste remains as it always does during pre-launch, but his swirling habit soothes him somehow. He presses against his restraints in an effort to look behind him. Leaning as far as his harness will allow, he peeps in on Williams, a young first-time explorer who exhibited signs of anxiety in

Prep for this jump. Her distant intense expression could be a deep daydream, but Fernando seriously doubts it.

"How you doing, Bec?"

"So far, so good, Cap…a little chilly, though," she replies with a touch of unsteadiness in her delivery.

Rhoan advises, "That's because we're idle on the rail right now."

Shanee adds, "That's true. Once we burst through the birth canal, we'll warm up."

"Birth canal?"

"That's how my senior peers describe it. They warned me about the chill on the rail."

Becca glares at Abs. "My senior peer neglected to mention anything about the chill or the bursting."

Abs pretends to not hear any of the conversation.

To call out Abs, Becca lets out a grating "Ahem!"

Abs finally answers, "Yes, Rebecca, dear. Is there something I can do to help you?"

"No. No. I'm just clearing my frozen throat that will soon be birth canal bursting. It just may be a tickle coming on at the thoughts of freezing and then bursting!" She keeps emphasizing the word "bursting."

"Har. Dee. Har. Har."

Becca giggles.

Abs finally addresses her concern. "I hope you aren't thinking that I've addressed every little eventuality we'll face during this mission. That's not even close to what exploration is about. In this business, you have to be ready to bounce off of anything that springs up to derail your survival."

"I'm just messing with you, Abs."

"I know, but here's one thing that may offer you some comfort for now. We should have nothing to fret over on this flight. Dr. Wilson is with us."

"I like Shanee. She is comforting."

Shanee looks over. "Aw. Thanks, Becca. I like you too. I still can't believe my luck. I'm actually on a flight with the Marlagans and actually making friends."

Abs continues, "That's cute and all. You sound like a kid's show teaching us about the first day of school, but that's not quite what I mean."

Feeling a tad deflated, Shanee asks, "What do you mean then?"

"How do I say this? I like you too, Shanee, so please don't take offense when I say this."

Becca advises, "Sorry, Doc. That means he's about to offend you."

"No. No. Well. Maybe. Maybe a little."

"Spit it out already, Abs," Rhoan chimes from the back in his mixed African/Caribbean accent.

"All I was going to say is that Shanee is basically good insurance."

"What? I don't get it," Becca replies.

"Think of it. Of all the flights that take place this week, we're the only one with one of the launch team aboard. I'm sure her team will do everything they can to get us all through this hop safely since one of their own is with us."

Shanee notes, "That's pretty cold, Captain Abernum."

Becca says, "That's just wrong, Abs."

A few chuckles fill the cabin.

Abs adds, "Then again, they do like you, don't they, Shanee?"

Even louder laughter erupts.

Shanee replies, "As far as I know, but the crap they gave me this morning after learning I would be riding with the Marlagans, I might have been misreading the depth of our friendships."

Abs snaps, "Not helpful, Doc! We're trying to ease the lieutenant's anxiety. Comforting her may have just taken a turn in the wrong direction. But if nothing else, we all may be about to find out how they really feel about you."

Rhoan adds, "I'm sure they have to love someone as adorable as you, Doc Wilson."

Shanee almost smiles.

"Romeo!" Abs calls in an attempt to rein in Rhoan's course of conversation.

Knowing Abs will embarrass him if he keeps flirting, Rhoan immediately changes course without the usual banter, "No. No. It's not like that. Come on! I can't even pay a compliment?"

Abs replies, shaking his head, "Not even a simple compliment, Romeo."

Shanee suggests, "To be honest, I think they care much more about getting the Marlagans up to the station safely far more than they care about me. So, Becca, you have nothing to worry about. This team has celebrity status. Trust me, extra precautions are being taken today."

Abs counters, "Well, you are going up to advise the Mayflowers. They are legends, our only remaining all-female team. If you're working with them, that's a mega high honor."

"I'm not sure it's that big a deal. Major Patki and I will discuss the extent of my assistance today."

Rhoan casually remarks, "I sure hope you were born on Mars."

"Why?"

"Were you?"

"No, but my family moved here when I was a baby."

Abs interrupts, "From Mom?"

"Hope1."

"You must have been one of the first infants to make the journey from an orbital station. What was that, twenty-four years ago?"

"Exactly twenty-four years ago."

"That has to mean something to Patki, and I'm pretty sure he already knows your origin story. Still, you may not want to bring that up. That stuff matters to him far too much."

"Why wouldn't I bring up where I'm from? I've basically spent my entire life here on Mars."

"Let's just say he has a predilection for Martian natives."

Zin chimes, "Basically, he sounds like a potential Earth-style racist like our dad."

Becca asks, "What's an earth-style racer-ist? Is that like if I have a predilection to vanilla ice cream and hate people who like strawberry ice cream?"

"Yeah. Pretty much, but it deals with bigger things that people have no control over."

"Well, I don't like strawberry ice cream, and I can't help that."

"Well, that's true. But back on Mom, it usually has

more to do with ancestry or gender for some people, though."

"You can't help where, how, or from whom you're born."

"Too true."

"Then that's stupid."

"I know."

"Are you saying we have those on Mars?"

"Well, from what I've heard, Patki sort of confessed to being like that."

"On Mars? No way. Nobody can really be like that."

Abs chimes in, "Humans, man. No matter the circumstances, human flaws always seem to find a way to infiltrate any gathering, large or small. We could be in paradise and just ruin it for no reason at all. Wait. We've already done that…just because we're human."

Becca asks, "Okay. This is going to sound stupid and naive, but why in this great existence would someone choose to be a racer-ist anyway?"

Rhoan notes, "Not racer-ist. Racist. It's about a person's race and ethnicity. And I can't answer that question for you, but our dad is one of those people."

"He is?" Abs remarks. "I never knew that."

"Yeah. He's a genuine piece of turd muscle."

"He's a Caribbean living in the UCA. Who could he possibly discriminate against?"

"I was just a kid when I realized it. And he didn't really discriminate as much as feel everyone was inferior to all native Africans."

"I didn't know he was a native African."

"Then again, I guess I have seen him mistreat certain

people just for coming into his shop. Mostly people he called colonizers."

"We're all colonizers."

"That's a whole different, longer, and more personal story, that is. Don't worry. None of it rubbed off on me, fortunately. I can't imagine hating myself as much as my dad did and not realize it. So he took it out on other people he didn't even know. Me, I love myself way too much to look down on others to inflate my self-image. There's just too much greatness going on up in here," he grins and points to himself in a limited vertical motion.

"Zin, did you know this?"

"I don't know that donor nor have I ever cared to. My mother never talked about him, and when I asked as a child, she just said I'm better off not knowing."

Abs notes, "Wow. This conversation took a turn. Being that you lived with a 'racer-ist,' Rhoan, how do you suggest the good doc here handle Patki?"

"Just be you. Screw that big baby."

Shanee gives them a nugget. "I actually feel prepared for someone like that. Believe it or not, I've studied human societal sciences and psychology for a few years now. I understand how over human history, racists and those perpetrating racism have done so much damage to themselves and others. Just go back to how they justified greed, possession, and genocide in the UCA and the UAC centuries ago by creating a narrative that they were helping or at least not hurting the 'stupid' native savages or that savages were the aggressors. In the case of Euro, they were committing genocide on an unbelievable scale by claiming a whole made-up brand of humans was a threat to the rest of civilization. In the Middle Eastern region of Earth, they've been killing brothers and sisters for minor differences of belief for eons. It's one of the sicknesses of being human."

Becca notes, "That's actually quite sad to me. I feel sorry for people like that and can't imagine being on the receiving end of it when you didn't even do anything wrong."

Rhoan asks, "I've seen it from my own dad. It's disgusting. Then kids would treat me like shit because of the things my father did. It really created major personal and social problems for me back then."

"Oh, that makes me so sad."

Rhoan asks, "So, Doc, what are you, some kind of history nut or something?"

"I just love human studies almost as much as engineering. I love watching old historic streams. They used to call them doc-human-trees or something like that. I even gave a lecture on rising civilizations once. So maybe I'm a history nut or could be just a nut. But my parents were born on Earth, and they mentioned some stuff they endured in their youth."

Becca continues, "It almost seems like a mental illness to me. Imagine not loving yourself on your own merit but needing to believe you, a simple human, are superior to any other simple human. Even people who claim royal titles are no less or more human than their toilet scrubbers. Yet you're describing a scenario where royal toilet scrubbers can convince themselves or be taught to believe that they are superior to other humans who may even be of royal descent simply because that person is different from them. It's sad, pathetic, and frankly mental."

Abs replies, "I don't think it was always about self-image, though. Sometimes, it served a personal or political agenda too. And to think, even now as Mars is on the precipice of expanding surface living, we may be on the verge of a scourge like this. That's unacceptable. And you know what they say about roaches and blarks. If you see one in your home, there are likely hundreds more that you don't see."

Shanee asks, "Do you really think there are others?"

"Crazy, right? Martian isn't even a race of people. Yet even on this planet composed of all kinds of societal mixes, doltishness finds a way. Historically, wherever there are humans, we tend to find dumb-ass ways to screw up our own harmony. Fortunately, on Mars, we still rely on one another too much for it to be a bigger issue than it is. For now."

"I wish I hadn't heard any of this. It's going to be hard to respect him now. How do you know any of this, Sergeant Romero?"

"We shared a mutual friend who warned me about him. Apparently, they got drunk one night, and Patki wouldn't shut up about it. He is good at hiding it at work, though, probably since it's so deeply in opposition to our culture on Mars. Just be aware and understand if he lashes out at you for no reason or seems to behave badly, it's not necessarily you unless you're actually screwing something up."

"This sucks. I wish I knew this before I accepted this gig."

"Now I feel bad for bringing it up," Rhoan admits.

Abs adds, "Don't let that dissuade you, Dr. Wilson. You're obviously important to that mission. At least this isn't planet Mom. I hear that insecurity in the form of racism runs rampant on that planet."

Rhoan agrees, "Indeed. Besides, I'm pretty sure his logic for being like that is he believes in order to be for Mars, one has to be from Mars. It sounds racist, but there's a chance it's just that."

Shanee demands, "That's still prejudicial, and he still may not see me as 'from Mars.'" She tries to use air quotes, but the harness limits her ability to raise her hands fully. "Let's talk about something else. This is not making my day merry and bright at all."

Eager to get it off of her chest, Zin jumps in, "Okay. What's the probability of you joining the Mayflowers?"

"Wow! Talk about a gear shift."

"Too abrupt?"

"No, it's good. Well. No one has talked to me about that. Not even a little. I'm just helping them with an engineering issue."

"They still don't have a permanent engineer, do they? They may make you an offer if you do a great job."

"Believe me, I'm going to do a great job, but I'm just an engineer, not an explorer. Exploring is only for a special breed of person. I'm not of that breed."

"You sure sound like a good fit to me. The Mayflowers are a confident and highly capable bunch. You obviously are too, otherwise you wouldn't be working with them."

"Nope."

Befuddled, Abs presses, "They're not? You don't—"

Embarrassed, Shanee explains, "No. No. Not no, the Mayflowers. No, me. I'm not a good fit because I'm not interested in doing what you explorers do. I'm not built for being that unsure about my day when on mission. I like my days as they are, routine and predictable."

"What if it's a routine mission with no surprises?"

"No explorer joins for routine missions. All missions are full of unexpected surprises."

"Good point."

"I sure wish I hadn't heard that about Major Patki. It's going to be stuck in the front of my mind every time I look at him or hear his voice."

Rhoan says, "He is usually pleasant even to an Earthling like me, so don't let it worry you. Fortunately for me, I've never had to work directly with him, though. So good luck with that."

"How is that helping?"

"Sorry."

"Why would they promote someone like that to his position?"

"Probably didn't know."

Rhoan observes, "Becca looks distracted enough now."

"I was. Thanks, Romero."

"My pleasure. Now that that's all behind us, the only thing we can do now is sit back, relax, and enjoy the ride, kids!" Rhoan says with a revived pep, hoping to ease Becca's tension beyond the conversation of the past minutes.

Shanee notes, "Rhoan, do you just bring up things to disturb people then walk away without helping them come to resolution all the time?"

"I don't understand the question."

"Ugh!"

Rhoan smiles. "What?"

"Staff Sergeant Romero, how do you put up with this brother of yours?"

"By largely ignoring him like I am now."

"Smart."

Abs sits quietly as Becca, Zintia, and Shanee playfully give Rhoan a hard time and takes note of a couple things that just happened. First, he finds it hard to believe how easily he was able to curtail Rhoan's flirting with Shanee. It's never been that simple before. The other is that he has not been very successful, if at all, in rejiggering Becca's intense and anxious expression even through her forced chuckles and yelling at Romero.

Once Abs starts paying attention again, he hears Shanee ask, "But I do have a question, Rhoan."

"Shoot."

"I hear you're putting on a demonstration at the tournament today. Is that right?"

"How did you hear that? No one is supposed to know that outside of the team."

"It is leaking in a million places then. Everyone is talking about it."

"What the hell?"

"So it is true then?"

"It's true. Just a demonstration, though."

"You just won the MAEMA tournament two weeks ago. Is that why you aren't competing?"

"I'm not able to participate in this rung of competition. It's two rungs below mine, so they asked me to give them a demonstration of what's possible if fighters at this level stick with it."

"What time is your demonstration? I'd love to catch it."

"Oh. You're interested in combative arts?"

"I could never do it, but it's a very beautiful art form in my eye. Even more than ballet."

Rhoan puffs up, "Oh really. Would you like to go as my guest?"

Abs warns sternly, "Romeo."

"I got it, Abs. Just offering."

"Thank you for the invitation, but I'm not sure of my schedule yet. If I'm available, I'll stop by and watch."

"Hope to see you there."

When things quiet down in the cabin again, Abs advises, "Bec, once we begin the launch, it helps to keep your eyes on the rail as long as you can. Concentrating on that can take away some of the anticipation of what's coming and can distract from nervous thoughts. It can be difficult to do, but the challenge of it focuses your thoughts on the moment. But most of all, enjoy what you are seeing and doing. Launches and missions are full of fun and wonderment if you allow yourself to take the time to enjoy them."

She nods repeatedly and silently without any change in expression, almost seeming aloof now as the reality of what awaits seems to seep in.

The rail about which he speaks is the mag-rail track system that lay ahead of them. As they look straight out of the panoramic lightweight window skin of the craft, about five hectometers of perfectly linear lighted track is visible. Not visible is the next two and a half hectometers of continued flat track followed by the gentle bend upward that leads to the eighty-degree vertical exit from the sealed cave. Smartly, the lighting engineers have designed the launch rail's lighting system to incrementally increase or decrease its lumens as flights get closer to the launch tube's exit to match the natural light of the outer atmosphere to prevent a jarring transition to the Martian sky. During nighttime operations as the lighting decreases, the track glows a pleasant neon lime green.

Several minutes pass before a sound is heard in the salt84-insulated titanium capsule. It seems each passenger is in his or her own world of introspection.

Fernando considers that Becca may be reflecting on a thought he had on his maiden flight to orbit: "This six-passenger vessel is so light that two anybodies can heave it onto the launch prep site before installing seats and equipment, and yet WSX trusts this hollow shell with our lives against all the elements in the upper atmosphere that want to kill us."

"Abs?" Becca calls.

Abs snaps out of thought. "Ma'am?"

"How do I meet you all in that calm place the rest of you appear to be in?"

Shanee debates, "Don't lump me in that category. This is my first hop too, and I'm shaking like a bald Chihuahua. We're in this together, Lieutenant Williams."

Williams replies, "Are your thoughts out of control too?"

"Not so much out of control as they are focused on what options we have if something goes wrong."

"What options do we have?"

"Do we kiss our asses goodbye on the left cheek, right cheek, or center crack?"

"Ha! Good one, Shanee. I think I like having you aboard," Abs laughs.

Her jape breaks some of the tension. The cabin becomes more jovial for a time, but Abs notices Captain Slight still seems somewhere else. Within minutes, the cabin falls back into stillness and contemplation. The hissing white noise from the launch control's cooling system becomes the only sound permeating through the cabin.

Abs realizes he never answered her question and says, "Bec, to answer your question, at the onset of this career, I tended to think reassuring things like if one person survived it or achieved it, I can too. As you should remember from our many conversations, I called that the 'If they can do it, I can do it' pep talk."

"How could I forget? Every time—"

Eager to stop her from bringing up something embarrassing from their childhood, Abs cuts her off, "Ahem. As I was saying, now that we've done this quite a bit, one of my many considerations is what thoughts you and Shanee may be entertaining. Shanee just explained her deep contemplations quite deeply. What are you thinking?"

They talk for a little more than a minute before the calming effect of their conversational repartee is shattered by the jolt of a sudden transmission, "Okay, *Nigeria*. Checklists complete. All systems check! We're ready to resume the countdown on your call. What's your crew status?"

"This crew is always ready. *Nigeria* is go!" Jim answers with vim.

The crew's earlier unease has been amplified by the unusual voicelessness and distant behavior of Captain Slight. He has hardly spoken more than ten words outside of radio communications. He's barely sighed or even grunted since breakfast (his excessive habit of grunting has commonly been the subject of humorous moments. So much so that he doesn't even acknowledge the pokes anymore).

Fernando looks around as much as his restraints will allow and thinks, *At times, this whole crew seems to be somewhere else today. At least Jim seems to have found some personality again. But still that was only during a transmission and not interaction with the crew. He is never this stale, and his peculiar quietude is not helping the crew's confidence in this launch. It's obviously having some impact on the rest of the crew. Even Rhoan has been stoic most of this morning, which is so rare that it actually may be the first time ever.*The crew will soon notice that radio transmissions are Jim's only words during the fifteen-minute flight until they near the station.

Zintia, on the other hand, loves technical conversations, and earlier, she has been unusually chatty with Dr. Wilson about the specifics of the ROD failures and how they plan to correct the shortcomings and reimplement the ROD system in the future. It's like the world is upside down. She actually seems the most at ease about this launch. That somehow has a calming effect on Abs. Yet he still can't help wondering back to how weird this whole morning feels.

Abs goes back into contemplation mode with the rest of the crew and makes a silent entry into his journal:

* * * * *

Abs Diary Entry 72B:

Mom, Dad.

We are about to blast off to MOS4. As we sit on the launch rail, the inside of *Nigeria*'s cabin, your second favorite vessel, has been disturbingly quiet, almost eerie at times. You may not have heard that two of the last five orbital rail launches ended in disaster. The jugheads, including Dr. Wilson, who is hopping with us, tried explaining it to Captain Slight, but he's satisfied just being an explorer. He didn't understand much after the acronym ROD. It's been good practice for him to force himself not to get too deep into the minutia of these missions and trust everyone to do their parts. One of the many things he says he is learning as he gets older is that too much unnecessary info leads to too much unnecessary confusion and forgetfulness. So he has adopted the exercise of staying in his own lane, where he's needed and most effective. I overheard the big brains say it had something to do with errant capacitor energy levels on the mag-rail ROD system causing explosive derailments. Jim convinced himself and us that it won't happen this time since they removed that experimental upgrade. He's been so quiet today I bet he's running through those calming and distraction practices he made up for himself. He repeats these eight things over and over in his head: wind, sea, rain, sun, beach, track, Marsh, Dreens. He told me yesterday that he misses Marsha and Drena (his family in orbit) more than he realized. I'm happy they will be together soon even if only for a short while. I miss them too. It'll be good to see them. Guess we'd better focus on this flight now. There was a mic click. I know I wrote you a long, heartfelt farewell earlier in case that entry was my last. Now maybe this one will be. Happy thoughts. I still love you both as much as I did this morning. Wait. I just checked the meter. It increased a tick. Lucky you. Who knows, maybe I'll see you at MOS4. Here's to hoping. All my love.

# Chapter 2

# Jump

AFTER A few more communications exchanges, Launch Control resumes, "Twelve, eleven…" launch control continues the countdown over the comms in the otherwise hushed rail capsule.

The rail charge motor starts to whine. Then the whine quickly swells to the insane banshee screams of the turbines.

"Here we go!" Rhoan yelps in excitement, rhythmically slamming his fists on his armrests.

To Abs, the anticipation that accompanies the howling engine noise is a massive improvement over the previous five minutes of silence and concern for Becca.

"Three, two, one…launch! *Nigeria* has cleared the locus en route to Mars Orbital Station Four (MOS4) on mission to explore the Jupiter moon, Io!"

Fittingly, there is no MMG (Magnetically Manipulated Gravity) utilized on these hops to orbit. For one, it lowers weight. Another benefit is that Mars natural gravity (MNG) is safer for orbital launches than Earth's pull. The 9MNG load during the launch has killed only once before, but updates to the launch vehicle's passenger cabins have supposedly addressed that issue. That does not mean it's painless. In fact, common complaints seem to circulate concerning discomfort in the sternum, shoulders, and crotch regions during orbital launches. Despite their discomfort, there is a barefaced sense of relief as they escape the Von Braun (VVB) Launch Site, Mars's second largest underground tube, which has been repurposed for orbital launches. The largest, Musk (EM), is humanity's first and largest of the seven colonies on Mars, which are connected through a system of bored tunnels and mag-rail transportation systems. It's also where the Slight's family home is.

"For Mars!" Sgt. Rhoan Romero yells as the *Nigeria* escapes the VVB and safely enters the Martian atmosphere. He is usually in a jocose mood during the moments leading to countdown, but he too has been having a rare quiet morning. And that whole soft flirt thing still has Abs mystified.

The crew echoes, "For Mars!"

Rhoan yells, "Woooo! Yeah! That never gets old!"

"For Mars!"

The entire crew is all smiles and chortles knowing they won't be the sixth of the recent launches to meet their fates in the tubes. Becca joins in the celebration for a brief period before the crew recognizes a familiar sound as she retches in her helmet and fills a bag with liquefied chunks of her breakfast donut sandwich and orange juice mixed with a little internal Becca sauce.

"You okay, Bec?"

"I think so. How do I release the bag again?"

"SBE button on the right side of your helmet display. And just snap the next one in its place."

"Thanks, Zin."

"Been there, sister."

As their craft enters the Martian atmosphere, Abs looks for Earth and Luna as he always does when the sky is visible. He describes it in short order using an app in his eye. Watching it fade in the distance, he cogitates humanity's recent achievements and future: *Just five hundred years ago, humans were merely Earthlings on that faint blue twinkle in the sky. Now, we have several colonies throughout the neighborhood of our solsys, and these missions could help us expand our reach even farther. We're starting to lay the groundwork for an orbital station around Io to maximize the production of siolens. Heck, we'll be orbiting Sol and Pluto in the next few years. It's a truly exciting time for a species that just left the ground for the first time just over six centuries ago.*

As the craft smooths out on its upward trajectory, the rush of incredible speed is still intense. But the crew becomes distracted as the capsule begins to waft with the aroma of Becca's breakfast and innards. Abs looks over, shaking his head and laughing.

"Seal that bag!" he exclaims.

Even Becca can't stifle her giddiness through her gagging tears, "I'll get to it after—" She continues to vomit.

After the raillery subsides and confirming Becca is in a better state, Abernum goes back into his own head, moving on to another app. He loves solving complex mental puzzles on apps he has created over the years. This is kind of standard practice for him in concerning times. Sometimes, he thinks it keeps him sharp; sometimes, it helps keep him calm by amusement; other times, he feels it keeps him from overthinking things. After watching Slight this morning, he now wonders if the crew sees him as being distant and antisocial during these elsewhere-focused moments in their presence. Fortunately, times such as these are few, but now he feels a new sense of angst from the tricky balancing act of being second in command. The age-old struggle of trying to maintain authoritative control while not alienating your crew. Despite being in his head about a great many things, he can't wipe away his fixed expression of jollity knowing that his crew has survived into the open Martian air.

His thoughts are abruptly halted.

"Hey Abs," Romero calls.

When the crew is alone, they are much less formal than in public settings. Romero calls him again.

Once it registers that Rhoan is trying to get his attention, he disconnects from his internal apps and streams of thought and responds, "Yeah, Rhoan? What's up?"

"When we get to the station, I have a favor to ask."

His sister, SSgt. Zin Romero, chimes in, "Uh oh. Here we go."

In a reluctant and tortured tone that seems in agreement with Zin's concerned response, Abs sighs, "Oh no. I don't like the sound of that. How may I help you, Romes?"

"I'm gonna take that as you're excited to help a friend in need. So—"

"Go ahead with your question, man!"

"Okay then. Since you're friends with Farheeb in Engineering, right?"

Shanee speaks, "Oh no. Please no!"

Laughter explodes.

Abs replies, "You know I am."

"Would you introduce me to her and put in a good word?"

"Don't do it, Cap," Shanee begs.

Rhoan asks, "What? Why not?"

Shanee answers, "Cam is my friend. We all know your game very well."

Abs chuckles. "Well said, Dr. Wilson. Now why would I do that, Romes? Weren't you just hitting on Dr. Wilson a few minutes ago? No wonder she turned down your invitation to the tournament."

"No. But. Because. Come on, man. She might be the one."

"Dr. Wilson or Cam?"

"Seriously, Abs. Tell her all the good stuff about me."

"Dr. Wilson or Cam?"

"Cut it out, Abs. Sure I think the good doctor here is quite attractive in many wonderful ways."

Shanee smiles. "Really?"

"Sure, but she's already made it clear she's not interested. I'm talking about Farheeb this time. Just talk about my good stuff, you know?"

"What good stuff? Your combat skills? I doubt she'd be overly impressed with that."

"Well yeah. That and what a great guy I am."

"You are boxing me into a corner here, Romeo. There's nothing good I could say if she were to ask about your love life. And I use the term 'love' loosely there."

Laughter fills the capsule along with the now familiar and lingering stench from the contents of Becca's bag. The entire flight crew knows Rhoan has a fear of commitment, regardless of how he feels about the women he has dated.

Williams chuckles. "He's got you there, Romero."

"Becca, don't you have another bag to fill?" Rhoan snaps.

Zin says, laughing, "When it comes to dating, bro, I'm gonna have to go with the Cap and Doc on that! Besides, Farheeb is going through a tough breakup, you'll definitely make things worse. Completely, totally, and undoubtedly."

Since she is a rare instigator, her comment causes another round of ribbing and sidesplitting at Rhoan's expense.

"Seriously? That makes it even better. I was planning on stealing her from that loser, Krase, but now my path is clear. She is painfully single, all alone, and in need of some tender loving comfort. It's fate that we will be together during her tender time."

Abs attempts to end Rhoan's pursuits. "Her tender time? What is wrong with you? That's my friend you're talking about, not some prey to be outsmarted."

"I didn't mean it like that."

"Sure you didn't. Even though she is single now, she's also in a lot of pain and your brand of comforting is not what she needs right now. Besides, your own sister wouldn't vouch for you. Stick with the professionals and BTR (Better than Reality) lovers until you are truly ready for a real relationship and leave Farheeb out of your mess of a love life forever."

Shanee chimes, "Thank you, Captain."

Annoyed by Shanee now, Rhoan states, "Not helping, Doc. Come on, Abs. Deep down you know I'm a good guy. How long have we known each other?"

"Knowing you deep down is one of the reasons I'm gonna look out for my sweet and sensitive friend. I'd set her up with Elf before you."

Zin howls, "Ooooh!"

Shanee asks, "Who's Elf?"

Zin dotes, "Oh. Elf is my baby. I created him. He's my ultimate smart pet robot and companion. I just gave him a few new updates you guys will appreciate."

Shanee guffaws and slaps her leg. "That's a terrible testament of their belief in you, Sergeant Romero. Maybe you should—"

Jim interrupts with a grunt, "Uhm. Okay, Squad, enough chitchat. Time to focus on the capture."

"Whoa. That was fast. Each hop seems to get shorter and shorter," Rhoan notes.

The vessel's casual tone immediately becomes all business.

Abs inspects his console for a moment. "That's called getting old, Romes. We're in the green, Grunt." Abs jabs at Jim's grunting habit. "Switching to your control…" There's a pause as he waits for the proper indicator to glow steady green. "Now!"

"Green light. I have control."

This is the only portion of the flight that Captain Slight opts to control manually. It can be a nail biter depending on experience level of the pilot. Abernum has performed manual capture three times. This is Jim's fifth, so the crew has justified confidence that this capture will be uneventful. Most flights utilize the auto-capture function, but the capture system on MOS4 has a reputation of not performing as smoothly as other orbital stations.

"Approaching final vector…and…intercept…and… capture," Jim announces.

The crew lets out a gasp and a short reserved cheer.

"*Nigeria*, capture is good. Welcome to MOS4, Marlagans. Enjoy your stay," the controller says over the speaker.

"Thank you, Command. Good to be back."

The crew then releases a more energetic cheer as they begin shutting down the systems aboard the craft.

After the shutdown procedures are completed and the airlocks are unsealed, the hatch opens.

One of the Evac crewmen cries, "Welcome! Whew! That is rather whiffy. Smells like you had a party in there. Fun ride?"

Rhoan replies, "You have no idea."

The Evac member laughs as he assists Rhoan out of the vessel, "Who gave up the goods this time?"

They all point to Becca, who is embarrassingly hiding her face behind a full bag of evidence against herself. The Evac crew assists the flight crew out of the vessel one by one.

After successfully disembarking, Slight's squad receives a merry greeting from the MOS4 Station Executive Officer, Colonel Kimba Djoibjin, and Administrative Officer, Major Kadaf Patki.

Djoibjin greets, "Welcome to MOS4, Marlagans. You remember Major Patki."

"Good morning, ma'am. Of course. Good morning, Major." Jim nods.

Djoibjin begins, "First, I'd like to again extend our sympathies for the loss of Lt. Dr. Banthira."

Djiobjin is a statuesque, fit, slightly bandy-legged, exceptionally beautiful Togolese with perfect mocha skin only betrayed by the newly forming crow's feet at the corners of her eyes, but they go beautifully with her cute dimples when she smiles. She looks so exquisite in her custom-fitted uniform that it appears she was designed for it as much as it for her. Her promotion to colonel was contingent upon her accepting the duty as XO on MOS4. As a result, she is the first of her family to venture out to Mars. She is one of only a handful of humans in the universe who have lived the trifecta—a resident of Earth, Luna, and Mars.

Jim nods. "Thank you, Colonel."

"Respect. He was a good man and a great Medical Officer. Sorry for your loss. He is missed by all of us here on MOS4."

Rhoan removes his WSX cap to reveal a wild gold Mohawk. The Marlagans bow their heads in remembrance for five seconds, something they have done since they lost their first crew member, Sergeant Steven Thoes, four years ago.

Abs looks up and asks, "Romes, what's the theme of this hairstyle?"

The colonel chuckles.

"It matches my medal from the MAEMA tournament two weeks ago."

"Congratulations, Sgt. Romero," Patki acknowledges. "I watched the tournament on The X Stream."

Major Kadaf Patki, who works directly under Colonel Djoibjin, is a short man of about one hundred sixty-five centimeters with near perfect olive skin and a slightly expanded belt line. His uniform compliments his widening figure. Though balding, he keeps his hair neat and professional at all times. His posture is slightly compromised by a mission injury years ago which causes him to stand and walk slightly bent forward at the waist.

"Thank you, sir."

"I understand you will be putting on a display shortly."

"That's correct, sir."

"I will certainly try to catch it."

"That would be great, sir. Please bring the good doctor with you too."

Patki looks at Wilson. She smiles and nods.

Patki answers, "Sure. We'll do our best to be there."

"Hello, ma'am," Zin surprises everyone by sounding off. "Do you happen to know how Elf is?"

"Hi there, Staff Sergeant," Djoibjin smiles. "I have no reports of damaged equipment. I'm sure he's fine. They loaded all of your advance gear onto your ship yesterday. If there had been any issue, I would have been alerted."

Zin smiles, nods, and replies softly, "Thank you, ma'am."

"Of course. Now let's talk about the future, your upcoming mission. It is my duty to brief you on a couple changes to your mission."

Slight interrupts, "Wait. Changes? What changes?"

"Major, I think this is a good time to take Doctor Wilson with you."

The major bows. "Yes, ma'am. Doctor Wilson, if you'll follow me."

Shanee breaks ranks. "Sure, sir. Marlagans, thank you for helping me feel welcome and making my first hop fun. I hope to see you again."

Abs smiles and gives a slight bow. "Great riding with you, too, Doctor Wilson."

Zin says, "I'll be in touch with you, Doc."

"Please do. Bye, friends."

She and Major Patki dismiss themselves.

Col. Djoibjin, replies, "I have news, Captain, friends. Your mission just got much more interesting."

"In what way?" Slight presses.

"You've just arrived. Take a few hours to get your feet under you, grab some refreshments from the galley, perform in your tournament, and meet me in Briefing Scif 3 (BS3) for a classified briefing later tonight. You are familiar with the protocol for that, correct?" She intends her question for the first time mission medical officer, Lieutenant Williams.

"Yes, ma'am," Jim answers.

She turns her attention to Jim. "Good. Please brief any members of your team who are not familiar. I'll send you preliminaries and specifics about the briefing shortly."

Abs smiles at her and chimes in, "I look forward to hearing more."

Djoibjin smiles back seductively (or at least what seems seductive. Everything about her screams sexy), "I look forward to sharing more." Then she looks around at the entire crew. "Look, Marlagans, I am aware that this is irregular. You've only had two mission overhauls sprung on you like this in the past. On the bright side, this is not your first rodeo in that sense. This mission update was received by us only twelve days ago, and very few of us have clearance or NTK (need to know) status. That's all I can share here in the open. I'll see you in BS3 tonight. You're dismissed." She bows, about-faces, and catwalks away.

Rhoan remarks quietly to Abs as the colonel walks away, "There's a sight to blind a wandering eye. She is the queen of all goddesses ever. Good Lord. Help me! That woman is a slice."

Abs elbows him in the side. "Calm down, killer. You were just begging me to introduce you to Cam."

Rhoan replies, "I might be thinking of an upgrade now. I don't remember her looking that good."

"That's probably because you had your hands full making a mess of so many other people's lives."

"C'mon, man. Give me some credit."

"Okay. Why do you think you never noticed her before?"

"Maybe the mission was on my mind. Probably."

"No. That's not it. Try again."

"Whatever, Abs. Don't we have something to do?"

Zin asked, "So, Cap, what do you think this is about?"

Rhoan chimes in, "It's probably about the ridiculous mission patch the Cap designed for this mission."

Slight is shaking his head. "Har. Har. Rhoan, you're the only one who doesn't like it, just because this one doesn't explicitly highlight your combat skills. This patch's theme is more about unity in loss than it is about individual talents this time."

Rhoan replies, "I still don't understand why this patch couldn't explicitly show muscularity in mourning. Strength in bonded mourning. There's your patch. The two are not mutually exclusive, you know. It would have made it easier for me to heal. Did you think of that? Every other patch made it plain that our team unity was our strength. Or vice versa."

"Vice versa? What? Our strength was our unity?"

"Close. My strength keeps us unified."

Zin sighs heavily. "Rhoan, have some respect. Your ego can't dominate everything."

"But it should." He smiles.

Jim shakes his head. "Zin, you were saying…"

"I don't even remember. His face flapper dominated that conversation too."

"I still got it, sis!" Rhoan exclaims.

Jim remembers, "Rhoan, stop talking. I remember, Zin. You were asking about this newly added alteration to our mission. I have no idea what's going on. This is the first I've heard of it. But I'm sure whatever it is, we're up for the challenge. It can't be more difficult than putting up with Rhoan. Guess we'll know later tonight. Any questions on protocol?" He looks specifically at Rebecca since she's not done it before.

Abs volunteers, "I've taught Becca about that process already."

She nods.

After verifying there are no other questions, Captain Slight nods. "Great. Let's dump our gear and grab some grub."

They load their bags and equipment into their

respective AC14s (autonomous carts) that will deliver their personal effects to their quarters.

* * * * *

Abs Diary Entry 72C:

Hi, Mom and Dad,

Just a quick update. We survived the launch up to MOS4. Haven't seen any sign of you two yet. Becca puked her guts on the hop. And not just a dram. Almost overflowed the bag. Poor kid. She was a trooper, though. She laughed through the whole thing. Like I said before, since this will be her first mission as part of the Marlagans, I promise to look after her as you told me. Khan was a little nervous sending his little sis deeper into space. His fear of heights even applies to flights. He's such a wuss sometimes, but that's my mans'enem, so he gets a pass. Headed to grub and a briefing. Sounds like our mission parameters have already changed. Kimmie greeted us and will be briefing us. Can't believe how we were able to keep our emotions in check when we saw one another a few minutes ago. It was very professional, and I don't think we gave anything away. We are excited to spend more time together later today. It's been four months. Hope I don't break her when I…uh…give her that first hug. I really miss her. I'm so glad you like her too. That has become so important to me (that you approve of my girlfriends) because you warned me about

Candy. We know how badly that went. Thank you for always knowing what's best for me and being brave enough to tell me. I will certainly be glad when you get back home. I'm always wondering if something happened to you during your mission if I would ever be informed or left in limbo. Time for me to get to the mission at hand. Love you both.

# Chapter 3

## Demo

AFTER UNLOADING the *Nigeria*, the Marlagans walk toward the galley together, meeting and greeting several familiar faces along the way. There are dozens of autonomous carts overhead silently scurrying along invisible routes. An obviously astounded and wide-eyed Becca observes as she watches them through the clear ceiling, "This place is busier than I expected." She pauses before declaring, "And the engineering is astounding. That's pretty ingenious how they use the lighting above and on the carts to light these areas below."

Abs joins her in looking up. "Yes. The lighting engineers did it that way for security. No one can sneak around up there without everyone seeing it. When the engineers are up there working, their shadows are very easy to detect down here. Notice how as the carts pass they don't interrupt the lighting down here but a person up there absolutely does. Somehow, the carts' undercarriage lighting matches the overhead lighting to give us constant undisturbed lighting. It's quite brilliant."

"I didn't think of that. Very clever. And it works so well."

"That's why they're the lighting engineers and we aren't."

"Incredible. Why so many carts? Are they just traveling because they have nowhere else to go or are they all carrying stuff?"

"None of those are idle carts. There are a couple hundred people here on the station and most are transitioning to or from a mission, another station or the surface. Those things load quarters, ships, supply stores, deliver mail and packages to personal units, meeting spaces and offices, and probably other things I don't know about. Imagine if all of those carts were people making those deliveries. This station would be much more crowded."

"I never realized so much happens up here."

"And it's constant. If you think this is something, you should visit MOS1. They are the port of entry and exit for travelers of all sorts."

"I had no idea these were so large. Sure, we learn about it in school and in training, but the scale of it was never something I gave much thought."

"Not even in your preparations to come up here?"

"I just went by the things I learned in training and what you and the team told me that I felt were relevant to succeeding on mission. Didn't consider the station operations much."

"Bad move, Bec. Missing the details can be deadly. You have to take a little more initiative to research things for yourself. If we all do our own research, some elements of said research will stand out differently to each of us, and the frontal memory of that knowledge could save a life."

"Guess I never thought of it that way."

"Now is the best time to start. Actually…never mind."

"Okay, boss man, sir."

"Your Highness will suffice."

"Good luck with that."

They continue walking under the clear lighted ceiling area. Lots of bowing to and fro with others along the way. Bowing has been adopted as the main form of greeting on Mars to reduce the chances of spreading disease. Physical touch is primarily reserved for friends, family, and more intimate relationships.

As they continue their walk, Becca notices the warmness of the station's design. To cozy up the atmosphere in some of the common areas, the titanium floor has a very thin veneer of hardwood, and warm soothing wall colors have been added to feel less sterile than mostly bare titanium-drenched offices.

Abs queries, "Romes (the crew sometimes calls him Romes and sometimes Romeo dependent upon which of his character flaws he's exhibiting. It's also useful for easier distinction from his sister when they're in close proximity), are you still struggling with your unit on the ground?"

He looks back at Abs. "Heh. It's gotten a little better. I guess they're starting to accept that I'm experienced enough to be the unit sergeant."

"It wasn't experience as much as age, though. Right?"

"Right. I can't help that I'm good enough to be where I am at my age. But I think as the Marlagans' reputation continues to grow, they seem to show more respect."

"Who wouldn't? I mean look at us. We're awesome!"

"That, we are," Jim adds, "but we're not as bulletproof as we wish we were, so keep your heads."

"Well said out of left field, Captain Buzzkill? Why so serious today?" Rhoan finally cracked opened the investigation everyone has been reluctant to peek into.

Jim ignores the question and keeps walking.

A few minutes later, Becca interrupts the other conversations with a question, "Does anyone else notice a surfeit of people looking at us in a disturbing way?"

Abs asks, "How so?"

"I'm not sure, but it gives me a sense that everyone else on this station knows something that we don't."

"That's possible, Bec. But when you say stuff like that it reminds me that this is your first mission with us. People always show respect for the crews going on these types of missions. Besides, we recently lost a couple Marlagans. That's probably why it's a little more pronounced than usual, I'm sure," Abs says, trying to remain nonchalant as he starts to notice she's right.

"Okay. That makes sense. Yeah. That's probably all it is."

As they continue walking, Abs begins to grow more uncomfortable as to why so many eyes are seeming to follow them without words today.

"Yeah, don't get yourself worked up about something so small. Save that energy. I get the feeling we're going to need it at some point in the near future," Abs says in a poor attempt to keep her calm. He vouched for her to be on this squad, knowing she is capable of being the best medical officer in the Corps when she is able to control her anxieties, the same anxieties that nearly kept her from successfully completing some portions of the WSX Officers Training.

As they arrive at their destination in the galley, Rhoan spots the stocky, blonde, and bespectacled SSgt Darren Ylinen, a good friend from his Martian colony, Tsiolkovsky. They run to embrace at the sight of one another. "Hey, Ylinen, how are things up here, my friend?"

In his thick Scottish accent, he replies, "Voyager! Long time, my man. I was happy when I first heard your team was coming up for another mission."

"Yeah, we're heading back out in a couple days. How's the station treating you?"

"You know. Really can't complain much. It'll probably just get me into trouble anyways. They promoted me to Gunny. More pay, more responsibilities."

"More pay can't be bad."

"Not complaining about that. But friendships do tend to change when you become the boss, though. How are you, Voyager? How are things back home?"

"Big D, you still calling me that? I haven't heard that in quite a while. I guess since the last time we spoke. Home is home, and I'm still me, so all is well. Congrats on the pay raise, though. Drinks on you?"

Ylinen replies, "Same old Voyager."

Rhoan smiles. "Couldn't change if I tried, but I get the whole boss issue. Dealing with that myself."

"This, too, we shall overcome."

"Yes, sir. We should talk later."

"We definitely will. By the way, my team was lucky enough to win the draw for arming your mission."

"Finally! About time. Got anything special in mind?"

Since they have a strong friendship that goes back several years, Ylinen uses Rhoan as a test bed for experimental weaponry unbeknownst to the WSX. But this secret arrangement has made the production of three current WSX weapons upgrades and accessories possible.

Ylinen answers proudly, "A few floaters wandering around the old noodle just for this mission."

"I look forward to a very special surprise."

"I know you're going to like either of these contraptions I'm considering for you. Have I ever let you down?"

"Not even once." Rhoan pulls Ylinen to the side and tries to ask his next question quietly so the rest of the squad doesn't notice, "D, is Farheeb around today?"

"Voyager, my voyaging friend. Especially with the dating it turns out. I'm only going to tell you this because I care. Leave Farheeb alone," Ylinen admonishes.

"What? Why? What did you hear about her?"

"She is good egg, my friend. She is not the problem here. I care about her well-being, everyone on this station does. So I don't want you doing to her what your reputation says you have done to so many others."

"Ylinen? Really, man? You too?"

"Farheeb is very sweet person who has been deeply hurt. She needs time to heal. You would not help that process."

"But I'm a comforter. Like a blanket. You know that."

"I do know that. You start with the comforting, then you become the reason they need comforting again. A wet, dirty, stinky blanket that won't come clean and the smell gets into your skin. And no—"

"Ouch! What the hell, man?"

"I know, right? You've made quite a name for yourself. Besides, she already knows your reputation too well. She is far from interested. Sorry, my friend. It's what's best for everyone. Even you."

"Me? How?"

"Imagine what people would do to you up here if you hurt her with your renown for hurting so many others. You're a very good friend, but when it comes to the dating, you leave a wake of devastation everywhere you step."

Rhoan drops his head in defeat but then briefly looks for hope, "But what about—"

Ylinen lowers and shakes his head. Then he raises his head to look into his friend's eyes. He puts his hand on Rhoan's shoulder and states, "No, my friend. Not this one. Choose another. There has to be at least three lovely ladies in the solsys who are not aware of your reputation."

Rhoan slowly nods. "Ooh, Big D. You took an axe to my heart right there. But that's okay. I see everyone is on the same team, here. It feels I'm like trying to score a goal on the whole station while everyone is shielding the ball and playing goalie. You leave me no choice but to move on…for now. Not because I'm defeated, only because I'm too young and too sexy to change my ways. Gotta use it while I still got it, you know?"

Zin happens to walk by at that moment and overhears Rhoan. She says in exhaustion under her breath, "Ugh. This kid…"

Rhoan looks at her and snaps, "I heard that!"

Zin keeps walking without a reply.

"So, Big D, are you participating in today's tournament?"

"No. I gave up competing. Thought I told you that."

"Why? You were so good at it."

"No, I wasn't. I'm better at the ranging weapons. I'm just focusing on that now."

"I was hoping you would be there."

"Truthfully, I didn't even know it was today. Are you competing?"

"I'm ineligible because of my rung, but they asked me to give an inspiring demonstration."

"Are you doing it?"

"Yeah. I said I would since it won't interfere with mission stuff."

"Then I'll be there just to see you inspire the lower rung."

"Cool. Thanks, D. Guess we'd better go. See you at the tournament."

They embrace again.

Ylinen bows. "See you then, my friend."

Rhoan bows in return.

Though their leader is still aloof in disposition, the Marlagans enjoy a meal and many conversations together before making their way to the tournament. By the time they arrive at the arena, the tournament is nearly at halftime. Rhoan dashes to the dressing room to prepare for his halftime demonstration as the rest of the Marlagans stand at the side entrance of the completely full performance center. The atmosphere is eardrum-exploding, electric, and contagious.

Zin screams, "That huge billboard of Rhoan will not help us in our efforts to rein in his ego any time soon!"

Becca cites, "I must admit, it is an impressive image

of him! I didn't realize he was such a big deal in this sport!"

Zin yells in reply, "He's the best there is! But please don't go fan girl on me!"

"Don't let that be a concern in the least!"

"Good to hear. He doesn't need any more fawning fans helping his ego balloon further. Our work will be hard enough following this tournament."

Becca hollers, "Goodness! It's loud in here! I'm starting to lose my voice already!"

"Not a party goer, huh?"

"Not at all!"

Abs yells, "Dang! Did you see that??"

Jim replies, "I hope she didn't break anything! That was brutal!"

Zin adds, "Oh no! Here comes the stretcher! Hope she's all right!"

Announcer: "The winner by TKO, Julie Pasquale!"

The crowd erupts in noise as Julie is praised and awarded while her opponent is carried away by the medical team.

Announcer: "Now for the halftime show we've all been waiting for. We have arguably the world's greatest martial artist of all time here with us tonight! Right here! On MOS4!"

Cheers and stomping nearly drown out the announcer.

Announcer: "He is part of the world-renown Marlagans Excursion Team, who are all with us right now! I see you over there. Let's bring them out!"

Jim shakes his head, hoping the announcer won't… too late.

Announcer: "MOS4, show your love and respect for Captain Jim Slight! Come on over."

Jim jogs over to the announcer, waving to the crowd.

Announcer: "Captain Fernando 'Abs' Abernum! Their newest member Lieutenant Doctor Rebecca Williams! And our favorite Tech Mech, Staff Sergeant Zintia Romero! She's sister to our guest of honor, the incomparable, undefeated, and greatest of all time, Sergeant Rhoan Romero!"

Crowd goes berserk as Rhoan runs out from the back to join his team at center mat.

Announcer: "Captain Slight, thank you and your team for all of your amazing discoveries and constantly putting yourselves in harm's way to further the cause of humanity! Respect, MOS4! High respect and honor to the Marlagans!"

The crowd's noise overwhelms the Marlagans as they stand in the center of the arena. They wave to the crowd as they quickly return to their corner against the wall. Along the way, many fans stop to bow as they pass.

Announcer: "Now for the halftime show you've all been waiting for."

The Marlagans finally retreat back to their spot near the corner door.

Announcer: "Sergeant Rhoan Romero will take on twelve! That's right! Twelve! Twelve of MOS4's finest. You heard me right, a full dozen attackers at once. If any of our artists hits the mat not of their own doing, their fight is over. This is not staged, this is not choreographed. Sergeant Romero doesn't even know who the attackers are or where they will come from. The attackers will be outfitted in protective gear while the great Sergeant will remain unprotected. Are you ready for Sergeant Romero, MOS4?"

The crowd's noise is outrageous!

Announcer: "Sergeant Romero, are you ready?"

Rhoan nods and takes his stance.

Announcer: "Attackers, attack!"

The crowd's noise spikes again as action-themed music begins to blare throughout the venue, lights rise throughout the entire venue, and the attackers come from the audience, the lockers, and the entrances. All twelve lightly protected opponents converge on Rhoan at once. As the first attacker reaches him, Rhoan wastes no time dipping his left shoulder to lift the charging attacker, spins, and tosses him at two wide-eyed opponents charging from the opposite direction. Attackers two and three catch the flying attacker with a thump to the torso, and all three hit the mat as Rhoan grabs a fourth attacker by the collar and somehow drops between his legs still holding his collar. Rhoan contorts his body in such a fluid motion that he is able to kick the attacker with both feet as he falls toward Rhoan, sending the fourth attacker breathlessly into the upper torso of the fifth attacker. Startled, they both crash hard onto the mat. The sixth attacker roundhouse kicks at the side of Rhoan's head while he is still seated on the mat on his way to gaining his footing. Rhoan blocks the kick and swings upward with his right fist at the attacker's groin, then rolls to wrap number six's leg between his own and brings him down with a small wrench of the leg. That same rolling motion allows Rhoan to pop into an offensive stance just in time to dropkick the seventh attacker. Then leaping immediately to his feet again, he chases down the eighth attacker, who's in retreat to regroup with other attackers. Rhoan blocks a flurry of rapid punches from number eight and catches him by the collar, pulling him down to the ground as the ninth attacker lands a solid roundhouse kick to Rhoan's lower back. Rhoan spins swiftly to face the ninth attacker without any indication that he even felt the strike to his back. The attacker stands frozen and stunned for only two seconds as he realizes his well-placed kick had no effect, then he misses Rhoan with a jab and follows it up with a right hook. This is all the time Rhoan needs to step inside the punch, grab number nine by the right arm, drop to his knees, and use the momentum of the attacker's follow-up punch to throw him over his head high into the air and slams him onto the mat right beside the eighth attacker. The crowd's noise rises to meter-shattering levels.

Seeming to observe all that has happened, the remaining three attackers break from a huddle and decide to work as a team. They encircle Rhoan and all three lunge at once. Two attack with punches while the third strikes with a spinning drop kick. Rhoan grabs the sleeves of the two punchers, drops to a split before either punch can land, and dodges the kick intended for his head. The force of their momentum and Rhoan's weight combined with his strength bring number ten and eleven's chin first onto the mat. Audible cries escape number eleven's breath as his teeth crash together. Number twelve attempts to stomp-kick Rhoan before he can get up, but Rhoan stuns the attacker with a flurry of punches to his lower extremities as they fly toward him. The surprise and pain are audibly evident as the attacker yelps and hobbles back on his muscular quivering twigs. Rhoan pops back into an offensive stance as the attacker tries to recover. Unwilling to give the final opponent the recovery time required, Rhoan lunges, but the attacker retreats for a little more breathing time. Rhoan appreciates the quick respite to catch his own breath. The attacker sees Rhoan inching closer and mounts a major offensive. Rhoan dodges and blocks five quick successive kicks before delivering a roundhouse kick which sends the screaming final attacker three meters back before thudding to the mat on his back and slamming his head. The crowd oohs in astonishment!

The stunned announcer walks in Rhoan's direction with a mesmerized expression before finally speaking, "Holy! My goodness! Did you see that? I'm not even sure I could describe what we just witnessed! Best in the world, folks! Unbelievable! I need to catch my breath!"

The crowd's noise level at the packed venue is beyond bearable as Rhoan's arm is lifted by the referee and the attackers who are able bow to Rhoan in respect.

Jim signals. "Let's get out of here."

As the Marlagans press through the crowd between them and the exit, Abs overhears a debate about the authenticity of the demonstration. One side feeling the short duration of the exercise, which lasted only slightly more than four minutes, proves it was all staged. The counter argument comes from a female voice claiming to be an avid fan who has seen Rhoan dispatch more opponents in a shorter amount of time with greater ease. This debate seems to harbor the only doubter to Rhoan's superhero-like abilities in combat among the thousands of spectators, many of whom hopped to MOS4 just for the tournament.

As the Marlagans near the door, a brunette boy of about eight years asks, "May I please have your autographs? I want to be a Marlagan when I grow up."

They all smile and give the boy encouraging messages as they each sign his small poster of Rhoan.

Once outside of the performance center, Becca still yells, "I don't think I'll ever be able to use these ears again, but that was really cool!"

Abs agrees, "Yeah. Have to admit. Rhoan was amazing in there."

Becca replies, "No. Well, yes, he was impressive, but I was referring to how cool the reception you got as Marlagans in there was. I didn't realize you guys were such a big deal."

Jim warns, "It's hard earned, but don't get caught up in it. It's a lot to live up to, Becca. You sure you can handle it?"

"I trust that Abs would not have brought my name forth had he thought otherwise."

"There's a tough mission ahead of us. Just don't let the accolades be a distraction. We need to stay focused."

Abs replies, "Jim, just stop and enjoy the moment once in a while. Relax. We're always ready."

"Okay. I just want us to stay sharp."

"We know. We get that, but today was Becca's first public acknowledgement as a Marlagan. It's a big deal, Jim. You remember."

"I said okay. I just want us to stay sharp."

Becca remarks, "Jim, I am fully aware of my rookie

status and that I may seem like an ingenue to you, but I feel very well prepared for the tasks that lie ahead."

"How many times do I have to say okay?"

"Don't feel bad. Your reminders to always be ready do actually inspire me to be at my best all the time. This team has done a lot to earn the world's respect and adoration. You have my word that I will do everything in my power not to mess that up."

"Thanks, Becca. See. Why can't the rest of you be more like Becca?"

Becca smiles as she feels this is the first moment of the day Jim has loosened up a touch, and he is actually acknowledging her existence.

Several minutes later, Rhoan appears from another side door back in uniform, and the crowd's noise blasts from the entrance until the door closes behind him.

"So, guys, what did you think?"

Praises for Rhoan's performance fly freely from his team.

Abs asks, "Are you even tired?"

"Not really. That was just a short demo."

"But that was a dozen dudes."

"Yeah. It's all about efficiency of motion. I rarely tire after a competition. I let the opponents do most of the work."

"There has to be more to it than that. You just took out twelve people in less than five minutes and look far less tired than they did."

Rhoan smiles.

"Good job, brother."

"Thank you, Zinny Girl. I must have been pretty awesome to get a compliment from you."

"The thank you would have sufficed and don't call me that."

Rhoan laughs.

Becca adds, "That was very impressive, Rhoan. You should be proud of all your hard work and training."

"Thank you, Doc."

"You took a pretty good hit to your back. Are you feeling okay?"

"I'm fine. I do a lot of impact training, so the pain during combat feels routine. My back is fine. Besides, dude hits like a flea."

Abs asks, "How'd you get out of there so quickly? There had to be a mob waiting for you."

"Not this time. I had security clear a path to keep me out of reach and snuck out this locker room door."

Jim notes as he looks down at his pyk, "Perfect timing, too. Djoibjin wants to meet with us in fifteen minutes."

"We'd better get cracking."

"Right. Let's head there now."

Rhoan notes, "I wonder if she was in the audience. Maybe she'll want more than an autograph. Know what I'm saying?" He nudges Zin with his elbow.

Zin huffs, "Geez. Turn it off. Will you?"

* * * * *

Abs Diary Entry 72C:

Hey, Da Mama. Hey, Da Daddy.

There's not a lot of time to chat. There's one thing I forgot to mention yesterday. While I was at the theater with Mustafa and Morrow, we ran into Mom's friend, Gladys. She told me to let you know she tried your recipe and it tasted nothing like the one you made. She wants me to ask you to send it to her again to make sure she got the right one. I told her I'd tell you, but your mission may be too long and too far away to get back to her. It made me sad to say that to her. It's like something bubbled up in me the rest of the night because I missed you more than usual last night since you weren't there for our farewell celebration before each mission. I know I'm a big knucklehead, but you two shouldn't be such great friends if you want me to grow up and be more independent. I'm putting all that on you, especially since you're not here to defend yourselves. My love's all over you today and always.

Becca sends love. She has quietly been a bundle of nervous energy since we met up at the launch tube. We know she'll do great; she just doesn't know it yet. To be honest, it's still weird going on a mission and not hearing that booming voice and laughter permeating throughout the vessel. As much as I love having Bec here, it really feels like we're not complete. No one has really spent a lot of time talking about him yet, but I'm sure it's coming. I know we all miss Hassan and his crazy comedic monologues. He was so much fun. I really do miss my buddy.

# Chapter 4

# Upgraded

THE MARLAGANS assemble outside of BS3 for the briefing with four minutes to spare.

Jim tries the door. He's surprised that it is open. "She must have opened it remotely."

They file in and grab seats around the medium-sized rectangular metallic table with a centralized built-in podium on one of the long sides. Fortunately, the metal seats are smartly cushioned and contoured for the average backside.

Right on the hour, the door cracks slightly, and the team chatter comes to rest in a uniform staccato as if they were being conducted. Col. Djoibjin's perfectly and permanently manicured fingernails are visible as she holds the seventy-five millimeter thick vault-like door slightly ajar. The crew hears her voice in a low murmur as she wraps up a discussion with a disembodied voice on the other side.

About thirty seconds later, she strides hurriedly

into the room with a small package and a lavender-adorned black briefcase until coming to a halt behind the small podium positioned front and center of the room. Her perfect posture and catwalk strut captivate every onlooker fortunate enough capture a glimpse.

While setting up her workspace, she begins, "Hello, Marlagans! What a silly name. Remind me. Whose idea was that again?"

They all point to Jim, who looks around with a dumbstruck expression of betrayal, then asks the colonel, "But it does grow on you, right?"

Abs speaks up, "When he recruited us, we were all asked to join the Marlagans. We had no idea the name was negotiable. Later, we learned the name has something to do with his childhood. That's about all he will divulge."

Rhoan instigates the matter further, "He won't admit it, but I believe he was kicked out of his teenage barber shop quartet or street corner doo-wop group and uses the same name to compensate for the a cappella dream that died in his youth."

Jim shakes his lowered head.

Djoibjin replies, "Ha! Don't let me find out that's true, Captain, and yes, eventually one does get used to it. I am not so sure I want that growing on me, though."

After a couple chuckles, Jim begs, "Yeah, yeah. May we please move on to the mission updates…please?"

Djoibjin starts, "Yes. Let's get to it. As you know, your harvesting missions are crucial to the WSX's ability to traverse the solar system and extremely important to the economy of Mars."

Rhoan boasts, "Thank you. We try."

She looks at Rhoan without any change in expression, blinks with her full eyelashes, and continues in her heavy Togolese accent, "First, I again offer my condolences for Dr. Banthira. He was a friend, a great doctor, a good Marine, and a good man."

Jim somberly replies, "Thank you, Colonel. We certainly do miss him. He was the very definition of a Marlagan and a wonderful friend."

"Of course. He certainly will be missed for some time to come, I'm sure. With that said, since you're sadly now a five-member crew this mission, you'll be taking the MS *JohnGlenn* on this mission."

"Wait!" Jim interrupts and grunts. "Why are we losing the *NeilArmstrong*? That's our ship. Is that what this is about? Kicking us while we're down?"

Anticipating resistance, Djoibjin maintains a phlegmatic tone. "No, Captain. That's not what this is about. As I just stated: You're a five-person crew now, and the *JohnGlenn* is newer, faster, sleeker and better suited for this mission. We've even outfitted a few new initiatives for this particular mission."

The tension in Jim's tone loosens slightly and turns slightly downcast, "But the *NeilArmstrong* is home. You could outfit her with the same initiatives, couldn't you?"

Ignoring the ship's gender slip-up, she explains with understanding, "Captain Slight, the *NeilArmstrong* is not lost to you forever. This change goes only as far as this mission for now. Nothing has been decided in that regard beyond this mission, and the sentiments you've expressed are duly noted."

"Okay." He slightly huffs. "But I'm still not excited about this."

"Once you're in the Mushroom, I think you'll feel better."

"What's the Mushroom?"

"That the nickname for the *John Glenn*."

"Should I even ask?"

"It's not moldy or fungus-y if that's what you're thinking. They only call it that because when looking down at it from the tower, its form is very much like that of a mushroom."

"Well, I certainly hope that's the only change you have for us, but I can't imagine a change of spacecraft would be classified."

Djoibjin unseals the small package and her tone turns serious, "What I am about to share with you is above top secret. The primary mission you thought you had is still your mission as far as the public knows. We still need all the siolens you can harvest for us, and this promises to be a major haul. The following details I'm about to share with you cannot be discussed with anyone at any time other than with the people in this room right now and others involved in an official capacity. And you will know who they are before takeoff. There will be at least one more briefing prior to departure. The only other time to discuss this outside of your mission will be at the formal debriefs upon your return. If you are to discuss it with anyone else at any other time, you will be thusly and officially notified by me or General Arms directly. Any questions or problems with that order?"

"No, ma'am!" Each fully attentive crew member responds in near unison.

"That's all well and good. As much as I trust you, the WSX doesn't, so I'm passing around this SAINT (shut-the-hell-up-about-it) agreement. After I have all of your DiNAs (digital DNA signatures) next to your names, we will begin the classified portion of the briefing."

They take about ten minutes to review and complete the form. After receiving the DiNA-signed digital documents, she waves her credentials over a sensor in the corner of the room near the entrance to "whiten" the room. By doing this, all forms of transmitting electronics other than her briefing devices and Abs's organic bionics inside the soundproof scif are disabled. However, Abs does lose his ability to record images or video and make contact beyond or within the "white" room.

Djoibjin continues, "Thank you, all. Now that the room is secure, let's begin. You Marlagans have been chosen for this mission because you're our most traveled Io teams and our most successful siolens harvesting team. It's also factual that you're the most capable at breaking new ground for the WSX."

Rhoan breaks in, "That's not classified, Colonel. Everyone knows we're the best."

Djoibjin stops to looks at Rhoan with a befuddled expression for about ten seconds before turning to Captain Slight and asking, "How do you put up with him?"

"You get used to it. Besides, he's the best there is. You saw his demonstration today. So he's not lying."

"If that's what gets you through the day…As I was about to say, until today you believed you were simply on another mission to harvest more siolens. What you and most of humanity, including the WSX, do not know is that we may have reason to believe siolens are somehow potentially linked to an unknown life form."

Zin sits up and queries in a tone of complete shock and disbelief, "A life form?"

"Potentially. We have reason to believe this may be the case. We did not have any indication of this until about half a year ago when something in the manufacturing process showed signs of life. All this time, everyone, including us, just thought it was simply a lifeless material left from the violence of Io's atmospheric conditions. Now, we know essentially nothing about the life form itself, if it is actually a life form. What has been reported did not seem to exhibit any intelligence, and there is no footage which clearly shows the short timeframe of the incident in question. The life phenomena witnessed has only been observed once. We're hoping this was just a mistake, a case of misinterpretation, misinformation, misguided belief, or even a hoax. We definitely prefer either of those scenarios over the prospect that siolens are living creatures."

Rhoan raises his hand.

"Sergeant?"

Rhoan asks his question, "Does this mean we might be going to war on Io for the rights of the siolens cache? How do we even kill them? Will we get experimental and specialized weaponry?"

"Romes, just stop being Romes for a minute and listen up. This is important," Slight advises.

Djoibjin maintains her appropriately professional demeanor, "No, Sgt. Romero, nothing that you've just said is even close to what we have in mind. This is not a seek-and-destroy mission of any kind. Neither is it an invasion of another species. This is primarily and officially a harvesting mission but with the side mission of seeking and capturing several, specifically five, live specimens for further research. Fortunately, most parameters of your mission as previously briefed such as your drop site, primary objective and time table remain unchanged. The original drop site was chosen because of its high density of siolens material as your orbiter observed on your last mission. This also seems the likeliest location for life if it actually exists. There may be a nest or den of some sort in that region. You are tasked with confirming or debunking life on Io."

Slight grunts, "Well then. That is significant!"

"Yes, Captain. That is one word for it."

Abs discloses, "Colonel, I've never mentioned this to anyone before. One, because I thought I was mistaken since we never entertained the idea of life on Io. And two, because I didn't want to bring any more attention to the fact that I'm a good candidate for a psych review."

There are a couple gasps and chuckles in the room. Jim grunts again as he turns to face Abs.

"Is that true, Captain?"

Abernum continues, "It happened on our second mission to Io last year, I could have sworn I witnessed a mass of siolens moving in an unusual fashion."

Colonel further inquires, "Please elaborate, Captain?"

"Sure. Of our many siolens missions, it has only happened once, and even then, I can't be one hundred percent sure what I saw."

"I'd like to hear it anyway."

"Yes, ma'am. We were passing an active lava pit outside of a tube in Cholcis. There was a load of siolens directly adjacent to the pit almost ready for harvest when it seemed as if something began moving within the pile. It felt as if something was watching us, but no one else said anything or even seemed to notice. But as I watched it for additional movement, something really seemed to be discomposing the pile slightly on one side. It did not appear to be the result of the load settling, it was more like something was upsetting the pile, but I didn't see anything. So I convinced myself that it had to be light shifts, lava motion, and globules playing with my peripheral vision especially when the crew asked me what was wrong. No one else admitted to seeing anything, so I simply chalked it up as an optical illusion."

"And you never reported this?"

"When we didn't see anything, there was nothing to report, ma'am."

"So none of the other Marlagans noticed the movement you thought you saw?"

"They did not confess it to me if they had."

"Interesting. I'll make note of that," the colonel states. "Thank you for sharing that. Has anyone else had a similar experience?"

The crew peruses the scif with anxious expressions, wondering if other reports of this type will surface. Abs held his breath hoping someone would report a similar experience. But none did.

"Thank you, Captain. Did you document that sighting anywhere?"

"No, ma'am. I didn't."

"Would you be willing to send me a brief statement regarding your experience immediately after this briefing?"

"Aye, ma'am."

"Thank you. It looks like Abernum is our only potential eyewitness to this phenomenon. Is that correct?"

Rhoan barks, "I didn't see it."

"Very well. Captain Slight, please escort Captain Abernum to Psych immediately." Barely able to get it out, she burst into laughter. "Just kidding, Captain."

Abs lets out a high-pitched sigh. "Not funny, Colonel. Good thing you broke so quickly, I was actually growing concerned."

Still chuckling, Djoibjin admits, "I've never been good at jokes. Some days, I laugh so easily that I have a tough time making it to the end of a joke. Any questions or statements before we continue?"

Zin is feeling quite intrigued and it's showing by her unusual chattiness during this briefing, "Colonel, let me just get this straight. You are telling us that our mission is to capture a totally unknown to mankind, never known before life form on a planet not believed to contain life throughout all of human history. Am I right?"

"Staff Sergeant Romero, it would not be the first time the Marlagans discovered new life."

Almost sounding like a narrator, Zin continues with a tone of wonder, "True, but that was by accident. No one expected to find cribules on Europa. But this time, we are actually going on a mission to seek out new life. Is that right?"

"That's correct, Staff Sergeant. Are you going to be okay with that?"

"Oh. I am better than okay with this mission. It's fascinating! I could bring back a new pet."

Caught off guard, Djoibjin can only eke out, "Well…"

Rhoan counters, "Elf will not like that."

"He'll be happy to have another brother or sister."

Abs jumps back in, "Colonel, is there a plan for capturing any living creatures? How are we even supposed to know what we're looking for other than movement among batches of siolens?"

"Good questions. Great segue. It's time to get into that. One thing that was observed in the case at the warehouse was a fluid-like motion without any known external force—possibly comparable to a slight bubbling motion, then it hardened momentarily before seeming to evaporate or disappear."

"Now my mind is racing with all sorts of random thoughts. Since that pit near the harvested siolens was bubbling, it has me wondering if there were creatures in the pit making it look as if it were bubbling. Is it possible that all active lava pits on Io are harboring living beings?" Abs inquires.

Djoibjin replies, "Nothing is off the table at this point. These two encounters sound strikingly similar, considering they are all that we have to go on about this phenomena. Hopefully the details of this report help you feel less bananas about what you saw, Captain."

"Doesn't hurt."

"The lab brains theorize that the bubbling described could likely have been some form of pressure release though it has never been reported before or since. They think this is only a possibility because, though raw siolens material is too firm to bubble like a liquid itself, it is airy enough that when air is introduced from below, above or any direction, that air escapes through other areas of the material. The biggest hurdle to this theory is the fact that the raw batch observed had no liquid through which to bubble. The nearest known liquid was more than twenty-five meters away. And the brains were never able to repeat the reported observation without liquid."

Abs asks, "Excuse me, Colonel."

"Yes, Captain?"

"Is there any report of gurgling sounds or anything?"

"It says here that observation seemed to occur in silence or at least not loud enough to hear in the facility. The engineers were right next to the shipment, so they should have heard it if there was a sound. Why did you hear a sound?"

"No, ma'am."

"Are you sure?"

"Yes, ma'am. Thank you."

"Okay. So. It's still quite a mystery. I have here numerous test reports regarding this matter and a few others. Regarding the bubbling effect, we don't know. One theory they've put forth is that the fluid was a foreign agent of uncertain origin, but we just don't know. Moving on to the subsequent transition to a solid as described, that too is not a natural siolens property. As you are well aware, siolens never solidify without processing. And after processing, air can no longer penetrate it either. It's just a steady state gelatinous substance. Of course you already know all of this as much as you have worked with siolens."

Slight waves, "It's good to hear this, Colonel. Please continue with their research."

"Very well. Since the reported incident is beyond what we know to be definitive properties of siolens, the brains hypothesized that if the report is accurate, what was described has low to medium odds of being an actual unidentified life form with the ability to alter states from liquid into solid. It may even have the capability to change its form as it wills, which would be extremely fascinating in one sense and just as terrifying in another. Remember the stream, Hollow Heart, or the classic *Terminator* movies with the liquid metal assassins?"

"Not helpful, Colonel. But if that is the case, what's the plan for capturing creatures with the gift of metamorphosis? It could stand in front of us one sec and just flow around us the next. It could just soak itself into the surface or even spread itself too thin for us to gather it up."

Zin notes, "Or even worse, soak itself into us and get into our bloodstreams."

Rhoan barks, "Oh! That just wouldn't be fair! Can you imagine that?"

"Those are the kinds of things we need your team to figure out."

"A million scenarios come to mind making your proposal to capture one of these things near impossible. If we capture it in solid state, wouldn't it just river its way out?"

"The brain jockeys eventually considered all of your concerns among others and believe they came up a plan which you will hear about at a later briefing. Another point we must stress is we do not know what it takes if the need arises to defend yourselves against them if something happens."

"Need you ask? I'm all over that. I've always wanted to bag a terminator. Can we call them that?" Rhoan boasts.

"What if they're harmless? Terminators aren't harmless."

"Then let's call them Hollows until we find out they are Terminators."

Zin challenges, "What is your tactic if they just absorb into you? You gonna shoot them off?"

"That's a Hollow if there ever was one. That's what I'm calling them, Hollows."

"Sorry to interrupt your important work of naming the probable creatures, Sergeants. But if I may…"

"Yes, ma'am. Sorry."

"While we're on that subject, we absolutely mandate that there be no unnecessary violence…" She pauses, looks up, and emplaces her gaze on Rhoan before calling him by name, "Sergeant Romero. In self-defense, of course, but if you figure out how to 'terminate a hollow' as you say, please refrain from that modus operandi when attempting to fulfill your mission of capturing them. Please be intentional about capturing every detail of each interaction and outcome of any unusual creatures, situations, optical illusions, sightings, etc., that you face. Record everything. We do not want to frighten, piss off, or harm any life forms you may encounter. We only want you to harvest the material and bring back a few live specimens for study. Debunking their existence would be the best possible outcome for all of humanity."

Their eyes remained fixed on her, and she easily senses their deep contemplation of this proposal.

"I know this is a lot to absorb in such a short time. But as you do, don't lose sight that all of this is above top secret!"

"Yes, ma'am!" A couple say in response.

Williams inquires, "Do we know if they have a pulse, heartbeat, or things we would recognize as signs of life?"

"Unfortunately, the incident report and investigation did not uncover enough evidence to verify any of that. The reported specimen apparently did not live or even exist in a useable way long enough for anyone to do any detailed study. After several witnessed the event, it must have perished shortly thereafter. It never repeated the actions that alerted the processors nor demonstrated any other signs of life. Nor did anyone find anything foreign or unusual in that batch that may have been a corpse. When our lab analyzed that batch of siolens, they did, however, report a very unusual red substance with faint traces of a chemical compound unfamiliar to humans. Could be environmental but it was unlike anything we've ever seen in a batch of siolens. That's the only tangible evidence to give this claim any legitimacy. Otherwise, this would not be taken so seriously. It can't be coincidence that the batch in question is the only ever to have such a report and such a strange substance."

Abs requests, "I'd like to see their report on the substance if possible."

Djoibjin rifles through a series of files and concedes, "Surprisingly, it's not readily available in these files. I will have to get back to you on that."

"Okay. Another question. Was that batch from a previously untapped region?"

"It was not. We had harvested that region twice before the harvest in question."

A hushed contemplation fills the room before Slight asks, "Are you at liberty to disclose which region?"

"Yes, I believe so. Stand by."

Djoibjin seems to scroll through digital files for permissions or information. Moments later, she looks up and blurts, "Cholcis."

"Probably a stupid question, ma'am. Why aren't we going back to Cholcis?"

"That's not stupid at all. It would make sense to do that. We considered changing your destination, but the region where your mission was already destined has proven to have a noticeably higher density of siolens. We're hoping that correlates to a greater chance of encountering or debunking life."

Jim grunts. "Thank you, ma'am."

"The next portion of our discussion is what you've been waiting for. Trapping the creatures. Since we don't have any information on the capabilities or physiology of these potential creatures, our lab created self-adjusting ionized transparent salt84-infused TiCordel (TiCordel is a clear, stronger than steel, and lighter than glass material invented by WSX engineer, Cristof Craven, nearly a century ago. This salt84-infused combination is also employed for face shields and clear elements on the Universal HAS4/LGS7 series space suits and helmets) boxes for the purpose of trapping anything that comes near it. Its internal temperature can be set to conform exactly to the surface on which it is placed. Temperatures can also be dialed in manually. That inner temperature will be maintained as long as the trap detects that something is held inside it. And since they are infused with salt-84, they can be easily carried by hand and dependent on the environment, the captor can be viewed from outside regardless of its interior temperature."

Williams asks, "Ma'am, is there any estimate on the size of the phenomena observed? Do we even know that?"

"Another good question, Williams. It is Williams, right?"

"Yes, ma'am."

Djoibjin answers, "We only have an estimate since this incident occurred in a large carted pile of siolens and the potential life form did not distinguish itself from the rest of the pile other than the motion and property change or changes. That specimen was estimated by the observers to be about a quarter meter long. No estimates on width. But like I said, the traps adjust their size according to their cargo. At full size, they can hold a creature as big as let's see…" She scrolls through documents. "Here we go, one and a half meters by one meter by one meter."

"Well, that isn't much of a fight, but at least we know we can take 'em," Rhoan whispers to Abs.

Overhearing him, Djoibjin reprimands, "Sergeant Romero, please do not let me hear about any unprovoked hostility toward these creatures, siolens, or anything in the Io atmosphere! Is that understood?"

"Aye, ma'am," he replies with an embarrassed fluctuating grin.

"But, Sergeant, if the shit spins up, do your thing," she says to boost his spirits.

"Yes, ma'am!" he replies with a big smile, a nod, and an easily recognizable expression of his own puffery without words.

Zin remarks, "Dang, I can smell his ego brewing all the way over here."

Djoibjin, who seldomly breaks with professionalism, giggles. "Yeah, it is getting a bit funky in here. Smells like burnt popcorn."

Zin laughs out loud to her own surprise.

Williams raises her hand to get the Colonel's attention.

Stifling her smile, Djoibjin asks, "Yes, Lt. Williams?"

"As Medical Officer, will I be equipped with any special equipment to detect them or medications to cure them if they become ill or seem to be losing life or any safeguards to protect us from them?"

Abs senses Becca's growing anxiety over the possible challenges facing the team, but more likely, the potential new challenges to her own role.

"I'm sorry, Williams, we just don't have enough information. We have, however, outfitted the *JohnGlenn* with a lollipop dispenser for good patients, but beyond that, you'll have to improvise," the Colonel offers half-jokingly and failing at trying not smile. Then she pretends to look through notes, "Oh my apologies. They scrapped the lollipop dispenser for a medical frost. Sorry. You'll just have to improvise."

"Thank you, ma'am," Becca nervously replies without enthusiasm or any acknowledgment of the colonel's wit.

"Improvising is what Marlagans do best, Lt. Williams. I know you have no expedition experience, but you are one of the finest Medical Officers to ever graduate our program. If anyone can improvise the hell out of this thing, I'm absolutely encouraged by the fact that Captain Abernum recommended you to replace Lt. Banthira. You will do great!"

"Thank you, ma'am, and thank you, Cap. I'm

sure we'll figure something out." Becca tenders her gratitude but appears no less apprehensive after those endorsements.

Abs knows Becca's fallen face of insufficiency, and it is becoming more and more undeniable as this briefing proceeds.

Colonel Djoibjin continues, "You're quite welcome, Lieutenant. Now. For more details on the trapping apparatus, General Arms will brief you on that along with the trap's creator tomorrow at 1030Z aboard your mission craft, which is docked in D4. He will explain every detail you need to know about that thing and any other elements of this mission that are within his purview. I don't even know the name of the contraption. That's not my area of expertise, so I have not concerned myself with such details. Let me see. Is there anything else?"

"Colonel, I have a question," Jim states.

"Yes, Captain Slight?"

"Is there any sense of the population we may encounter? Or specific precautions we should take?"

"Good question, Cap. No and no," Djiobjin snaps. "Sorry. As of this moment, you know as much as I think I know. We want you facing this mission with all pertinent information we have, and unfortunately, that is only an iota more than bupkis. All we can arm you with is what I've told you and what you will hear tomorrow. Any other questions I can try to answer?"

No one chimes in.

"Okay, Marlagans. There's one more note here that says, and I quote, 'Should they,' meaning you. 'Should they accept this mission and return with or without live specimens, the entire crew will receive an incentive of 25 percent hazardous pay increase over their current salary.'"

The Marlagans sit quietly, but uncontrolled squirms of excitement with a few gasps and irregular breathing sounds betray the indifferent front they're attempting to portray upon hearing the Colonel's last statement.

Finally Slight boasts, "That's nice, but we're not in this for the money. We're in this…FOR MARS!"

Everyone in the briefing room including Djoibjin echoes, "FOR MARS!"

She eyeballs them all and smiles, "I love it. If there's nothing else, best of luck, Marlagans. Bring back something amazing, even if it's just proof that there is no life on Io. Oh, and don't get killed. Dismissed!"

Rhoan raises his hand. "Oh wait, Colonel. I have a personal question."

"Yes, Romero?" she asks.

"Is Farheeb on duty today?"

Abs interjects, shaking his head, "Ignore him, ma'am." Then he swiftly turns his attention to Rhoan. "Romeo, you do know Farheeb is the colonel's niece, don't you?"

A squeamish "Oooo! To the nuts!" is heard from Zin above the rumble of voices in the gallery. Apparently, Abs was the only one aware of that fact.

Rhoan turns drunk red and drops his head. "Sorry, Colonel, ma'am. I mean no disrespect."

Her tone turns serious and threatening, "Young man, if I get one tiny itch in a single hair on my ass indicating you are trying to mess over my niece like you have so many of my other friends, I guarantee that you will remember the way your ass feels after I'm through with you for the rest of your life." She glares daggers through his soul.

The crew gasps are accompanied by a few expletives and exclamations as Rhoan stands mortified knowing that there are rumors of her practicing voodoo.

"Are we clear, Sergeant?"

Looking straight ahead, he mutters, "Yes, ma'am."

"Good." The colonel releases him from her terrifying voodoo death glare and turns her attention to the remainder of the crew and asks, "Are we good here?" Then she glares hard at Rhoan again.

Jim answers, "Yes, ma'am. Not sure about Romeo over there, though."

Romero answers, "Oh. Yes, ma'am. No problems here. You've been unnecessarily scary and very clear."

"Good. Rest up. Big day tomorrow."

Jim stands to dismiss as the colonel waves her credentials over the same corner sensor before she exits, but she makes a parting statement at the door. "All right, Marlagans. Please keep this information locked tight. Don't get too wild tonight while we are on the station. Lips tend to loosen under the influence. Enjoy your evening. Maybe I'll stop by and see you at pre-flight tomorrow morning."

The colonel makes her exit.

Jim notes, "I guess that says it all. Let's go."

Rhoan stands and demands, "Don't say a word! Anyone need me, I'll be working some of this out in the gym then headed to the BTR Lounge for the next rest of the night."

Zin roars, "I'm not saying a word about the eyeball beatdown you took a minute ago, but don't you get enough of that BTR weirdness at home. We're on MOS4. Take in the sights. Besides, you're gonna lose yourself in that thing one day if you keep up this pace."

"Everyone seems out to destroy me today. I may be forced to give up my dream of Farheeb being my lady tonight, but don't take this from me too."

Abs consoles, "Romeo, no one is trying to destroy you. We're trying to keep you from doing that. We care about you, man."

"Well, it sure doesn't feel like it at the moment. At every turn, somebody has given me grief today. I just want to go to the gym and work out some frustration."

Jim says, "Okay. Go ahead, Romeo. In retrospect, it has been a tough day for you. Go work it out and feel better tomorrow."

"Bye, brother! Don't die." Zin waves and blows him a kiss as she walks past him to exit the briefing room. "I love you."

Rhoan stands befuddled in the doorway as she walks away. "Die? Why wou…what? Wait!" He runs to catch up to her.

Abs turns to Becca. "Hey, Bec. You okay?"

"Sure. Why do you ask?"

Jim pardons himself. "I'll see you guys a little later. I'm going to try to catch up with Djoibjin."

After Jim leaves, Abs continues, "You seem more concerned about your role on this mission after the briefing."

"Suppose you were responsible for everyone's survival in this crazy unprecedented circumstance. Wouldn't you be worried?"

"Bec, I'm always responsible for everyone's safety

and survival in unprecedented circumstances. All of us are. That's what we do."

"Abs, I'm not sure. It's getting really real now, and this is scarier than I prepared for mentally."

Abs puts his arm over her shoulder and walks out with her. "Sis, if we all do our jobs, you just get to sit back and explore with us. If you need to spring into action, just do your best. You're the best doctor there is for this or any other team. Remember that. You're the best doctor we could ever have, especially in the unknown circumstances. You are to medicine what Rhoan is to martial arts. Remember, only the best make the Marlagans. Okay?"

"Okay. I'll do my best. Maybe it's the anticipation more than the actual journey that's getting the better of me. Then to hear the colonel lay all that heavy stuff on us. I can't help but feel a little…no a lot unqualified."

"Maybe you think I brought you on this team as a favoritism thing. That would be incredibly stupid and irresponsible of me to do that."

"What?"

"You don't think I brought you along because of our relationship, do you?"

"Well, not really."

"Bec, we could all fail miserably and die if that's the case. The Marlagans get so deep into the shit that any person who doesn't belong is more of a threat than the crap we face out there. Everything wants to kill us. Atmosphere, temperature, terrain, creatures, the unexpected anything everywhere. It's what we do. Bringing you on this team because you're like family would be like taking your child into a live battlefield.

Think about that. Now that you see firsthand the kinds of missions we tackle, think about why I would bring you on this team. Really think about it."

"Yeah. That's making sense. Besides, I am a damn good doctor."

"Hell yeah, you are!"

"I'll be okay by the morning. Can I ask another question since it's just the two of us?"

"Sure."

"Have you noticed Jim being cold and distant toward me today?"

"He's been that way with everyone today."

"Is that normal for missions? Does he always get distant with the team at the start of missions?"

"No. Not usually. Not sure what's going on with him, but everyone is entitled to a hormone day every now and again."

"Yeah. I guess that could be the case. I'm more concerned about him changing his mind about us now that he's up here with her."

"Please do not drag me into that muck."

"Who else can I talk to about this? You're all I've got."

"I really wish you two had not done what you're doing. It's such a knife's edge for all of us."

"It will only be a little while longer until he finishes out this Union term, then we can be official."

"Bec, I just don't want to see you hurt. And this one could be really bad."

"I know. I know. Don't worry. I'm a big girl now."

"Okay. Where are you headed?"

"I think I'm going to change up and join Romero in

the gym. Maybe he can teach me a thing or two. Care to join us?"

"No thank you. I need rest."

"I'll be headed to bed after the workout, so I'll see you in the morning."

"Have a good night, Bec. Don't hurt yourself trying to keep up with Rhoan."

"Aye, sir. And, Abs."

"Yes."

"Thanks for…well, everything."

"Of course, sis."

He kisses her on the forehead, and they head in differing directions.

* * * * *

Abs Diary Entry 72D:

Mom, Dad,

Our orbital launch was a wonderfully uneventful success. Given the recent failed launches, it was a great relief that we did not encounter any issues whatsoever. We docked on MOS4 a couple hours ago. We just found out that our mission has changed to a highly classified one. Needless to say, no more detailed information about the mission can go on these personal pages. If you were here on the station, I'm pretty sure I'd know by now. But deep down, I'm still hoping this mission brings us where you are, and we can be on this adventure together. Silly pipe dream, I know, but how amazing would that be? The only thing that kills that dream for me is that they haven't restricted our access to the outside world, at least not yet. Jim, Rhoan, Zin, and Becca send their regards. There are a few unnatural feelings I have about this mission. First, is that we will only be a five-person team this time. First time ever. It's also going to be weird going on our first Marlagans mission without Hassan and Li. Just being on MOS4 without Hassan is painful, but no one is really expressing their emotions yet. When we stopped by to see Li a couple days before we launched, not even then did we allow ourselves to tackle the subject of Hassan in detail, but I expect all of our hurt to come out at some point during this mission. Who knows? This could be a unified effort to move on and focus on the future. Could be that it is still too hard for us to discuss out loud together. The latter seems most likely. Gotta scoot. Loving you.

# Chapter 5

## Dawn

R EVEILLE SOUNDS throughout the quarters.

Abs muscles his stubborn sleep-filled eyes open at 0630Z as the station-wide alarm sounds and notices the familiar decorative overhead mirror installed at his request. That and the figure he sees next to him in that mirror's reflection remind him that he is not waking in his home on Mars nor is he in his station quarters. He gently lifts his head and begins to move around gingerly in hopes of not waking up Djoibjin, whose head is resting on his shoulder. Fortunately, she splurged for the aerated cooling mattress which allows them to sleep so closely without sweating, but his shoulder and right arm are both bloodlessly dead from the weight of her head resting on him all night. He attempts to gently slide his arm free without waking her. He fails. Her eyes spring to life, and she lifts her head to free his arm, then comes to rest on his pillow facing him.

Gently resting his head back down on his pillow to

face her closely, he looks at her and moves a curl of hair out of her eyes. "Hey, sweetheart. Good morning. Go back to sleep. Reveille just sounded. I'm going to grab a quick shower."

In her sexy gravelly morning voice and mild Togolese accent, she replies, "Okay. Wait. You need any help with that?"

He growls, "Rowr! You even wake up super sexy. I would love some help with that, but if I'm late, who will I blame? I can't pin it on you just yet. Besides, that lava motion may have broken your boy toy last night."

He sits up.

She smiles. "Ha. Lava motion. That was awesome." She reaches for his cheek. "You know you're not a boy toy to me. Why would you say that? You're far more than that to me."

"Am I really now?" He leans back to give her a passionate kiss.

"You absolutely are."

"You sure that's not that Valentines fever talking?"

"Absolutely sure."

"Hmm." He smooches her and says, "Get your rest, Kimmie. You have a big day today. I'll come by your office and say goodbye before I leave."

"That had better be the least you try to do before leaving on the only days I've see you in so long."

"If I wasn't so sore, we could have another farewell/pre-Valentine's Day celebration like we did last night."

"Don't feel bad. I'm quite tender myself."

Abs leers at her seductively and suggests, "But another round of farewells like last night would be well worth walking wide-legged and sore the whole mission."

"Ha! Hit the showers, lover man. You have a very important morning yourself and need to be on time."

He throws his head back and mumbles, "Buzzkill."

"I heard that. I tell you what. Sometime today, I will to try and stop by to bid your whole crew a safe journey prior to departure anyway. If we can sneak away for a private farewell, let's do it."

"Yes! That'll work. I might find it hard to keep my hands to myself in front of everyone, though."

"You'll figure it out. You had better. We've been keeping us under wraps so well this long, you'll behave."

"It's not as easy as I make it seem, madam. When you're in your uniform sometimes, I'm instantly teleported to Shaboingin, Idaho."

"Why are you such a silly person?"

"Who's sillier, Kimmie? The silly person or the one sneaking around with the silly person? Think about that."

She smiles and shakes her head. "Ridiculously silly. Go take your shower."

"Aye, ma'am."

They smile and kiss.

"Did I ever tell you that I love it when you call me Kimmie?"

She never told him that Kimmie is what her mother called her as a child before an untimely accident took her from her family just days before her twelfth birthday.

"Do you now? Then you can expect me to do it more often. And I'll call you Kimmie while I do it too."

She laughs and hits him with his pillow as he sits at the edge of the bed twisted to face her.

He laughs and asks, "Since you're up, would you like me to make you anything for breakfast?"

"So sweet. Just leave me some coffee, Tiger."

"Aye-aye, ma'am." He kisses her again and heads toward the shower.

* * * * *

Upon hearing reveille, Captain Slight reaches for his personal alarm before realizing that the sound isn't coming from his alarm but the overhead speakers. "Damn. I thought I turned down the station alarm."

His union mate of nineteen years, Captain Marsha Slight, says, "You did. I turned it back up to make sure you got up on time."

"Marsh, these are our only nights together for the past three months. Why would you interrupt our love and tranquility by making me get up early?"

"For one, we were asleep. That's not loving tranquility. That's you snoring for the whole station to enjoy. And two, it's not early, it's on time. Big day, remember?"

"Any time I'm sleeping next to you is loving tranquility to me."

"Yeah, I know. Me too. But you have been talking constantly about how important this mission is. You don't want to set a bad example for your newest Marlagan, do you? You're always teaching people to be the exampl—"

He interrupts, "I know. I know. You're right. See, this is why I'm nothing without you. I really have missed you far more than I had realized."

They kiss with overflowing passion, and eventually,

they each open their eyes to soak in this moment through deep longing gazes that will never be enough to fulfill either of their longings for one another.

Jim dotes, "I love you so much, Marsha Slight."

"And I, you, James Slight," she reciprocates.

"I wish this could last forever. Even if it did, I don't think I could ever get enough of you."

"Oh, James. What's gotten into you?"

"What do you mean?"

"It's like you're worried about something."

"I guess I've just missed you so much, and it didn't really hit me until I saw you."

She offers, "This distance has obviously done something to you this time. I'm not complaining. I love it."

"I love you."

"I love you too, James. Now get a wiggle on."

"You're the boss, Marsh."

"Don't ever forget you said that. I'll make some breakfast. Sausage or bacon."

"C'mon, baby, you know I don't like to make choices like that…both. It hasn't been that long, has it?"

"Haha. Just checking to make sure you're not an imposter. I'm really excited that you get to stay here for a week after the mission. Feels like it's been over a year since I left home."

"Yeah. The months we've been apart have been long and lonely without you. Good thing we were able to convince General Arms to advance our mission. Now we get to spend time together on MOS4 during your rotation up here. We should go station hopping when I get back."

"That would be lovely if I can pare down this workload I have. It's been very busy here, but that hasn't stopped me from missing you. Enough stalling now, Captain. Get a move on. Your destiny awaits."

"Marsha. Marsha. Marsha."

"Git now."

"One more thing."

"Stop stalling."

"I'm not. This is serious. I have something to tell you."

"Yes, James?"

"I'm thinking of making this my last excursion."

"What are you talking about? No, you're not!"

"I really am."

"Why? You love these missions!"

"I do. But I think it would be better for us all if I stayed put for a while to spend more time with you and Drena."

"Honey, Drena is practically grown and away at school. As nice as it would be for us to spend more time together, I don't want you to give up something you love doing so much with people you love doing it with. Besides, what would the Marlagans be without you? They wouldn't be Marlagans anymore. Abs might even change the name to something ridiculous like the Fabs."

"Not funny, but it's working. Hmph," he grunts. "Let's pick this conversation up over breakfast."

"Okay."

They kiss and part.

In the NCO quarters, Rhoan and Zin wake up in their own spaces.

Rhoan heads to the gym after grabbing a supplement shake and a gallon of water from the frost.

Zin calls for Gnat, her tiny AI bot pet she fashioned from a micro-drone. Gnat flies from the kitchen into the bedroom, "Good morning, Gnat. What's on my agenda today?"

"Meet Jamie for breakfast. Meet crew at DB4 at 0800Z. Departure briefing. Fly to the moon. See Elf after successful launch."

"Thank you, Gnat. Keep me company."

Gnat follows Zin into the bathroom. "Gnat, play my wake-up music."

Gnat lands on the counter near the sink and plays music.

"Thank you, Gnat."

The music pauses. "You're welcome, Zin." The music resumes for only thirty seconds before Gnat alerts her, "You are being contacted by Shanee Wilson."

"Answer."

"Hi, Shanee. Thank you so much for dinner last night. How are you this morning?"

"I'm well. Thanks. Last night was so great. I love talking tech like that."

"You have no idea how refreshing that was for me. My crew for the most part is very uninterested until it effects them or something goes wrong. It was so nice just talking to someone who likes talking engineering."

"You are so good at what you do. If they don't appreciate your skills, that's a real shame. I'm always excited to hear about work on your level."

"Thanks, Shanee. It feels better to hear that than you can imagine."

"Well, it's true. What are you doing for breakfast?"

"Nothing really. Supposed to have breakfast with a person who might not show up. I'm finishing a shower now, but I have a little over an hour before I'm scheduled to be at a briefing."

"Oh. I guess you have plans then."

"Who, Jamie? She usually has more excuses than appearances. I absolutely have time for breakfast if that's what you're asking."

"Great! I can be at your place in five minutes. Let's grab a bite."

"Sounds great. I'll be ready in ten but will set the door to open for you in five minutes."

"Perfect. See you then."

Williams wakes up alone in her bachelorette pad in the officers' quarters. She sits up in the temporary bed perusing the dimly lit, mostly empty room suffering from loneliness, uncertainty with an air of melancholy. She will eventually learn that her mood lingers into the entirety of the day.

Becca wraps herself in her blanket and slowly tootles her way to the shower, humming her favorite crying love song, which she tends to do when trudging through her brand of depression.

After her shower, she practices her occasionally successful practice of smiling in the mirror repeatedly for five minutes to lift her mood. It does help slightly when she laughs at how stupid she feels. Then she continues preparing for what she feels could be the most important day of her young life, but dreading that the mood she finds herself in right now may not soon go away.

Meanwhile, back in Djoibjin's quarters, Abs has

completely packed and prepared for today's journey. He has even remembered to leave Kimmie a perfectly brewed cup of coffee just the way she likes it. Now that it's time for her to get up and for him to leave, he quietly enters the bedroom to gently wake her with kisses, but finds she is already climbing out of bed.

"Hey, you."

"Abs. Good. You're still here. You were so quiet, I thought you had gone already."

"I wanted you to sleep, so I did my ninja thing." Then as he looks at her, he is overcome and quickly closes in on her. "Wow. I really, really am happy to be with you, Kimmie." He plants a surprisingly deep kiss that lasts much longer than either of them anticipated.

She catches her breath. "Oh. Abs."

"I'm a little sad we won't be together in person on Wednesday for Valentines. I just hope we are able to BTR most of the day."

"You'll still be in transit, so you should have lots of time. I'm more concerned about my schedule. But if nothing else, I'll be yours all that night."

"Sounds wonderful enough."

"Good." She kisses him.

He tries to shake himself back into normalcy. "Well, guess I'll see you in a little bit." He can't stop himself from gawking at her with utter desire and adoration.

She becomes emotional. "Why do I miss you already?"

"Uh oh. Sounds like someone's catching a feeling. Better be careful. There's only one cure for that."

Oh yeah. What's that?"

"Marriage. It's clinically proven to cure all signs of

feelings for one another. That's probably why it's mostly outlawed."

"Ha. Ha. You may have just stumbled onto another cure."

"Which is?"

"Terrible jokes like that. Don't you have something to do today?"

"You're right. I have to grab a bite too. I'd better get going, but that will just make your love bug worse."

She shakes her head, kisses him, and pushes him toward the door. "Go! Go now! So I can miss you."

They enter the foyer together where most of his hand-carry gear is already packed near the door. He steals a look at her door monitor to check for nosy crew members, kisses her again, and departs.

She cheers, "Go make history, Tiger."

About forty minutes later, Abs arrives at the entrance of Docking Bay 4 at 0752Z to find most of the Marlagans assembled.

"Good morning, everyone. You're all nice and early. Anyone seen Jim yet?"

Rhoan remarks, "Don't worry about Jim, playboy. Where were you this morning?"

"What? What do you mean?"

Rhoan replies, "I rang and banged on your door and tried to pyk you this morning. You didn't answer anything."

"Pyk" refers to a line of personal intelligent devices created by PYK Universal Intelligence, Inc., which creates and produces the latest technology in HAID devices (Holographic Artificial Intelligence Dark Matter Devices and Communicators)—operating on dark matter and ZiP crystal technologies. These devices have hundreds of years of self-recharging battery life and unlimited range of communication through the Matternet (dark matter-powered extranet, which is 3×103,000 times faster and more powerful than the Internet of the twenty-second century) throughout the universe as proven by the exploration launch of SDSP2 in 2392. The Matternet has the ability to give each user their own personal internet (personNet), which is un-hackable unless a person you've granted access to any portion of your personNet betrays your trust, in which case, you would know right away who the culprit is. Most pyks are wearables, worn on the wrist, as part of clothing, tucked away visors or eyewear, while others opt for integration into preferred body parts, and still others are crafted into furniture, such as tables, seating, beds, walls, etc. The very few cyborgs like Fernando often have their pyks integrated into their brain circuitry, which is the route Fernando has chosen. Since he's a brilliant programmer and engineer, he keeps the software in his eye ahead of the latest trends and limits of commercial technology.

Abs wears a goofy expression. "What? What door?"

"You know what door, C310."

"What time?"

"Around seven."

"Oh, I met a friend for breakfast this morning and silenced my pyk. I turned it on and saw you pyked me, but since I was on my way here, I just figured I'd see you now."

"What friend? We are your only friends."

"Haha. Very funny. Just about everyone up here is a friend in one way or another. Mind your business!"

Flashing Abs a super grit and nodding sarcastically, Rhoan replies, "Oh. Okay. I see how it is, Mr. Popularity. Keep your secrets. For now. You know I'll find out. I always find out."

With a revealing burst of laughter, Abs says, "What about you? Are you feeling better today? I know yesterday was rough for you."

Just ahead of the appointed time, Jim joins the group looking refreshed and giddy. He grunts and cheerfully greets, "Hey, crew. Looks like everyone is here. We ready to do this?"

Rhoan grunts back. "Um hm. Yes, sir."

Zin and Rhoan laugh.

Jim turns to Zin. "How are you doing today?"

"I'm great and super excited to see Elf today. It's been a rough couple weeks without him."

"That would be such a weird answer from anyone else, but it's totally understandable coming from you."

With an ice-cold and slightly angry continence, Becca glares at Jim with death rays and snarks, "Good morning, Captain. How is the lovely Mrs. Slight?"

Jim, who has noticeably been trying to avoid making eye contact with her this morning, looks at her with incredulity and a little frustration while trying to seem as if nothing is out of sorts. "Fantastic! She's great. Thank you for asking."

"Hm. That's fantastic," Becca mumbles under her breath as she releases him from her sharp gaze. Looking down and away, she folds her arms.

Though he tries to gloss over her pained disposition,

Jim conspicuously shifts uncomfortably in his skin as he hopes someone else will break the tension.

The rest of the team notices the awkward exchange as their eyes wander to and fro in bewilderment while shrugging to indicate that no one is up to speed on this situation but not interested in probing further.

After that instant of tension, Abs brings everyone back to mission. "The general should be ready for us about now. Let's head on…"

Jim's relief is palpable as his respiratory system reengages.

* * * * *

Abs Diary Entry 74A:

Hola, Madre, Padre,

Waking up to another day of seeing Kimmie is as special as anyone could ever hope. I know we are supposed to live with our parents until we Unite, but seeing her has really given me thoughts that I may not be living with you two forever. I'm not saying anything happened. No one proposed to anyone else or anything like that, but this is truly the closest I've ever felt that a Union could actually be in my future. How can a person be so perfect for me? She allows me to be silly. Everyone knows I have the worst jokes and am not funny in the least, but she lets me be me and even pretends to laugh sometimes. It's as if I've won a prize of some sort. On the flip side, Jim seems to have totally destroyed Becca's hopes of them being together forever. Since yesterday, he's been awkwardly distant and cold toward her. Almost like he flipped a switch and is hurting my sis. I'm conflicted on whether to break his face before the mission to get them back on track or keep him away from her, or if I should let them work through it, or if I should convince Becca to get over him now and treat him as if he doesn't exist and she feels nothing for him. I wish you were here so we could talk it out. But for now, I think I'll just keep my face out of it and let this be their problem until grows beyond the borders of those two. Here I go, minding my business. Thanks for your wisdom even in your absence. Love you both. Adios.

# Chapter 6

## General

ALMOST ON perfect cue, Abs spots Farheeb's beautifully wild, dark, and fluffy mane in the distance dancing toward them alongside the general.

"Well, speaking of General Arms. Rhoan, shut your hole and stay focused."

Rhoan, who was facing Abs, turns to look where Abs's eyes are fixed. He jerks in surprise, then quickly gathers himself, hand pressing his clothes and mussing about with his hair.

"Oh mercy! Showtime! C'mon, Abs," he attempts to whisper.

"Lock it up, Romeo. General on deck!" Jim orders, standing at attention.

The Marlagans snap crisply to attention.

"At ease, Marlagans," General Arms directs. "Captain Slight, I've asked you before not to do that."

Jim laughs. "I know, General. I just do it to watch

my team act disciplined for a change. Sorry, that's the last time I'll use you for that purpose."

The General nods with a smirk and shakes Jim's hand. "Captain, we are proud to send you off on this new adventure. I know you all are familiar with our top wizard of everything, Cam Farheeb. Her team created the new technology you will be using on this mission."

In her beautiful strong Egyptian accent from her parents, who arrived on Mars when she was a child, Farheeb greets, "It is a pleasure to see you all again."

She shoots a bright smile at Abs as she comes to a halt.

Abs returns the pleasantry.

Rhoan takes note of the silent exchange.

"Shall we?" the general asks, signaling the direction of the docking bay.

"Hi, Farheeb," Rhoan lets out a high-pitched slur accompanied by a dumb-founded expression of goo-goo.

"Hello, Sergeant Romero," Cam responds with regimented seriousness.

Abs bumps Rhoan in the chest with his shoulder as he walks over to give Cam a kiss on the cheek. "Hey, Cam, it's great to see you. Proud of your work on this, but you've always been brilliant. I'm not at all surprised that you were the one they pegged for this."

Though all of her speech therapy throughout her life has successfully corrected most of Cam's speech impediments, she still pronounces most "th" sounds with "d" sounds. Most find it adorable and endearing, making her genius less intimidating.

"It's really good to see you too, Abs. Dank you. But you know you could have figured dis out much sooner dan my team." Then she addresses the entire Marlagans team, "It brings me happiness to know dat dis team is de first to try my new devices. It would have been hard to trust any udder team to give us an honest and true assessment as much as we trust de Marlagans to do it. We are expecting a substantial list of critiques and suggestions for improvements from you at de end of dis mission."

Arms interrupts with sarcasm, "Aww. Now, isn't that the schweetest t'ing? Let's get to it! Time's short, folks!"

Slight agrees, "Of course, sir."

Abs walks over to Rhoan as the team enters DB4. "Watching you. I will mess you up then tell the colonel so she can mess you up too."

"C'mon, Abs. I just said hi. It's not my fault if I'm the only polite person on this team who is willing to greet our dear and oh so incredibly beautiful engineer," Rhoan snickers.

Abs pushes Rhoan in the door ahead of himself.

As they approach the vehicle, unusually regimented guards salute, the general and crew reply in kind.

Zin asks, "General, can you tell me what that bulge is in the hull there? That's new, isn't it?"

Arms replies, "Caught that, did you, Staff Sergeant?"

"Of course. If there is a speck out of place on my ship, I'll notice."

"This is a new ship for you."

"I've already studied everything I need to know about every ship in our fleet, including the *JohnGlenn*, and that bulge was not there before."

Arms grins. "I love that preparedness! Gets me right here," Arm says, holding his fist to his chest.

Slight gloats, "Only the best make the Marlagans, sir!"

"I see. That's still a stupid name, though. Sounds like a school of fish," Arms quips. "You'll learn more about that bulge inside, Staff Sergeant."

Zin replies, "Thank you, sir."

As they enter the craft, the general asks the security detail for the comm channel in case they need to reach him.

"Sir, Channel 3 is your designated channel this morning,"

"Thank you, Sergeant. Channel 3 comm check." Arms checks his pyk to ensure the frequency is correct.

After hearing his voice echo on the guards' pyks, he orders, "We are not to be disturbed. If there's an absolute emergency, then call me on channel 3 before approaching this craft. Understood?"

"Sir, yes, sir!" They both acknowledge.

The general closes the inner hatch to the airlock, which doubles as a sonic decontamination chamber, enters the garage area, and turns to the crew, all of whom have formed an arc facing him and Farheeb. Most are standing at parade rest.

Arms starts, "Okay, let's cut the formality for the time we're in here. I hardly understand any of this stuff, so I'm just going to spurt out my piece, then you can take it from there, Cam."

The crew and Farheeb nod and murmur.

"Good. You guys are going to be capturing live siolens."

"We call them Hollows right now," Romero offers.

"What? What are you—"

"Please continue, sir. The sergeant is having an off day."

Arms admonishes, "Get it together, Sarge. Short on time, here."

"Yes, sir."

"Now if I may."

"Of course, sir. My apologies."

"Yesterday, Colonel Djoibjin probably already told you more than I know about this matter, so a lot of what I have to say may be repetition. Blasted! Months ago, no one even had the slightest inkling Io could possibly host living creatures. Personally, I still don't think there's anything to these reports, but here we are. You could possibly make history, but I think we just simply found the perfect material, and haters gonna hate. Harvesting this substance has been our planet's greatest trading leverage with our solsys counterparts. And since learning that there could possibly be living creatures involved, which I sure hope is all a huge misunderstanding or scandalous plot, well, that has potential to impact our harvesting methods, which could impact our production, which could impact our shipments to Earth and Luna, which could impact WSX Earth's income stream, which could impact our funding support from WSX Earth, and we definitely don't want them talking about defunding any of our programs. They're all too important if humanity is to survive as a species."

They all stand in silence as the general continues.

"Anyway, if these things are alive, when you return, no one standing in my presence right now is permitted to utter a single word of it to a single soul in any single situation. Not your mother on Mother's Day, not your brother on Mars Day, not even your pillow. It may be bugged. The only exception is the scif debrief upon your return. At the debrief, you will be given specific circumstances and orders where discussing this find is approved and appropriate. These orders will be updated periodically. But for now, just save us all a heap of trouble and just don't! Understand!"

The team replies, "Yes, sir!"

"Okay, Mechanic, you asked about the new device in the hull. I'll let Cam handle that. If you have no more questions for me, I have a meeting," the general declares, looking like he wants to be anywhere but in this particular ship at this particular time.

When no one proffers an inquiry, Arms quickly states, "Good luck, team. Make us proud. FOR MARS!"

"FOR MARS!" they repeat in unison.

The general opens the hatch and exits so quickly, no one has time to ask a question, salute, or say goodbye. Abs closes the hatch behind Arms.

Becca says, "Did anyone find it strange that he did not even mention the amazing possibility that we may be on the precipice of discovering a new life form on a moon of Jupiter, where none thought life could thrive. How is he not excited about that prospect?"

Abs sarcastically answers, "Calm down, Senator Leandra (Senator Davonna Leandra was a naturalist who fought for legislation to outlaw hunting of any kind since it was not necessary to feed the increasing population. The bill eventually failed by a slim margin, but it did pave the way for more common-sense hunting laws and preservation of dying habitats). I did notice it, but we know Arms is more concerned about his career and the success of WSX Mars than almost anything else."

Slight agrees, "Yes, but Lieutenant Williams is right. He did seem strangely unfazed by the notion of life on Io, but then he has probably had time to process that possibility already."

Becca tries to insert her view, "Yeah. Maybe. Bu—"

Abs continues, "Don't worry, Becca. If we bring back life, the implications that come with that discovery will be bigger than the general. There will be nothing he nor anyone else can do to keep it quiet for long if that's what you're worried about."

"I suppose you're right."

Zin rings in, "Farheeb, you're awfully quiet today. Are you okay?"

Cam finally speaks, "Dare's so much going on. Sometimes I just get lost in dought. Since standing here, I've dought of tree improvements I wish I had time to make on de Cam Traps."

Abs smirks at her. "Cam Traps? Really? You named it the Cam Trap?"

"Haha. No. Not really. Dat would be silly to have my name on my own invention. Why would I do dat?"

Zin asks, "So what are they called?"

Cam blushes and burst in laughter. "Cam Traps! But dat is just until de WSX actually comes up wid an official name."

They all laugh.

She guides them toward the cargo area where ten traps are stacked neatly against the hull. Zin notices a small digital device above them intruding on the hull's smooth shape, which is creating the bulge she saw on the exterior.

"Dese are my babies," Cam points to the ten traps. "De exterior surface of de traps are whatever de ambient temperature is to de touch. De interior temperature has de ability to match de air temperatures of any planet, moon, or star or you can dial in a manual temperature wid dis device." She points to the small digital device built on the bulkhead.

She continues, "Day can maintain any temperature for up to tree months. Day detect de outer atmosphere troo dese sensors and use its energy accordingly" She points to tiny nubs on the bottom of the trap. "Full features are operated remotely. Even dough battery life is tree hundred years, I added basic manual operations just in case."

She opens the trap. Rhoan takes a step back, expecting a brutal temperature change from the interior of the trap.

Cam laughs at his cautionary reaction. "Don't worry. It's just matching de current air temperature right now. You need dis remote to adjust temperatures manually."

She pulls the remote device from a housing unit built into the hull that Zin noticed earlier.

"We integrated a housing system in de hull, so de remotes and traps won't be easily lost by misplacing dem elsewhere inside de craft, so please always return dem here when not in use. All equipment here is prototypical and priceless. And patent still pending."

Zin says to the crew with satisfaction, "I knew that protuberance in the hull wasn't part of this ship's natural design."

Rhoan answers sarcastically, "We know, sis. Good job." He physically pats her on the back.

Cam goes on, "It operates like so. Do not stand directly in front of de trap when you press dis button." She gestures for them to clear the space in front of the trap.

The crew hustles to stand beside Cam.

Cam hits the button and there's an audible *bwoosh*! Then silence and an incredible arctic blast fills a small but growing area of the vessel. She depresses the button again to turn it off.

Rhoan remarks, "Yup! That's ridiculously cold! And fast!"

Abs adds, "My goodness! That's crazy!"

"It is, but look inside it now."

They all look and gasp as they observe it looks exactly as it did before she turned it on and is back to the room's temperature even though the air still holds magnificent chill.

Zin asks, "How on Mars did you do that?"

Cam smiles. "Like I said, patent pending. As you will see in de field, dese are designed to mimic de surface upon which it sits as well. Arm a trap on the surface, and it camouflages right in. Day are capable of matching de heat of active volcanoes and hotter. I believe it's possible for dem to reach temperatures hotter dan our sun. Hasn't been tested yet, but de mad looks good. So you will set dem in strategic locations manually or remotely, hit dis button to arm it, and de trap will do de rest. You'll know it has captured a specimen when it is closed and dis green light illuminates on de physical trap or on de remote right here. Den just carry it by dis handle or call it to de remote with de homing feature. It's pretty simple. Any questions?"

Abs asks, "Do they not have intelligence to place themselves?"

"Future models will. Dare wasn't time for dis batch, so day need to be set in place manually, but like I said, day can home in on de remotes."

Slight says, "After saying 'it's pretty simple,' I'd feel like an idiot asking my question."

Cam, embarrassed, replies, "Oh. I'm sorry. I didn't mean it like dat."

Slight pretends to walk off and throws his hands up. "Too late. Damage is done. No questions."

They laugh.

Cam whines, "Ohhh. I'm sooo sorry. Please ask any questions."

Zin asks, "Does the battery life of the remote match the traps?"

"No, de traps are ZiP Crystal–powered like most of your equipment. No batteries. No dark energy. Just crystals, so unlimited power, tree-hundred-year battery life. De remote, however, uses a rechargeable pin battery for now because of time constraints. A fresh charge, which dese have, should last about tree months. De housing unit has built-in charging for longer missions, but de patent is for ZiP Crystals."

Zin gives a satisfying "Wow! That's amazing, Cam."

"Dank you, friend. Dat means a lot coming from a fellow engineer. I'm really proud of my team. Any questions before we begin handling my babies?" Cam scans the crew for inquiries. So does everyone else.

"Okay. If dare are no questions, dat's all I have to

present. Since your flight is in a few hours, let's take a quick few minutes getting familiar with de equipment so you can get to your other pressing matters."

They spend about ten minutes using the traps and realize the genius of their design and ease of use.

Cam finishes up, "You guys are quick studies."

"No, Cam. They're just very well designed and easy to use."

"Dat's what we always shoot for."

Zin cheers, "Bull's-eye!"

"You're de best. I love spending time wid dis team. You get me."

Abs admits, "You get us and our needs. Wish we could make you our personal lab tech."

"You're so sweet. Wish I could stay and soak up more love a while longer, but sadly, I'm already past my allotted time wid you. General Arms was not unclear about my time restriction here. It was really good seeing you again." She bows and begins to walk away.

Rhoan responds, "Terrific job, Farheeb! Stellar work! It was incredible seeing you too. How do we get in touch with you, you know, if we have problems with the Cam Traps?"

She turns, walking backward, and unable to disguise her suspicion. "Danks. De captains know how to reach me. Just have one of dem contact me if something comes up."

Rhoan replies sheepishly, "No problem. Okay. Thank you. Nice seeing you." He bows.

Abs informs the crew, "I'll be back, guys. Just escorting Cam out." He quickly walks to catch up to her.

Abs says to her in a moderate whisper, "Cam, you

should be really proud of yourself. I know I am. This is an incredible creation especially with such a rushed deadline."

She turns to him and whispers, "Diving into dis project actually helped me get troo de past few monts. A wonderfully productive distraction."

He wraps her in a warm embrace as he would his own daughter for what only seemed a few seconds, trying to transmit all of the comfort he could from his being into hers.

He notices she begins sobbing softly and strokes her hair.

With her head wrapped in his chest, she wipes her tears and whimpers, "I really wish you could stay here longer dan just today."

"I promise we will hang out when I get back."

"We'd better. Hopefully, I'll feel better den. Today's just been one of doze days."

"I'm sorry, Cam. I promise it's going to be fine soon. And don't worry if you still need support when we get back. That's what I'm here for."

"Danks, Abs. You're de best uncle friend a girl could have."

"Remember, he doesn't deserve you. He never did. And he's not worthy of your grief and pain, but I know all of that is easy to say."

She slowly and reluctantly pulls from his embrace. Wiping her face, she stands up tall and chuckles. "Yeah. Much harder to feel 'dat' way when I feel 'dis' way."

Abs looks into her eyes. "Cam, you're an amazing person. Look what you did here, and there's so much more inside your big head."

"What? No, you didn't just call me a big head," she laughs.

"Ha! Yeah, I did. At least I got a giggle out of you."

Cam does appear slightly cheered up by his jest. She looks up at Abs and says, "True. Danks, Abs. You had better get ready for your trip."

"Are you okay?"

"I will be. I wish I could tell you about my latest project. But you know…"

"I do know. I bet that one is amazing too."

"It truly is. Cam Traps are nudding compared to dat one," she says with an excitement that seems to improve her mood.

"Love you, Cam. Let's do dinner when we return."

"At de very least! You'd better remember dis time. You still owe me a game of EVR Ball."

"I ain't scared of you. It's on! But you know that missed dinner was Kimmie's fault last time."

The rest of the crew join them in the entryway.

"I know. Love you too, Abs. Come back safely. Dat goes for all of you."

Rhoan pipes, "What? You love all of us?"

She laughs, "Good one. Come back safely and bring us back some-ding amazing even if it's just proof dat dare is no life on Io."

They all bid farewells as she exits the craft.

Abs turns to Rhoan. "Hey, Romes. You deserve credit for keeping it casual and light with Cam. I think I detected a little growth there."

"You did hear Djoibjin's unnecessarily uncouth threat, right?"

"I did indeed."

"I don't see any need to continue this course of conversation then."

"Like I said, growth."

Jim says, "Well. I'm gonna take off too. Our next thing is at 1600 at Pre-Flight. See you all in there."

"Where are you headed?" asks Becca sharply before she realizes words came from her mouth.

Jim mumbles to himself, "This is going to be a long mission." Then he grunts a reply, "Uh. I have a few things to wrap up before the fight. I'll see you there."

The rest of the crew turns to Becca to see her reaction. Only Abs is fully aware that she and Captain Slight have been having a secret affair, but her recent slips of the tongue and her behavior this morning may have tipped off the other crew members.

Abs puts his right arm around her. "Come on, Bec, let's grab a quick snack, a quick pack, and get on back. Jack."

Zin rolls her head to Abs and says with exhaustion, "Ugh! Please don't make this another rhyming mission!"

He throws his left arm up and replies, "What? You love my rhyming."

Rhoan barks as he passes, "No one loves your rhyming, Abs!"

A giggling Becca looks up at him and says, "I don't know what they're talking about. I thought it was cute."

"Cute? And with that, my rhyming career is over. I've got a better idea. Since Becca is here, we can do some Olde English for you."

"What do you mean by that?"

"For fun, sometimes Becca and I speak Olde English. Ever since the first time she read Shakespeare, its period vernacular has fascinated her, so we have been having Shakespearean-like conversations since she was a kid."

Zin gives a look of befuddlement. "What?"

"Yond wouldst beest most wondrous!" Becca exclaims with excitement.

"It wouldst beest excit'ment, wouldst not it?"

"Oh stinking goody," Zin snarks.

Abs laughs at how annoyed Zin is.

"What's wrong, Zintia?"

"If you're going to torture me with your annoying artistic side, at least do a period we can understand."

"We're open-minded. Give us a challenge."

"Most of our streams begin in the twentieth century. Do twentieth century slang. I get that century if you insist on putting us through your creative crap again."

Abs replies, "Done. We'll put you through some twentieth century creative crap, and you know the twentieth century was the best century in my opinion." Then he turns to Becca. "What chu got on that, homie?"

"Totally tubular, dude!" She laughs and continues, "That is one of the few valley phrases I remember from the twentieth vids, but I'll give it my best."

"Two of you, huh?" Zin sighs. "This is going to be so fun."

Abs cheers, "Up top, bruv!" He and Becca guffaw while high-fiving,

Zin walks away, shaking her head. "Goodbye. See you in Pre-Flight."

Abs yells back, "Groovy! Three's company. Want us to join you?"

"Not even a little bit!"

"See you at the nine-to-five then!"

Zin plays along, "Good grief, Charlie Brown. Later, dudes!"

"That's the ticket, Zin!" He chuckles and shifts his attention. "C'mon, Bec. Let's grab a bite before we pack."

"Sorry, Abs. I have a lot to do before the flight. I'll see you at Pre-Flight too."

Slightly dejected, Abs says, "Okay. You're figuring all this out, aren't you?"

"Thanks to your preparations over the years."

"Good. Good. Well, get to it then. We don't want to be late."

When Becca is out of earshot, Abs turns to Rhoan, "Looks like it's me and you, buddy."

Rhoan jokes, "After watching you get shot down by those two, I am not gonna be seen with their reject."

"Dang. That actually had a bit of sting to it, Romes."

"What? You've been whipping up on me this whole trip so far, and that hurt you."

"Whipping on you? What are you talking about?"

"How can you ask that? You've been riding me since I said hi to Doctor Wilson on the *Nigeria*. Giving me crap about Cam. Just making me feel like I'm some sort of head case all day."

"Rho, I'm just trying to keep you from messing over so many undeserving victims."

"Victims? I'm blessing these ladies out here, and you're blocking their blessings."

"I wish I could be the ghost of Christmas present right now."

"You're talking about the ancient movie of somebody's wonderful life?"

"No. *The Christmas Carol* with the three ghosts."

"I'm not sure…Oh the past, present and future thing?"

"Yes. I'd show you how your blessings are really impacting the lives of those poor women. You're leaving a wake of emotional trauma that not only hurts them, but it affects how people perceive you too, and none of it is good. Hopefully, you will see that sooner rather than later. I've just been trying to help you get there."

"Bull. You're just riding me to ride me. I'm like your little twerp brother, and you get off on giving me a hard time at every turn. Honestly, Abs, I'm getting tired of it."

"I'm glad this is out, Rhoan. We should talk more about this over a snack before we pack."

"I've got a lot to pack too. Maybe we'll pick this up never again. See you, Abs."

"Okay. But I'm just trying to help you."

"Don't. See you later."

"All right then. See you at Pre-Flight."

Abs is left standing and feeling all alone on the station of hundreds. He considers sneaking over to see Kimmie, but he knows she is in a big meeting. So he grabs a snack and goes to his room to pick up his already packed gear.

* * * * *

Abs Diary Entry 74B:

Hello, people from which I come.

Still on MOS4. Just got our first look aboard the *JohnGlenn*. It's nice but it isn't the *Neil*. It was cool, though, to see Cam and get a briefing from your favorite lab tech. She is just so sweet. She's still struggling to get over that douche who dumped her by video. How sorry do you have to be to post a video to dump a girl you've dated for almost a year? I don't know if that makes him a coward or just a waste of space. No humanity in that, and all of the station saw that at the same time she did. The great thing is how the entire station has rallied around her and have shunned him to the point where he is rarely seen outside of his workspace or his unit. I have yet to see him since we've arrived. Most people say they haven't seen him since the day the video was posted and he was confronted by an angry mob in the Docking Bay. Not sure if he worked today or not, but Cam walked into that Docking Bay like she owned the place. Everyone spoke to her as we went into the vessel, and she didn't seem afraid to leave on her own either. That girl is fierce even in her pain. Her inventions are second to none too, as you already know. Guess I'd better get to PiF. We are so close to departure time that I feel like I won't get to see Kimmie again to say goodbye. That makes me really sad. She has such a busy day, I doubt we'll have time. Speaking of not having time…gotta scoot. Fare thee well.

# Chapter 7

## PiF

A FTER THEIR break, Abs passes through the decontamination hall leading to Pre-Flight (PiF) at 1018Z to find Becca is the lone crew member to arrive before him and is already partially dressed for the flight.

"Wow, Bec! You got an early start."

She replies in a trembling moan, "Hey, Abs. Well, I got nothing else to do, might as well beat the rush."

Karen, a wise and respected forty-eight-year-old Pre-Flight engineer, observes, "Uh-oh. I know trouble in paradise when I hear it."

Abs lends Becca a wordless eye of compassion as he begins to greet the Pre-Flight team, "Hey, Karen. How've you been?"

He gives her a kiss on the cheek. This is one of the few areas on or orbiting Mars where physical touch is common. Since there is so much physical contact involved in dressing the crews, the entire area is constantly sterilized through ventilation and automated means.

Karen smiles, kissing him back, and answers, "I'm good, darling. How have you been? Some rumors going on around here about you."

"What?"

"Yeah, that's old news now. I anticipate a fresh one will soon find me regarding the li'l lieutenant over there."

"Karen, I'm surprised that you even entertain the notion of 'rumorisms,'" he says with air quotes and a smirk.

"Baby, I don't start 'em, but somehow, they always seem to find me. It's like we're some sort of hub or something. Every flight goes through here, and a lot of people have a lot on their minds, and we listen. So, baby, we're just here to serve…" she pauses, "the information… to the people."

Abs chuckles as he greets the next Pre-Flight engineer, "Come on, Karen. You're better than that. Hey, Michele. Don't tell me you partake in such things too."

He greets her with a kiss too.

Michele replies, "Don't fool yourself. Karen is not above 'rumorisms,' and somehow, those same rumors that find her make their way to me too. I'm not quite sure how the physics of all that works in orbit, but it works."

Abs laughs. "The physics? Really? It actually seems pretty simple to me. My guess is a small station plus farting humans equals ten to the twentieth rumors. Can't really expect much to stay hidden here. Hopefully, rumors can at least stay true and secret information can remain classified."

They both laugh. Karen says, "Not likely! But if hidden ones do exist, we just don't know about those yet! Haha!"

"Hey, Michael!" Abs greets the third Pre-Flight Team member with a loud hand grab and half hug. "How do you put up with those two all day?"

"I drink on duty."

Everyone bursts into laughter, including Becca.

Abs walks over to Becca, who is being attended by Pearl Kim. "You gonna be okay?"

"Of course. Why wouldn't I be?" she says with a forced smile and obviously clutching a welled tear.

He kisses her on the cheek also and rubs her upper back just above her flight suit, which is slumped and gathered just above her waist.

"Hey, PK. You seem really focused," Abs observes as he reaches to kiss her on the cheek but decides it would be less distracting to her work if he simply pats her on shoulder. So he pats her on her right shoulder.

She nods but never speaks or releases her eyes from the tedious netting and stitch work to fit the suit perfectly which has her full attention. If she misses one loop, she'd have to undo it all and start over, and at the moment, she is three quarters of the way to completing the most arduous part of fitting during pre-flight. Fortunately, this custom fitting procedure only has to be done to fit the suits to the crews. At the end of the flight, they simply remove the suits, leave them in their cabins, and the suits are returned to PiF through the Post-Flight (PuF) team.

Karen informs, "This is your spot today, dear," pointing to the Abernum nameplate above his pre-flight position. "Let's get a move on before—"

Just then, the remaining Marlagans enter the room about two minutes before 1030Z.

Karen comically interrupts herself, "Disregard my last. Here comes the rush."

Jim gleefully announces as they walk in, "Hey, PiF! Time to party!"

Rhoan echoes, "That's right! Marlagans have arrived! Please hold your applause!"

Karen snarks under her breath, "Hmph. That will not be a problem."

Michael is the first to greet the incoming crew. "Welcome, Marlagans. Now sit your asses down. Camel (a longtime nickname Michael gave Rhoan because he says he wants to ride him all day and night through the desert, for some reason), my love, bring that hard body over here to me."

Zin urges seductively, "Go get yourself some Michael time, Romeo. You know you want some." While teasing, she pushes him toward Michael's station.

After the force of Zin's pushes subsides, Rhoan meekly scurries over to Michael's station with his head lowered and without a word. Rhoan and Michael have an ongoing amusing game of Sexy Cat Chase Daunted Mouse—one of the few times Mr. Martial Arts (Rhoan) allows himself to reveal his timid side. Michael is always making passes at Rhoan, fully aware that he is heterosexual. But they both enjoy the fun of the game... as do the rest of their units.

Michael says as Rhoan approaches, "Camel, I saw you kicking all that ass yesterday. Quite impressive."

Michele asks, "Oh yeah. What happened?"

"Camel here took down twelve dudes at one time, and they weren't scrawny scrubs either. These were serious fighters."

"He did? You did?"

Michael continues, "Yeah. You should have seen my man. Kicking ass all over that arena. It was incredible!"

"Wow. Good for you, Sergeant Romero."

Michael contemplates aloud, "Yes. Now we have to figure out how to put that skill to the best possible use in our dungeon."

Confused and slightly frightened, Rhoan chirps, "What in the world?"

Rhoan attempts to stand. Michael presses him back into the seat.

Michele yells to the rest of the Pre-Flight team, who are readying themselves in the back room, "Let's go, Pre-Flight! The whole crew is here! SSgt Romero, you're with me."

Gerard enters the fitting room from the supply warehouse with gear in his arms. "Good day, Marlagans. Captain Slight, I'll be your butler today, sir. We're right here."

He points to the station as he reaches it. His station happens to be right next to Pearl Kim's station, which is where Becca has been assigned.

Abs looks on with a touch of concern as Jim settles in, hoping there will be no more inappropriate exchanges between Jim and Becca. His apprehension eases as he realizes Becca intends to ignore Jim. It seems she even refuses to look in Jim's direction. Considering the rumor mill in which they are being fitted, his concern-o-meter is on high alert.

Rhoan quickly grabs everyone's attention when he shouts, "Ow, Michael, not so rough!"

"Michael? Michael?" Michael gets louder with the second call of his own name.

"Please don't make me say that."

"I'm waiting."

"Sheikh Michael. Sorry," Rhoan whimpers.

Michael quips, "That's better, Camel. And you weren't complaining about the roughness last night because, baby, we all know you like it rough."

Rhoan jokes, "Can I get a new concierge, please?"

Karen answers, "You surely don't want to come over here. It'll be much more painful and then I will probably put you in stasis."

Most laugh at the banter between the two. Slight and Williams seem so wrapped up in their own tension that they don't appear to notice the other exploits of the room nor are they amused by much of anything right now. The rest of the crew immediately know why Karen threatens stasis. Karen's daughter, Nikki, was one of a string of hearts Rhoan has broken with his sexual over-indulgences. But Rhoan hardly remembers her from three years ago until Karen reminds him before every trip since then, with the exception of the past two missions when Karen was vacationing on the surface.

Surprised, Rhoan asks, "They figured out the stasis problem?"

Karen says bluntly, "No." She never breaks stride or looks up while working on Fernando's pack.

"Oh, that's cold, Karen. I thought we were cool."

"Stasis is the only way you would be cool with me."

Rhoan adds, "I'd also be dead."

"More than likely," she says as she pauses the pack fitting to look up with narrow eyes and glare at Rhoan.

Immediately upon seeing Karen's face, he remembers Nikki. "Oh. OH! I'm just going to stay here with Sheikh Michael and shut my mouth now."

Karen gives the Southern American female response, "MM HMM. Not even a sorry from your sorry ass." Then she removes her hand from her hip and resumes fitting Fernando's equipment.

"Karen, I'm sorry," Rhoan offers.

Don't try selling your sorry to me, son. Nikki is the one you hurt. You hurt my baby. Treated her like some rollercoaster just for your amusement. I could give two toilet turds in a swirl about your sorry," Karen verbally jabs and uppercuts.

"You're right. I'll talk to her when we get back."

"Don't bother. She is finally over it. To be honest, I get that the planet down there doesn't contain millions of young females, but that doesn't mean you have to destroy the few there are," Karen admonishes.

"Yes, ma'am," Rhoan mutters in an attempt to end the conversation with no serious intention of changing anything.

"Stop being such a childish selfish boy. Figure out what a man is and be that!"

Rhoan sinks into the chair a bit more. "Yes, ma'am."

Michael leans down and gets close to Rhoan's face, "Sit up, Camel! It sounds like I may need to take you in the back and give you a well-deserved camel spanking."

There are a few hesitant chuckles, but more attention is focused on Karen's reaction to see if she is willing to permit a less dense atmosphere.

She is. She smiles. "Take him in the back, Sheikh

Michael. I'll cover for you. Show him what a real man can do."

Laughter and chatter permeate the space again. Abs hopes to himself that since this needed exchange between those two has finally taken place, there will be no more uncomfortable moments during the remainder of today's pre-flight.

PK has been a quiet observer to this point, but now that she is finished the netting, she asks in her strong Taiwanese accent, "Jim, Bongo and I wish to have dinner with you and Marsha upon your return from this mission. Bongo has some new dish he's been wanting to make for you since the last time we dined together."

Abs, realizing his hopes of a less uncomfortable prep session were just destroyed by PK's invitation, thinks, *Why?*Jim steals a fleeting glance at Becca, who is seated directly in front of PK and looking away from him, as his gaze makes its way to Pearl Kim and acknowledges, "That would be great. You guys can arrange that while I'm gone. Tell Bongo I look very forward to it with much excitement. How is his band doing?"

PK responds, "They're still gigging regularly. He's happy, but I hardly see him on gig weeks. Just in the mornings before work. I'm just happy they aren't more successful. I don't think I'd ever see him if they made it big."

Karen commands, "Be very still, Captain. This is the very delicate part."

Abs apologizes, "Sorry."

The entrance to Pre-Flight opens. A large secured AC7 (autonomous flatbed cart) labeled Classified enters Pre-Flight. The entire facility has been built with a network of magnetic smart rails for autonomously moving large objects and baggage. Swiftly in tow are General Arms, Cam Farheeb, and Colonel Djoibjin. Fernando notices an animated excitement in Cam's air. Big improvement over yesterday.

General Arms commands, "At ease, everyone. Are we at a good breaking point here to take the room? We need to speak with the Marlagans about a sensitive matter, so we need to commandeer your room for a moment, but only if it's a good stopping point. We wouldn't want to cause any misfittings now."

Karen, who notices Arms's excited nervousness, replies, "Good morning to you too, General Arms."

"Oh. Did I forget again, Karen?"

"You did."

"Apologies. A lot to do today."

"All the more reason to be cordial."

"You're right again, Karen. My mother raised me better than that. Good morning, everyone. May we please have the room for a few minutes? We need to speak with the Marlagans about an urgent confidential matter."

"Good morning to you as well, General Arms. Just one quick moment while I finish this portion of his suit and then the room is all yours."

Karen works to wrap up the last remaining strands of netting for Abernum.

The general nods and wears an expression that seems like slight embarrassment or maybe a slightly drinking blush. Either way, he does not look very comfortable as all the other Pre-Flight team members acknowledge that they at a good stopping point to leave their stations. One by one, they begin to peel away back into the warehouse.

Captain Slight starts to stand but finds that he is unable to make it to his feet. Gerard forces him back to his seat, pressing down on both shoulders. "Standby, Captain. Let me get that for you. You're still secured to the apparatus."

"Oh. Thank you."

Gerard frees Jim and heads through the Secure Door, where every other Pre-Flight crew member besides Karen has exited the room.

A couple minutes later, Karen announces, "You're good to go, Cap. General, the room is yours. Just let me join my team."

Arms bows as she exits.

When the room is secure and white, Arms begins as Cam remotely unlocks the classified AC7. "Our genius of all things here has cracked a critical code just in the past hour. She was able to outfit your helmets with prototype siolens detectors that will allow you each to clearly see the material highlighted regardless of the surrounding atmosphere. Your Harvesters have been upgraded with this feature and are being loaded onto your vessel as we speak. The primary purpose of this upgrade is to make siolens harvesting much more efficient, but for you, the most important advantage to this function is the ability to more easily detect any siolens movement and alarm the wearer of such movement even if the wearer is not looking in that particular direction. It's another amazing achievement from our lab techs."

Everyone turns their attention to Cam as she extracts a helmet from its case and starts the demonstration. "As you can see if you look closely, dare is a halo of needle cameras feeding information to your heads up display. De seamless integration is what took de extra time to code. Here, Captain Slight, dis is your helmet. Place it on your head if you would."

Jim obliges and, with the helmet on, looks around the room and says, "I don't see anything unusual. Should I notice a difference?"

Cam smiles. "Not just yet."

"Okay."

Then she reaches into a separate compartment in the container and pulls out a small receptacle of raw siolens.

While he's still scanning the room, the helmet directs him to look toward Cam. When he looks in her direction, the immediate sight of neon blue veiny product in her hand startles him. "Whoa! Now I see something different. Is that bright blue stuff the siolens?"

Cam boasts, "Raw siolens. Notice how it stands out. If you look at dis helmet…" She lifts up a standard helmet from the table. "Notice de shield, which is comprised of processed siolens and salt84, does not illuminate. It only illuminates raw siolens. Dat was anudder challenge in itself, but my team finally cracked it."

"It definitely does pop out at you but not in a distracting way. That's so wild," Jim observes excitedly. "How'd you do that?"

Cam explains, "Again, patent pending. We chose de bluish color because dare is nudding else on Io remotely close to its color. Even surrounded by all de wild and vivid colors on Io, dat blue should stand out enough to make a huge difference in harvesting efforts."

"This is amazing," Jim says as he continues to explore

the room and the raw siolens with the new helmet. "Well done, Cam. Let me guess. These are Cam-mets?"

Cam smirks. "Giggle. Giggle. No."

Abs looks at her and tilts his head. "What are they called, Cam?"

"Helmets. All-dough, Cam-mets does have a sweet ring to it. You know, since we have so much new camera technologies incorporated into de design."

Abs chuckles, "I see what you did there."

General Arms notes, "Okay, crew. These mining helmets are classification Bravo. They will be on your craft in secure bins. You will wear your standard flight helmets until manual flight is complete. Upon mission completion at Io, these helmets go back in those secure bins before the return flight, not to be viewed by or mentioned to anyone else outside of this room until mission debrief instructions. Is that understood?"

"Yes, sir!" they say in unison.

"Good. Good luck and bring us back some good data. FOR MARS!"

"FOR MARS!" the entire room echoes him.

Farheeb retrieves the helmet from Slight and repacks the AC7.

Arms, who's been patiently waiting by the exit for Cam to secure all of the classified equipment, gives Djoibjin clearance to dirty the room. She waves her credentials over the security sensor.

Once all of her equipment is properly secured in the classified crate, Cam bids the crew a safe flight, "Well, Marlagans. I'm conflicted about dis mission as always. I hate to see you leaving but am happy dat it is you who are on such a mission. Be safe, do what you do and come back so we can celebrate and party togedder."

Everyone, including Rhoan, receives a farewell hug from Cam. Soon after their farewell exchanges, Arms bows to the crew without any further words, and Cam and Arms exit with the AC7 leading the way.

Djoibjin walks over to a seated Abernum, bends down, and whispers in his ear for nearly a minute with her hand resting on his left quadricep. The Marlagans look on with intense curiosity and watch her with mouths agape as she catwalk struts to the exit.

Abs, who remained silent throughout the entire exchange, speaks up to break the agog silence filling the room, "Don't ask. Don't say shit."

Rhoan unable to comply, "Cap! The hell? She was definitely inside the safe zone. You holding out on us?"

"What?"

"Something is definitely happening there."

Abs, without replying or looking at anyone, walks over to the secure door to bring back the Pre-Flight team. "We're all done with the classified briefing. Welcome back."

Karen enters, saying, "Being kicked out of my own kingdom is not on my top ten list of favorite things."

They resume pre-flight preparations.

* * * * *

Abs Diary Entry 74C:

Pre-Flight was something else. More than ever, I wonder if bringing Becca to our team was a good or bad thing. She's extremely capable, but trying to help her and Jim manage their big secret is becoming harder and more annoying by the day. On MOS4, there is no getting away from the Slight Union, and it is taking its toll on poor Becca. I did the best I could to prepare her for this eventuality, but the reality seems to be more than she can handle. This mission has been very fluid. We received more top secret info during PiF, and new super-secret gear was added to our mission just a short while ago. I'm starting to lose hope that we will be joining your team unless we are bringing you new intel and equipment. That's the only spark of hope left for seeing you out there. Karen was a riot with Romeo. With her and Michael hitting him from different angles, he looked pretty hopeless. Even Zin joined in the bantering. It's actually been a tough day for poor Romes. He felt overwhelmed after Kimmie stomped on his shorts about Cam. On top of that, he really didn't appreciate my helpful advice to calm down on his wild styles earlier. He has been quite upset with me today. I hope I'm wrong, but if this keeps up, I fear he may be on the verge of a smaller version of the breakdown he had a couple years ago. Fortunately, the gym and BTR help him release a lot of his tension and should work to keep him healthy and avoid something like that from happening again. Short talk. Gotta go. Don't forget I love you both.

# Chapter 8

# Launch

THE PRE-FLIGHT team escorts the fully geared squad of Marlagans to the entrance of DB4, handing them off to the Pre-Launch team. The PiL escorts lead them to the entrance of their ship.

Along the way, Abs whispers to Rhoan near the back of the formation, "Rho, you okay?"

Seeming oblivious, he replies, "What about?"

"Karen leaned into you pretty hard."

"Abs, I'm sure you enjoyed that."

"No, I didn't. I actually felt bad for you."

Rhoan smiles. "I guess you wouldn't understand this life. That's part of the game. Mamas gonna mama. I'm surprised to see that you even care about that."

"Of course I care. And you're right. That isn't my life, so I don't understand getting threatened like that regularly. Just glad you are okay with it."

"Pfsh. Every day is a journey, Abs. Just gotta live it."

"If you say so."

Upon reaching the *JohnGlenn*, Jim greets the leader of the Pre-Launch team, "Hey, Mike! You got us today, huh?"

"Greetings, Cap! I requested to be your PiL Lead today. Hey, Zin," he says, turning to Zintia with the most goo-goo expression ever seen.

"I wonder why," Abs chuckles as he eyes them both.

"Hey, Mike," Zin responds sweetly. "How is the family?"

The rest of the Marlagans continue to interact with the rest of the PiL since Zin seems to be engaging in a lengthy discussion with Mike.

"They're fine," Mike answers. "You know our Union is almost up, right?"

On Mars, Luna, and most societies on Earth and its orbit, marriage has been replaced by United Mating since the divorce rate had reached nearly 95 percent of all marriages by the end of the twenty-second century. In response to the divorce rate, marriages have declined so sharply, leading to an entirely new societal epidemic of no family structure. By 2307, only 3 percent of the adult population was married causing insurance, inheritance, medical, and a number of rights issues and litigations. In an effort to protect the sanctity of family, the UCA (United Continent of Afrika) introduced the legislation of United Mating in which couples commit to one another for a two-, three-, five- or ten-year term. This new family structure permits couples to enjoy all the benefits and rights of marriage with the exception of divorce. In United Mating, which is a legally binding agreement, separation is possible, but divorce and adultery are illegal and punishable by law. At the end of the Union Term, couples can decide to extend for another term as many times as they wish with all legally binding obligations intact. If one or both decide to end the Union, it ends at the end of the term with the only fanfare being child custody, child visitations, and property settlements agreements, which are often decided before or during the Union in advance of the term's end. Beyond that, they just walk away with no further commitments to one another. One's relationship status on your PIC (Personal Information Chip) just changes to "Available for Union" from "United with (Partner's Name)." There is no hiding your Union since one's PIC is easily accessed via anyone's pyk devices.

Zin replies, "Yes. You keep me posted on your status every time I see you. Now that you have a baby, surely you're going to extend with Thakkura."

"Yeah. That's the thing. She actually has eyes for a coworker of hers, so she is considering coparenting while she unites with this old man at her job."

"Ooh. That's gotta suck a little," Zin sympathizes.

"It's not so bad. I'll get to spend precious time with my little girl and spend time getting to know you better if you don't mind."

"I do not." She smiles while twirling the low curl in her hair with her helmet in her other hand and swaying side to side. "You only have about a month left in your Union, right?"

"Actually it's three weeks, which is right around the time you return from this mission," he answers as they gaze into one another's eyes.

"Sounds like someone has been spying on me."

"Only because it matters to me...a lot."

"That is cause for celebration when we get back if I've ever heard one."

Slight yells from the craft's door, "Staff Sergeant, we'd hate for this little mission of ours get in the way of your major, important, universe-altering humanitarian conversation! But get in here! It's time to go!"

"Oh sorry. Coming, Cap!" Zin pops out of their euphoric moment.

Jim continues, "You too, Mike! Let's get a move on!"

Mike shouts in response, "Yes, sir!"

They both laugh as they run through the decontaminating airlock and into the spacecraft.

Inside the spacecraft, they find the PiL and Marlagans hard at work on pre-launch duties. Mike notices Cam near a couple massive secure cases labeled "CLASSIFIED" on the bulkhead near the storage room. Though it's irregular, he knows better than to question her about it. Even still, he can't help but wonder why Farheeb is inside the ship near secret equipment during pre-launch.

Rhoan, unable to help himself, yells to Farheeb as he is being escorted up to the Control Room by Gingy, "Hey, Cam, do you have dinner plans in three weeks when we return? It would be nice to celebrate all of your success and ours with you after this mission."

Cam pretends not to hear him.

Abs shakes and drops his head as Rhoan passes.

Cam sports a sour smile but silently continues inspecting the classified cases, ensuring the system is properly functioning.

Becca turns to Abs as they enter the lift. "The lighting here is very elegant and so smart. I noticed it last time we were here, but now that I see it again and with more people aboard, it's even more impressive."

Abs asks, "What do you mean?"

"I've noticed how it almost spotlights people and a small area around them as they move to save energy."

"Oh yeah. All vessels do that. We have to save as much energy as possible for propulsion systems, computing systems, and everything else we do aboard this thing. Some missions have lasted as long as five years with a massive crew, so energy efficiency is a major engineering consideration in the designs of our fleet."

She looks around in awe. "Wow. The things we don't know until we know."

Abs nods. "Indeed."

Up in the Control Room, Gingy, who is a good friend of Ylinen's, seats and straps in the sergeant. She then whispers in Rhoan's ear before she puts on his helmet, "I hear there's a special toy in the armory just for you."

Rhoan, who knows Gingy is off limits, remains professional. He turns to her and smiles. "Yeah?"

"That's what I hear."

"Thank you, m'lady!"

Zin enters the Control Room and asks, "Thanks for what?"

"Oh. Nothing. I was thanking Gingy for taking such good care of me."

"O-okay," Zin says pleasantly surprised and half suspicious since Rhoan is not usually the type to give personal thanks unless it's very necessary."

Zin inquires, "I didn't see Elf on the way up here. Does anyone know how Elf is doing?"

Mike, who is strapping her in, confesses, "He's fine. I've taken extra special care of him for you."

Beaming, Zin manages to whisper a throaty thank you.

Their eyes stay on one another for an extended second until an interruption.

"*JohnGlenn*, MOS4 Command, radio check" comes over the speaker system.

Jim, who's now in the Control Room, responds, "MOS4, *JohnGlenn*, loud and clear, how about me?"

The speakers reply, "Loud and clear. How about channel 2?"

Jim repeats as he is being strapped in, "Loud and clear, and me?"

"Loud and clear, channel 3 radio check."

Jim says, "Channel 3 is loud and clear, how about me?"

"Loud and clear, *JohnGlenn*. Standby for panel and alarm checks."

"Roger," Jim replies. "Abs, you're up."

Abs, who is being escorted by Cam, Becca, and their PiL members, Gracie and Kennedy, replies, "Yep, got it!"

As the PiL nears completion and the team and begins to exit, Zin is surprised when Mike sneaks up behind her, touches her shoulder, and plants a good luck kiss on the side of her helmet before making his exit.

Abs notices, but the rest of the team seems too busy to see it. He just continues his pre-launch work.

Cam follows suit by giving Abs a hug and a good luck kiss on the side of his helmet. Rhoan notices their farewell, and his mouth and eyes compete to open the widest.

As Cam leaves, she says, "Good luck, Marlagans! I sincerely hope you don't find any-ding out of de ordinary. But if you do, I'm happy it is you out dare."

Jim answers, "We are right there with you, Cam."

After she is gone, Rhoan can't help but ask, "What is the deal with you, Cam, and the colonel? What the hell is going on there?"

Abs simply says, "Don't you have work to do."

"Seriously, Abs. Is this a three-way thing?"

"Kill it, Romeo! Right now!"

"Jackpot. So exactly how—"

Mike pokes his head in before locking the hatch. "Have a great mission and come back safely, Marlagans!"

"Thanks, Mike!"

"Take care, Mike!"

"See you soon, Mike!"

"I look forward to it."

Mike locks the hatch. Now that the cabin is sealed, the Marlagans loosen their lips.

Rhoan starts, "I'll get back to you, Abs. You and Mike, huh, Zin?"

Zin responds, blushing, "Maybe. Doubt it. Who knows?"

"Mike's not a bad guy, sis. Nice pick."

"It seems being without Elf for so long is making me susceptible to all kinds of squishy emotions like a stupid human."

"Either way, I'm just happy to see you so brightened up the way you were around him. I haven't seen you like that in a while. And he's a good dude," Rhoan remarks.

Abs adds, "Right on. That's groovy. Happy for you, Zin."

Zin is so far in the clouds, she doesn't even notice Abs trying to irritate her with his twentieth century jargon.

Rhoan takes one final jab, "Speaking of squishy, he is kinda doughy, so don't break him."

Zin notices that and tries to punch him in the shoulder, but her restraints keep him safe this time.

Jim grunts and orders, "All right. Let's refocus, Marlagans."

Abs grunts mockingly, "We're three in the green, Grunt!"

Slight shoots Abs a rare glare of annoyance at the teasing before announcing to MOS4 Command, "Ready to resume countdown on your mark, Command."

Command quips, "Ready for your vacation so soon, Cap. Aw. And we thought you liked us. Now I'm sad."

Slight responds, "Ha. Yeah, the warm relaxing sandy beaches of Io await."

Rhoan shouts, "Hold up. They put my peanut butter crackers in my stash, right?"

Abs, knowing he can't reach him, pretends to swipe at him. "Man, shut your hole. I thought something was wrong."

"This trip would be all wrong without my PBCs."

Zin chimes in, "Just be silent until we get there, Romes."

"Abs would you like to say a couple short words before we take off?" Jim asks.

"Sure. Let's pray together. Lord, Creator of this amazing Universe, thank you for being our great protector. Keep us steady and true. Guide our paths and corrections. Help us be better for Your glory. Our lives are in Your hands. And it's in Your name that we pray. Amen."

A chorus of amens echo in the Control Room.

Becca, who has been pretty silent in the launch vehicle, asks, "Wait. Is everyone on the crew religious?"

Rhoan answers, "No. We just feel safer when he prays for us. Since he is a believer, we all are safe by default. Trust me, we have survived things that we should not have. So I personally believe his prayers somehow keep us safe. That's really all the captain is good for." He erupts in laughter.

Abs just shakes his head.

Becca continues, "So then why don't you consider yourself a believer? I don't understand."

"Okay, *JohnGlenn*, we will resume the countdown at two minutes on my mark…Mark!"

Rhoan whispers, "A conversation for another time."

"Mark. Resuming countdown at two minutes, Command," Slight replies over comms.

Suddenly chatty, Becca asks, "Will I always be this nervous before every launch or does it get better?"

Rhoan answers, "The first is the worst. After that, it becomes a rush."

Abs adds, "It does depend on the pilot, though. Jim's the best there is, so there are no worries."

Becca nods nervously and repeatedly. "Well, I'm glad to hear that. I don't want to feel like this every time we launch on a mission. If this doesn't calm down, I may earn a nickname with the word puke in it."

"Bag's on your right," Zin advises. "Been there, girl."

Becca, looking around, says, "Got it. Thanks. This may not be pretty."

"Yeah, we know that from experience. It sure wasn't pretty getting up here to the station, so we have some experience with your version of un-pretty."

"Hush-a-bye now, Abs."

Zin begs, "Don't start the jargon yet, guys. Please."

Abs chuckles and ignores Zin's request. "Don't fret, Bec. It's mostly butterflies the first time. Once we beat feet out of here, it'll be the bees' knees."

Zin rolls her eyes and growls.

The speakers announce, "*JohnGlenn*, twenty seconds to launch!"

Jim replies, "Green across, Command. See you when we return."

"Have a successful mission, Marlagans," MOS4 Command answers.

Jim calls to the crew, "All right, Marlagans, grip your grips and lock your lips. Here we go!"

"Two. One. LAUNCH of *JohnGlenn* on a mission to harvest siolens on the Jupiter moon, Io."

Inside the craft, the crew experiences five g's of silent thrust on takeoff, which mercifully ease after sixty-five seconds when the artificial environment systems can safely engage to give the sense of normal gravity and atmospheric behavior, although the spacecraft is under constant acceleration. Fifteen minutes after launch, the flight suits have done their job and the crew is free to move about the ship.

Abs leans over. "That was far out. Right, Bec?"

"You bet your sweet bippie. It was fun. Easier than the hop to orbit."

Rhoan removes his helmet, unstraps, and stands up while announcing, "I'm going to see what special toys they left us in the armory and then get some beauty sleep."

Zin rebuts, removing her helmet, "No, you're not. You're going to Olympia again, aren't you?"

"Sleep. BTR. Apples to apples here," he says, alternating each hand's height as if balancing a scale while his eyes move from hand to hand.

Zin pleads, "Just please be careful with that stuff, Rhoan. I recently heard about some kid who died in Olympia."

"Stop lying."

"It's true," Abs confirms. "He actually died of thirst and starvation because he lost track of time and was in there for five days nonstop."

"Of course, I know about that case. That was just some dumb kid—"

Abs interrupts, reading from his pyk, "Yeah, it says here, he was eighteen years old and was logged in for one hundred eighty-one hours when they discovered his body. That's the fifth Mars BTR casualty this year. I didn't realize you could lose the sensation of hunger or thirst when connected."

"Amateurs. All of them. Just set alarms. I've got it covered," Rhoan boasts as he heads through the portal and closes the hatch behind him.

Jim says, "Well, I'd better be settling in myself. Gotta take over in a few hours. You okay for now, Abs?"

Abs, who has duty flight, says, "Yes, sir. We're good to go up here. Enjoy your rest."

Becca stands and asks, "Captain Slight, may I have a moment?"

Jim looks at Abs, then at Becca. "Uh. Sure. Come on back. See ya, Abs."

"Aye, aye, Cap!" he replies, wondering if the Romero sibs will become further clued about their secret feelings for one another.

Zin unlatches excitedly and uses a husky voice imitating Liam Neeson to join in the artistic conversational game, "All right, Abs. I'm going to use my special set of skills to go release my best friend from bondage, take a look at the grub in our kitchen, and get some shut-eye. Need anything before I retreat, dah-ling?" She ends with a Zsa Zsa Gabor impersonation.

"Thanks, Zin. That was really good except the first part was twenty-first century. That was still awesome, though. A for effort."

"Geez. I give you gold, and you nitpick. Guess this crowd just doesn't deserve true talent."

He chuckles. "Now that was spot on! Well done."

"Thank you. Thank you. Do you need anything?"

"Nah. I'm good. Got my snacks, my water, my pyk, my puzzles. I'm good. Thanks."

"Roger that, Cap! Hey, I just want to say thanks for bringing me on this team," Zin humbly acknowledges.

"You've earned it. You're a perfect fit and prove yourself every mission. We'd be a much less effective unit without your onesies, Zin. Couldn't ask for a better mech tech." He smiles at her.

"Thanks, Abs. Even though it's been years, there are still times I can't believe my life." She smiles, pats his shoulder, and heads for the door.

"You're putting on your onesie now, aren't you?" He turns to ask Zin.

"You know this, man!" She laughs. "Now that has to be twentieth century."

"Haha! Nailed it."

"Thought so. And there's nothing better for space travel than a onesie and my Elf. It makes me feel like Santa in my happy place for some reason." Zin heads out the door.

"I'll have to take your word for it." Abs smiles before the door shuts. He turns back to the console, turns up the music in his headset, nibbles on a carrot, and settles in for hours of solo flight.

As Zin passes Captain Slight's quarters, she grows curious about the conversation between Jim and Becca and wonders if it's ongoing.

Inside Jim's quarters, he invites her to sit down.

"I prefer to stand for now. Thank you." She stands about two paces from the door.

He opens, "Why are we having a private conversation during the mission? We agreed no private conversations on mission."

"I know we did, but this can't wait."

"What can't wait? What's this about?"

"Jim, I need to ask if you still love her."

Jim swings his head in frustration. "Oh, come on, Becca."

She states her case for bringing it up, "You seemed so childishly giddy this morning when I saw you, and you have been so distant with me. I just want to tell you if you love her, be with her."

"I thought you wanted to…never mind."

"Wanted to what? I know you're not thinking what I think you're thinking."

"Doesn't matter. Becca, this is not the time for a conversation like this. What if someone hears us? We don't have privacy on missions. We discussed that. Let's talk about this when we get back to Mars."

"I can't live through a whole month of wondering about this. This is my life. My future. It's a simple yes or no, and I'll be on my way."

"It's not just yes or no. It's more complicated than that," he says, backing away from her and dropping onto his bed as if weakened by the weight of the topic.

"That is not the answer you gave last week. It was a solid no last week. What's different?"

She pauses to catch a glimpse of him with his head hung sitting on the edge of his bed and demands, "Why can't you look at me?"

He looks up. "Becca. I…I…" he stammers but never completes the thought.

"You what?"

"What do you want me to say?"

Feeling hurt by his lame response, she replies, "Just give me the truth, Jim. That's all I'm asking right now."

"I feel caught off-guard. I'm not sure what you want me to say here."

Broken by his weak response, she painfully concludes, "I've been a fool. A fool for getting involved with you. A fool for allowing myself to believe. I should have known better."

"No, you're not. Stop this."

Jim tries to reach for her hand, but she stands motionless and with her arms crossed.

"You've just been using me this whole time," she cries.

"No, Becca." He stands up and lifts her head to look into her eyes. "I love you."

She snaps back quickly, "Don't touch me. You can't love us both. I'm not going to prison for someone who just wants to keep me as freezer meat."

He takes a step closer to her. "C'mon, Becca, I really do love you."

She takes a step back closer to the door and reminds him sharply, "You did not answer the question, Jim."

"Not now, Becca. We just had a great day, a great launch, and everything is going so well. Let's not do drama right now."

"Oh. My pain is just drama to you now."

"No I didn't mean—"

"And by the way, Captain, I did not have a lovely day today! My day has been filled with speculation, nausea, heartache, headaches, cramps, and a wandering mind that just wants you to answer one simple question, so I can know how to move on with my life. By the way, that nauseated feeling I had a little while ago before launch really had very little to do with the launch itself."

"Okay, Becca. Listen. We have another year in our Union. I have to do what I have to just to make it through to that finish line."

"So you're saying you have to love her, and I'm just what you have to do to make it through the last year?"

"No. No. No. That is not what I'm saying at all."

"Then what are you saying, Jim? Because the question can easily be answered with a simple yes or no."

Jim notices her lacrimal wells beginning to overflow. "Becca." He reaches for and touches her hand.

She turns to pulls her hand away. "I said don't touch me."

"Please, Becca. Don't do this now."

She becomes disappointed in herself when she feels herself sniff. "Jim, how could you do this to me? I thought you really cared about me."

"I swear to you that I really do."

"Why can't you see that not answering my simple question is the answer that contradicts what you just said and everything I thought about us?"

Tears she'd been forcing back begin to stream down her cheeks.

"Becca," he whines with his head tilted and sadness painted all over his face.

Her pain becomes audible sniffs and whimpers as she sobs quietly, holding her face in her hands. "I've been such a fool. How could I have been such a fool?"

"Come on, Becca. Please." He looks on helplessly and with compassion inviting her to come closer or reach some sort of truce.

She wrestles mightily with her raging desire to just swallow her dignity, forgive him, and leap into his arms as he pleads for her to believe in him, believe in them again.

Sensing her hesitation, he tries to coax her closer to a softer disposition, "Becca, I really do care a great deal for you. Please know that."

She battles the insistent urge to betray herself and swallows the temptation.

"Don't say another word to me if you can't simply say no to that question or at least be a man and say yes, you love her," she cries while still covering her face as her sobbing becomes more pronounced.

Jim looks on with growing despair and ache but does not give her what she so desperately desires, a simple yes or no answer.

She turns away and motions for the door.

He stops her and says, "Becca, I have no choice."

Unable to control her rage at his weak response and in disbelief that she had the urge to go back to him just seconds ago, she whips around and barks, "You had a got-damn choice, Jim! You had so many fucking choices! Don't give me that shit! You could have left me out of your Union issues. You could have told me you still loved her and gave me that choice to make. You could have told me you were just lonely without her. You had a billion choices, Jim. Choices that would not hurt me or her so badly. Instead, you chose selfishness and disregard for my feelings, Marsha's feelings, and even Drena's feelings. Hell, you could have just said yes a few seconds ago, but it was your choice not to say anything, you fucking coward!"

"But, Becca."

"Screw you, Jim! The way I am feeling right now," she snuffles, "don't be surprised if I turn myself into the authorities the minute we get back."

"Why would you do that? Just to hurt me. You wouldn't just be hurting me."

Still standing with her back on the door facing a droopy Jim, her tone softens slightly but wears a heavy hint of snark, "You're right. I'm not a thoughtless and slimy weasel like you, Jim. I even care about Marsha and your own kid more than you care about any of us."

"Okay. Listen, Becca. This is not easy for me either, you know. We have renewed our Union four times. This is our nineteenth year United. You have to have feelings for someone to do that."

"Nineteen? You never told me you were together that long. You literally should stop trying to explain. You are doing a perfect job of making it worse."

"We have a daughter who is sixteen. I thought you knew." He reaches for her hand again.

"Goodbye, Jim." She sharply pulls her hand up to her shoulder and reaches for the door keypad. "Don't touch me. Don't smile at me. And avoid speaking to me on this trip unless absolutely necessary."

"I don't love her, Becca."

"Bomp. Wrong answer. Wrong time. And you are a piece of shit. Goodbye."

"No, Becca. Don't do this," he begs.

She walks out, saying, "You want me to leave now because you don't want to hear the fire that is on the tip of my tongue nor do you want me to do what I'm thinking right now." She slams his cabin door.

Fortunately, the salt84 insulation in the 2cm thick walls and doors has soundproofing properties so most of the conversation was muted to outsiders until she opened the door. And by chance, no one was in the hall to overhear it.

She beelines to her quarters stifling soft sobs and hoping not to encounter anyone in the corridor. Once on the other side of her door, she dives for her bed, buries her face in her pillow, and screams into it three times before breaking into wailing. She eventually cries herself to sleep.

In Jim's quarters, he hurls a few objects around the room, careful not to hit the walls. Emotionally exhausted, he plops down onto his bed, wipes tears from his face, and runs all ten damp fingers through his thinning hair. After he takes a while to review the entire encounter with Becca in his mind, searching for ways it could have gone better and wishing for a do-over, he drags himself into his private latrine (only he and Abs have private facilities), wets a towel with cold water, and washes his face. He does a few pushups and jumping jacks in his tight quarters and fast paces for an hour before attempting to sleep.

* * * * *

Abs Diary Entry 74C:

Mom and Dad,

My crew is turning into a bunch of dramatic lovesick teenagers. Zin, Rhoan, Becca, and Jim. They ALL want to be with people they shouldn't or can't have. This is starting to drive me nuts. If it doesn't end soon, I'm bailing. I'll turn this ship around, and no one is getting any ice cream! I do not want to be in the middle of all this secondary school drama. It's distracting and irritating. I'm just trying to explore, not play school counselor. Take a breath. Ahh. Our launch from MOS4 was as smooth as silk. Becca had jitters before launch but handled it well. No puking this time. We're taking good care of her, don't worry. I'm monitoring the flight for the first shift right now. Everything is going according to plan. Still hoping to see you on our "siolens mining expedition." Poor Rhoan was reprimanded so severely by Karen in PiF that I felt bad about giving him a tough time before that. He's still a touch upset with me, but c'est la vie. He'll feel better after BTR. He always does. Guess I'd better focus on mission. Lots of love.

# Chapter 9

## Into the Deep

A BS CHECKS the time, noticing Captain Slight is about five minutes late to the Control Room to take over flight monitoring duties. He doesn't mind Jim's tardiness yet because he is midway through watching a live Formula One race on the console's holographic artificial intelligence dark matter device (or haid). The life-like hologram size can be set from fifteen-hundredths to four times life size. He's enjoying it at two-tenths the size of real life or about a meter cube in the Control Room, but at home, he goes as high as half size or about a seven and a half meter cube. He often enjoys watching it with friends at sporting venues where the image is full size or larger using multiple cameras to capture the entire fields of play at those sizes. It's the closest he's come to seeing it in real life. His favorite racer, Delano Asbury, has a 2.3 second lead on the chasing pack. Abs is willing to give Jim another forty minutes, the remaining time left in the race.

Just as Delano Asbury crosses the start/finish line with nine laps to go, Jim pyks Abs from his quarters sounding as if he's just waking up. "Hey, Abs."

"What's going on, Jim?"

"Sorry. I overslept. Not really sure how that happened. You okay?"

"Yeah, I'm fine. The race still has about twenty more minutes to go."

"Oh, Phillip! I forgot the race was on. Are you alone?"

Jim has used the name Phillip as an expletive in contempt for his childhood bully/friend, Phillip Nichols, who was one of the worst human beings he has ever known.

"All by my lonesome."

"Okay," Jim says, "be right there."

Minutes later, Jim enters through the control room portal to join Abs. He's startled back into the door as the racers appear to run through him. "Whoa. Wasn't ready for that. I'm barely awake."

"Sorry, man. You want me to shrink it?"

"No. No. It just caught me off guard. How's the race going?"

"Asbury is still leading, Buchaka's in second, and Carrier is leading the chase pack with five laps to go."

"C'mon, Carrier, get up there," Jim urges.

Abs rebuts, "Keep your ass right where it is, Carrier. We need this one. Delano's doing exactly what he needs to do."

"He's won all but one race this season. Why does he need this one?"

"We're trying to break the points record for a rookie season. If he doesn't win this one, we're out of the hunt."

"Would you be such a fan if he wasn't your cousin?"

"Doesn't matter. He is. I am. And since I'm helping fund his team, when he wins, I win."

"How did I not know that?"

"Probably because it's not a big deal."

"Dude! That a massive deal! You have a championship leading team."

"I just see it as helping family. His parents couldn't afford it anymore, so I'm just helping my little cuz," Abs says without taking his eyes off the race at the front.

"Well, it looks like he's got this one in the bag," Jim acknowledges.

"A lot can happen in three laps. Don't hex it."

"No one's catching him," Jim insists.

"Cars break, but I hope you're right. Is anyone in the corridor?"

"Not when I came out. Why?"

Abs looks at Jim. "What happened with Bec?"

Jim grunts. "Shit, man. That was a Phillippin' disaster." Jim goes on to tell him everything that took place.

"How is she?"

"Not good when she stormed out. Not good at all."

"Damn, Jim! I ought to kick your ass right here, right now."

"Abs, I know. I've never even thought of doing anything like that before. Not sure what came over me with Becca. Just can't explain it. Now everything could be in tatters just because of me. I completely messed everything up."

"I couldn't agree more. You've broken my sister's heart, and this mission does not need this kind of distraction right now! I really hope this doesn't screw up the mission. That's the only reason I'm not kicking your ass right this second."

"Without a doubt, I would totally feel the same if the roles were reversed. I'm so sorry, man. I'm not sure what I'm doing or how any of this happened. I just flipped my whole world upside down."

"Not to mention everyone else's."

"What the hell is my problem, Abs?"

"Maybe you are doing the midlife thing and acting like a preteen in the process."

"That can't be. You know me. I'm better than that."

"Apparently not. Look at it from outside."

Jim takes a quick pause, then grunts, "Phillip. Maybe you're right."

"If this becomes a mission problem, you know this is on you."

Facing his compunction, Jim whines, "I know. I know."

"Guess I'll check on Bec before I go to sleep."

"I sure hope you can make her feel better because I sure am insanely screwing this up."

"What I don't understand is you knew this could happen. This is exactly why you created the no-fraternization rule among Marlagans. No domestics. Right?"

"Right."

"What is this, Jim? What are we dealing with right now, Jim?"

Jim interrupts, "I know. I know."

"No. No. I want to hear you say it. What are we dealing with right now, Jim?"

"A domestic."

"A freaking domestic, Jim, on your own team created by your own foolishness."

"Abs, I know. I really Phillipped this one up. When I think about how much impact this could have on the team…" He throws his head back and sighs deeply. "I can't be that guy. That's one major reason why this might be my last excursion."

"WHAT?"

"I've been thinking about it more and more since I realized she and I could become a problem."

"Geez, man. You just took all the fun out of Lano's victory. Who else knows?"

"I mentioned it to Marsha."

Abs, shocked, exclaims in an animated whisper, standing up, "YOU TOLD MARSHA ABOUT BECCA?"

Jim pulls Abs's arm down to bring him back into the seat so they could continue speaking quietly. "No! No! I just told her I'm thinking of making this my last excursion because I'm getting tired of being away from her and Drena. "

"Are you serious? Did she buy that?"

"It appears that she did. I don't know. We left the penny in the air and just decided to talk about it when I get back."

"For the record, Jim. I'm a whole lotta pissed at you right now. You let your little boy brain cause this mess. And leaving the Marlagans for such a weak reason as a domestic squabble is unacceptable. Here are the facts.

You will not leave the team. You will fix this mess you've made with Becca, and that's that! Do you understand?"

"What?"

"Do you need me to say it again?"

"No, no, no. I got it. Just how the hell—"

"I don't give a rat's tickle on the undercarriage of my balls. Fix it! And start thinking like the old Captain Slight that I followed through that clustered colon of a mission on Europa. Fix it!"

Jim grunts heavily. "Abs, really?"

"I am not toying with you, Grunting One. Fix it!"

"Damn. Okay. Maybe you're right. No. I know you're right. I'll figure something out."

"You need to be a Marlagan. Imagine a life without this."

"I would definitely be miserable without my Marlagans and our holiday excursions. Not sure what life could be like without this team. I seriously don't want to go back to the plant. Although—"

"Maybe this will up the stakes too. If you bail on us, I'm changing the name."

"Marsha said the same thing. She put the fear of your creativity in me."

"How so?"

"I'm not going to tell you the monstrous names she threw out, but suffice it to say, they were real incentives to stay."

"I doubt Marsha could come up with something to piss you off more than I can."

"Look, I said okay. You can stop with the threats now, sir. Captain. Sir." Jim pouts.

"Look at my little cuz on that top step again. Proud

of that little booger." Abs beams with pride during salute of Delano's national anthem.

"Have you ever even spoken with him?"

"Who?"

"Asbury."

"Yeah, all the time. He usually pyks me a couple days after every race. He's been doing that since we started him in hover carts."

"Dude! How did I not know this?"

"Don't worry about that. Just put all your focus on figuring out a way to fix this mess you've made," commands Abs as he stands up and rests his hand on Jim's shoulder.

Remorseful, Jim agrees, "I said I will, so lay off it."

Abs pats his shoulder. "Good man. And I'll let it go when you tell me it's fixed," Abs agrees as he starts heading for the portal and turns back to ask, "You good up here?"

"Yeah, butt pain. Thanks."

"Call me what you want as long as you TCB."

"Zin is not here to annoy. Don't have to do the twentieth century thing now."

"If it annoys you, I do."

Abs opens the door. Jim calls, "Hey, wait."

"Yes?"

"Did you have a name in mind already?"

"For what?"

"The Marlagans."

Abs stops. "No. Not yet but if I had to come up with a name right now, it would probably be Becca's Bunch." Abs smiles at Jim.

"Ha! That'll do it! Get out of here, Abs. See you later."

Abs walks down the corridor to the door labeled "Williams" and raps softly.

Becca opens the door as if she were expecting him. "Hey, Abs, come in."

He walks in. "Bec, how're you doing?"

She closes the door and falls into his arms, sobbing heavily.

He cradles her head and holds her tightly as she soaks his shoulder.

Minutes later, she is able to form staccato words through her sobbing, "Abs, I should have known better."

"Becca, we all do regretful things when we are young."

"Not you."

"Especially me. It may surprise you to know I have been where you are right now."

"What?" His statement seemed to shock her from sobbing into whimpering. "Okay. That would surprise me. You never told me about anything like that. What happened?"

"If I tell you this story for your benefit, it has to stay in this room," he demands.

She agrees by crossing her heart and holding up some finger thing that he doesn't understand.

"What is that?" he asks.

"That's the Girls Scout Promise. You don't know that?"

"I was never a Girls Scout, so no, I'm not familiar."

"Well, I promise not to tell a soul. Whip it out!" she says with a slightly brighter disposition.

"Okay, but you know in the twentieth century 'whip it out' means something completely different."

"Come on! You know what I mean."

"Okay. Here it is. I was in my final year of secondary school. There was this teacher who kept offering to tutor me beyond the school's standard curriculum to prepare me for higher education."

"Oh god. Don't tell me you did your teacher," she says with wide eyes and mouth.

"It was more like she did me."

"No way!"

"The funny thing is I hardly knew her, but she apparently knew of me very well. One day before graduation, which was my sixteenth birthday, she approached me from the opposite direction as I was passing her class. She wished me a happy birthday, which shocked me because I had no idea she knew who I was, and then she asked to speak with me about one of her struggling students after school. I agreed."

"Whuh oh! This is getting juicy." Becca brightens further. Then she crosses her legs as she plops down onto her bed, pulling Abs down with her.

Settling in, Abs continues, "So I stopped by her classroom after school. There were a few stragglers in there, so I queued up in the back and waited my turn. When they left, I was sitting in one of the front row seats. She asked if I'd walk with her and talk because she was running late for something. I can't remember if it was a meeting or—"

"Dude! Let's get to it," Becca's impatience demands.

"Okay. On the way to her vehicle, she offered me

a ride home, so I wouldn't have to walk and we could finish our conversation about the student."

"So there really was a student?"

"Yeah, there actually was a student that I helped pass her class."

"Oh," Becca looks bemused, "weird turn for a sex story. But what happened next with you and the teacher?"

"Let's see. Oh yeah. We were leaving the school. When we got in her vehicle, she started telling me how she has been noticing me growing into a man over the years and how handsome I had become. I was surprised because she was never a teacher that I encountered the whole time I was in that school, so of course, I felt like a stud. Then things went really fast after that. While we were riding to my place, she started touching me and making strong advances. Anyway, as much as I enjoyed being the object of her desires, it felt completely inappropriate, which actually added to the excitement of it all. But I felt powerless in that relationship when I shouldn't have. She had so much to lose if word of our relationship came out. She was United, had a baby, and was a teacher sleeping with a student. Well, former student. We didn't have a physical relationship until after graduation. I call that the summer of love because we were like two rabbits in heat. What eventually sobered me up was the realization that we both could have been criminally prosecuted if caught. One time we were going at it in her POV on a private turnoff of the rail behind a building when a cop stopped and told us to break it up."

"What?"

"Fortunately, he didn't ask any questions. And just allowed us to leave…probably after watching us for a while. I had fallen so deeply in love with her because she was my first real love. Almost immediately after the incident with the patrol officer, she became aloof and eventually tossed me out like a funky dishrag."

"What?"

"She did, and your boy was devastated."

"Ooo. I bet you were."

"It took a few months to recover from that heartache, but the trouble really started after I had gotten over her. She came back to me with talks of leaving her Union at the end of their term, which was a few months away and us getting United. I couldn't believe how happy that made me to realize I wasn't just another student she had used."

"Then what happened?"

"We saw one another for a few months almost every day. I was right back into loving her. I literally fell more in love with her the second time around, which I didn't believe was possible. She was beautiful, smart, and really seemed to love and care about me. Then she just disappeared. I couldn't reach her. She was never at the school. I thought something had happened to her. I feared her um might have found out about us and did something to her. Then a couple weeks or so later, she finally got in touch with me. She casually informed me that they had just gotten back from a second honeymoon after renewing their Union. She didn't have the decency to tell me face to face. She messaged it to me, talking about how sorry she was. I never saw or heard from her again."

"Oh no."

"Oh no is right. Boy! I was a messy pile after that.

It took me longer the second time to recover than it did the first time. It still feels a little sharp at times when I think about it."

"Poor dear. So you do understand! At least you never saw her again. My problem is I still have to work with Jim."

"You could choose not to if that's what you want. As much as I love having you on the team, if you need to leave, I would be sad but understanding."

"Maybe he should be the one to leave. At times, I just want to out us and face the legal ramifications just to see him go down. But that's not right, is it?"

"It isn't."

"How do you keep such a high level of morals all the time? You know where that teacher works, but you just let her be. How?"

"I pray for guidance and all I need to get through stuff the right way. I pray about everything, especially the tough stuff."

"Do you really believe in all that God stuff, even with all we know now?"

"It's funny that you say that. We are the only known earth-based species with the ability to learn from the previous generations, yet in so many ways, we're still the stupidest because of our own pride and willful ignorance. We make the same mistakes that history teaches us to avoid. We elect bad leaders in repeated cycles, seeming to choose worse and worse as time goes by. We still eat poorly even knowing the consequences. We begin the cycle of overspending as soon as we discharge our bankruptcies. Generation after generation, we just keep recycling the same small and significant mistakes and usually make them worse as time goes on. Sure, we improve things in our lives for a time, but we're only human. We're all temporary. If history has taught me nothing else, it's taught me that mankind is terrible at playing God, yet we keep trying to make ourselves God. God is eternal, we are not."

"What do you mean 'playing God'?"

"If you rely only on yourself and believe all you have is your own ability, if you think so highly of yourself and walk only to your own personal beat and that nothing else is above you, and if you believe, like most humans do, that you're the ultimate form of existence, you're your own God and need nothing else."

After a moment of contemplation, Becca asks, "Hmm. Isn't that what we all believe though?"

"We all start with the belief that life is only what we can see and we feel fulfilled in that, but then the majority of us reach the point where we feel like there has to be more to life than just being us for our own purposes."

"I have felt that. There have been times when it seems like I'm just in pointless and endless cyclical motion. Like a rut even though I'm doing important work for Mars. It just feels like I'm not really doing enough with my life."

Abs nods heavily. "Yes! And we try to fill it with things like relationships, working harder, building wealth, power, alcohol, drugs, or whatever. Some of the most powerful and wealthiest people are the saddest and lowest among us because that's all they've ever believed would bring them ultimate fulfillment. But when they get there, they're no more fulfilled than they were in the struggle. Most of the time, they feel even less fulfilled because they're not living out the most basic human need for connection and worship. People worship greed, power, and lust, but there's no real fulfilling connection there."

"So are you saying we are all missing God?"

"Yes. We are creatures created to worship. We just usually choose the wrong things like money, our homes, people, obsessions, work, and they help for a time, but then we end up needing to fill the void with more and more until we either accept the truth or just die having lived a good simple unfulfilled life."

"And you think all of that is because we are missing the God experience?"

"I do with all my heart."

"Hm. Can you prove it?"

"Only by what I've lived and seen but faith is not about seeing, it's about believing."

"That sounds like a cop-out."

"It can seem that way. In fact, most people choose to see it as exactly that. But I choose to have faith because I know what I know. At this point in my journey, I believe because I have seen."

"Seen what?"

"Seen God work."

"How?"

"First of all, I shouldn't be here. My mother describes me as half-born when I was born. Doctors said technology couldn't save me, but my parents prayed and prayed for hours, which turned into days, which turned into months. And that is why we are having this conversation. The doctors didn't save my life, God chose to save me and did."

"That's something I didn't know about you."

"Following Jesus gives my life deeper purpose and mission, and it helps to feel that I'm never alone in anything ever. I've seen so much evidence of my own prayers working, it can't be denied, at least not by me. Ask yourself why our team of supposed nonbelievers asks me to pray before each mission. They are closet believers who have seen the truth. In the times when I'm overwhelmed, praying helps me accomplish what I can't on my own. I know there's a Creator of our universe, and He helps me find my way through this world. He's far more wise and capable than me or anyone else I've ever known. I try to walk the path He lights for me, and I'm totally convinced life could not be better, and there has never been a tough situation than we could not handle together."

"That's intriguing when you put it that way. I never thought of it in the sense of never being alone. Why have we never talked about this before?"

"I have lost too many friends and even gotten into lots of trouble for talking about my faith."

"But we're like family."

"Also, Khan didn't want me talking with you about this stuff until you were old enough to decide for yourself, so I honored his request."

"Dang Khan. Always thinking I'm too young to live my life."

"He's just trying to do what he thinks is best for his younger sister."

"Does he believe what you believe?"

"Not really, but I'm just happy it doesn't hurt our friendship."

"Do you think I'll feel better if I pray right now?"

"I know you won't feel worse."

"That's for sure. Would you mind showing me how?"

"Well, to be honest, I've never taught anyone to pray before. It's a bit intimidated."

"Why?"

"It feels so personal and revealing. The work 'naked' comes to mind."

"Please. It's just me."

"That kind of makes the 'naked' part feel more uncomfortable."

"Be serious, Abs. I want to learn. Please. It might help me feel better."

"You'd better be glad you're Khan's little sister and I promised to take care of you," he kids, "It's kind of nerve-racking, but I'll do it for you."

"Guess Khan is good for something after all."

Abs chuckles. "I guess."

She continues, "So how do I start?"

"First, I like to lower myself before the Creator of the Universe, so I'm usually on my knees or bowing before God, but that's not necessary as you saw before launch."

They both get on their knees with their elbows on Becca's bed.

"Now I usually start with thanks."

She interrupts, "Just do it!"

"Okay. I'm more nerv…never mind. Let's just jump in. Our heavenly Father, thank you so much for bringing us to this moment together, which allows us to come before Your mighty presence…"

* * * * *

Abs Diary Entry 76A:

Mom and Pop.

Been forever since my last entry. I'm being sarcastic, of course. Is it illegal to strangle your captain if he deserves it? I guess that doesn't matter. He has really been pissing me off with this Becca thing. Now he's talking all kinds of craziness. I spent some time putting his head back on straight and putting Becca back together. In doing so, I actually taught Becca to pray a short while ago. She requested it. Our first prayer together. I was nervous, but I really think it helped her. She said it did anyway. It would be so incredible if she saw what we see and witnessed the life-changing miracles we witness along with us. We'll see how things shake out. People usually call on us in crisis but fall away when things are back to normal. Time will tell if she does the same. Gotta sleep. Chat again soon.

# Chapter 10

## Into the Deep

MEANWHILE, ZIN, donning her koala bear hoodie/ footie onesie, eagerly makes her way to the Garage to bring Elf to life. She arrives at and admires his bed box she created for travel. She flashes a quick frown upon noticing a new blemish on the well-traveled titanium case from this mission's shippers. She kneels to observe it closer and mutters an expletive before returning to the excitement of having her best friend and confidant back in action. She reaches into her fluffy pocket and pulls out a homemade key, which slips perfectly into the slot of her own design on the bed box. The coding of the key activates the bed and powers on her precious robot. Elf takes approximately ten seconds to boot up and survey the area. He then transforms into his cheery character as programmed, "Hiya, Zin!"

"Hi, Elf," she giggles and happily greets her favorite pet, "I have missed you."

"I missed you too, Zin. What do you want to do now?"

"Let's go inspect our equipment."

Zin and Elf start by inspecting the Marlagans' longtime hover rover named the Black Swan. As they enter the area, the automated lighting systems illuminate. She is delighted to see the massive vehicle is now dent-free, freshly painted, and cleaned to a sparkle. After a cursory perusal, she notes to herself, "Wow. They even put the captain's mission patches back on her. Ooh. Look, Elf. They have the new patch on here as well. They did an amazing job considering the shape she was in after the last mission. Do you remember that mission, Elf?"

Elf whirs behind her obediently, "Yes, Zin. It was a tough mission."

"It sure was, Elf."

She inspects the engine bay and discovers the engine has been completely rebuilt and looks brand-new. The dark matter processor has been completely refreshed along with the entire rack of gravitational systems.

"Oh yeah, the Swan is ready." She grins and looks around, but there's only Elf around to celebrate this joyous moment with her. She commands, "Dance with me, Elf. Let's celebrate."

"Okay, Zin!" Elf replies enthusiastically.

They dance for about three minutes before she commands Elf to stop. Then excited to share her giddiness with someone human, she runs up the stairwell to Fernando's door, but as she is about to knock, she remembers that he should just be getting his sleep now.

She shifts directions and runs to her brother's room and knocks, "Rhoan, come see."

Rhoan wakes up in his BTR lounger and thinks, *What the—How in the hell did I fall asleep so quickly? The Armory!*

He pops out of the lounger, grabs his pants, and answers the door.

"Hey, sis. Hey there, Elf. Bet you're happy to have him back."

"You have no idea."

Elf cheerfully replies, "Hi, Rhoan."

"Sorry, sis. I have to get to the Armory."

Her giddiness flies out, "You have to see the Black Swan and the improvements they've made. It's beautiful and perfect. They've even—"

Rhoan rushes past her and Elf and cuts her off, "I have to get to the Armory."

"Why? Did you get another secret surprise?"

"I think so. Let's go."

"On the way, let's check out the Swan."

"Armory, then Swan."

"Fine. Let's just go."

As they approach the Armory, Rhoan advises Zin, "You may want to stay out here until I know what we're working with, but you have to leave 'Snitchbot 5000' out here where he can't see or hear us."

"That might be a good call." She stands by the open entrance and powers down Elf.

As Rhoan surveys the Armory, he finds the routine armaments and row of lockers. He darts to his weapons locker, where Ylinen usually has the team stash his "special" weapons. After opening it, he immediately kneels to the bottom of the locker where he finds a package wrapped in plain reddish-brown paper, which in itself is a rarity. He remarks, "This must be it. Classy. It's wrapped in paper. What do you have for me this time, Big D?"

"Pretty paper? Is this how you get your fancy gift paper?"

"Some of it. I need to be really careful with this part. Let me concentrate. We don't want any incidents."

He gingerly unwraps the package in an effort to preserve the paper and safely expose the weapon. After the careful removal of paper and tape, he finds an ionizer pistol. Initially, he sees nothing special about it until he rotates it and sees something unusual under the chamber.

"Hmm. What's this thing do?" he wonders.

Zin pokes her head in and notes, "It just looks like an ionizer."

He flips over the weapon. "Not this part, but that's the beauty of his designs. They are not glaring improvements unless you know where to look. Let's see what this does."

Then he rummages through the wrapping and finds the note inside the packaging. To his delight, it is a handwritten note, another rarity.

He reads the note to himself: "Hey, Voyager, my team put together this gift for you. Notice that little addition to the lower chamber? Yeah. That is our own recipe that we call DAD. Don't ask what that stands for. Just know it has more than double the usual range and power and triple the usual blast duration. Just slide the lever under the chamber to the right, and the weapon becomes Godzilla or DAD, whichever you prefer. As usual, DO NOT stool me out if you're discovered using these modified weapons! Enjoy the voyage, V! This note will self-destruct in ten seconds."

He leaves it unsigned and is kidding about the self-destruction of the note, but Rhoan knows it's their code to burn or shred all evidence of Darren's involvement.

The glee on Sergeant Romero's face is undeniable, but he tries to keep his composure as he toys around with the weapon on safety. His joy is stirred with immediate disappointment since his many requests for an onboard range have all been denied, and there is no place onboard to safely put his new toy through its paces. He takes solace in the knowledge that all of his secret weapons up to this point have done very well in field tests sans one. He hopes this will not be the second to fail in a combat situation.

"So?" Zin queries anxious to show off the rover.

"So. It seems pretty awesome if it works as advertised."

"How will you know?"

"Have to field-test it."

"Ready to see the Swan?"

"Sure. Let me tidy up a bit in here first."

"I'm bringing Elf back now."

"Oh yeah. Go ahead."

"You have got to see all the repairs they've made to the Black Swan."

"Hiya, Zin."

"Hey, Elf."

Rhoan replies, "They just did what you requested them to do, right?"

"Yeah, and a little more. It's like brand-new."

"That's great, sis. Don't you want to know more about this baby here?"

"Why? I'm not ever using it."

"True. But don't you want me to get familiar with it?"

"Of course. But later. Check out the Swan."

"Let me take this to my room first. Don't want anyone else to see this too early."

"Geez. Okay. Let's go. Your quarters, then the Swan."

Zin turns to Elf, "Elf, let's go."

"Okay, Zin." He appears to perk up as he has been programmed to do based on Zin's tone.

She, Elf, and Rhoan secure the Armory and retreat to Rhoan's cabin.

* * * * *

Back in Becca's cabin: "Amen," Abs concludes his first one-on-one prayer with Becca. In fact, this is the only time he's prayed aloud outside of his home, where he and his parents often pray together.

"That was really good, Abs. Those had to be the most sincere and comforting words I've ever felt. Where did you learn to pray like that? You're not a closet minister, are you?"

"Ha. I'm definitely not that. My parents and I pray together from time to time. When we come before God, we should just pray what we feel. The words don't matter as much as an open and honest open heart. God already knows what we need before we ask. We just need to humble ourselves and come before Him."

"You really do sound like a minister from the old

days now, but I like the way you do it. I've always felt like God is there but never had anyone teach me anything about that stuff, except for the crazy fanatics everyone ridicules, and they are just a turn-off to me."

"Well, I have been thinking about getting a few interested and curious people together and form some sort of group to talk out the possibilities of God and how He is still relevant in our lives even now that we are beyond our home planet, which we once believed to be the center of the universe. Sometimes I wonder… since I'm being open and honest, I often wonder if those light orbs we see flying around are angels or God's army checking up on us just to monitor how horribly we humans are blowing it."

"You and a bunch of crazy people."

Abs flashes her a slightly pained expression.

When she notices his expression, she offers a veiled apology, "Oh sorry. That slipped out. But that's the general consensus."

"Not helpful, Bec."

"I know. I'm sorry. Speaking my mind with you is a force of habit." She grows serious. "But honestly, Abs, this time together really has helped. Thank you so much. In all my life or at least as far back as I can remember, you always seem to know how to make it better, no matter what I'm going through."

Exhausted from his flight duties and the seriousness that followed, Abs, wanting to lighten the mood, teases her by exaggerating a smile. "You're so welcome, Bec."

She fake hits him for mocking her. "Can I ask you a question and you answer it honestly?"

"Uh-oh. No?" he says timidly, looking afraid of what may follow her request.

"Come on, for real."

"I'll tell you the truth if I can, but you know there's a lot of classified—"

"I'm not talking about that kind of stuff. Be serious for just a moment." She pretends to hit him again.

"Okay, what do you want to ask?" He straightens attentively.

"Do you think I'm a fool for messing with Jim?" She pierces deeply into his silver-flecked hazel eyes. Her eye contact and stare can be intimidating.

"Yes," he answers matter-of-factly.

"Really?"

"Yes, I do."

Her visible anxiety quickly turns into an obvious twinge. "Damn. I guess I should thank you for your honesty, but it kind of hurts to hear that."

"Just being honest from a place of love."

"I know. Why do you say it so bluntly?"

"Because I love you, kid sister."

"Guess there's no hope for me and Jim ever, huh?"

Abs answers, "Bec, you know Jim and I have been friends for a long time. Most of the time I love him like a brother. He is loyal to a fault. That is why I was more than a little upset when you told me you two were involved. My discomfort and concern were mostly about you getting hurt. I knew he and Marsha had been United for a very long time and thought he may not have not have told you. So I confronted him about that. He told me you knew he was United for another year and were willing to wait. But I have known Marsha almost as long as I've known him. They have had issues this past renewal, so I thought they were…Why am I telling you all of this?" He stops himself.

"No, no. Go on. Please!" she pleads.

"The short of it is, I don't really think you are a fool. You foolishly got caught up. When I heard about you two, I'll admit I was seriously enraged, but you asked me to let you make your own mistakes."

"I guess I do appreciate that."

"Jim is a handsome charmer with the hair thinning just right, the eyes, and the British accent. Always has been. I think you were naive and your actions were age-appropriate, but lessons like these are what make us wiser if we learn from them. My advice…"

She listens intently.

"Would be to go through the pain of letting him go now and get over him. I care about what happens to you and don't want to see you hurt any longer than necessary. But you are hurt now because of this. I'd hate for you to prolong that or even go through it all over it again with Jim. You should also be mindful that the damage from this affair becoming known would extend well beyond you and Jim."

She remains silent and drops her gaze from his eyes to the floor.

He concludes, "That's it. I just think it's best for you, best for Jim, best for his family, and best for the Marlagans, which would in turn make it best for the WSX, even for Mars, if you just move beyond this experience with him."

She nods, still looking down. "Abs?"

"Yes, Bec?"

"I know you're right. My brain knows you're right. But my heart aches so much that it is totally confusing my senses."

He gently wraps his arms around her, "I know, Bec. It will pass if you let it. Prayer helps me when things are tough. It helps me regardless of the situation."

She pulls back from Abs and pops her head up. "Subject change."

"What? What is that expression about? Why are you grinning like that?"

"So what did the beautiful colonel whisper to you with her hand on your thigh earlier in PiF?"

Abs feigns a yawn. "Oh geez. Will you look at the time?" He starts to stand.

Becca pulls him back down. "Abs!"

He dons a stupid grin. "I already answered your question. What are you talking about?"

"Don't play stupid with me. Are you two a thing?"

"A thing? What thing?"

"Come on now. It's just me. No one can hear us."

"I don't know what you mean."

"I already know something's up. You might as well give up the goods. I already know."

"Are you saying there's no convincing you otherwise?"

"The truth, Abs. I want the truth. What's up?"

"Okay, between you and me, have you seen that woman?"

"She's definitely attractive."

"Attractive? She is a flippin' goddess. I will say she is a very, very, very (with each 'very' his voice gets more sensual) beautiful woman," he says, nodding with that same stupid grin.

"So it's official then?" she asks again.

"She is officially beautiful. No doubt about it."

"Come on, man."

"Okay. She was asking if we can talk when we get back…in private."

"Is that all?"

"That's what she asked?

"What exactly does that mean? It sure seemed to take a long time to just ask that."

"She's a professional. She had to make sure she asked it right."

"Bull! You're a fart. Why won't you tell me the truth?"

"What makes you think that wasn't the truth?"

They volley back and forth for a while, taking Becca's mind further and further away from her woes, but never moving the conversation about Abs and Djoibjin forward.

"Okay, Bec, I need to get some sleep," he says, genuinely yawning this time.

"Oh, that's right. Sorry for keeping you up so long."

"No worries. This was good. I hope it helped you."

"Abs, I'm so happy to have you here. I can't imagine how much worse this situation would be alone. Thanks for being here."

"I'm happy about that too, Bec. It would be hard for me to know you were out here dealing with this all alone."

"You're a really good friend to have as a brother." She hugs him and kisses him on the cheek, then rests her head on his chest.

He embraces her consolingly for a moment. "Are you gonna be okay in here alone?"

She lifts her head. "Yes, I think so. I'll be fine," she states the ending sentence with reassuring confidence.

"Okay. You know where I'll be."

"I do, and that's where I'll be if staying here alone doesn't work out."

"That's perfectly fine. Okay. I'm going now," he says with hesitation because she still has her arms around him. "See you in a little while,"

"Okay," she says while still holding him.

They clumsily sidestep toward the door, still embracing.

"Becca?" he says softly.

"Yes?" she replies softly, sounding as if she's almost sobbing.

"Do you need me to stay here with you a little while longer?"

"I don't think so," she whines and wipes her face on his uniform.

"Then you will have to release me in order for me to go."

"I will."

"Shall I just take my nap here?"

"No, you don't have to if you don't want to."

"I don't mind if that's what you need."

She finally releases him. "I'm okay," she manages as she mops the remaining puddles from her face using her t-shirt.

Abs reaches for her door knob. "I love you, kid."

"Thanks, Abs. I love you too."

"I will see you in a little while. Be ready for action."

"Yes, sir. I'll be ready." She salutes and forces a smile.

He moves closer to her and kisses her on the forehead

and then opens the door. As he exits her room, the Romeros exit Rhoan's quarters.

Rhoan speaks up first, wringing his hands and approaching Abs, "Well, well, well. What have we here?"

As he circles Abs, Abs replies, "What is wrong with you?"

"You and Becca, huh? You seem to be one hypocritical and insatiable love monkey." Rhoan continues circling Abs.

"Doofus, if I were going to have an affair with someone that I wanted to keep secret, why the hell would I bring her on our mission and then mess around on this ship?"

"Good question." Rhoan continues circling. "Maybe you couldn't help yourself or maybe so you could say what you just said."

Zin grabs Rhoan. "Come on, idiot. Let's go. Nothing to see here."

"Okay, Cap," Rhoan snarks. "I've got my eye on you, Cap. Something smells, and I'll find out what it is, Cap!"

"Let's go, Elf. Never mind him, Cap," Zin says, pulling her brother away.

"I never do." Abs smiles.

Zin yells back at Abs from down the corridor, "You should come down and check out the Black Swan. She's beautiful. All fixed up and upgraded."

"I'll see her soon enough." He waves as he opens his cabin door.

They wave back. "See you, Cap!"

Abs Diary Entry 76B:

Hey, Mom and Dad,

We are getting closer to Io by the day. Little of the drama has subsided since being on this flight. The Becca and Jim saga continues, though not as severe. At least they got out their feelings toward one another. We're still waiting to see how bad this gets. I'm hoping we've seen the worst of their drama. It feels good to be back in space with the Marlagans even with the dramas. We finally started telling Hassan's jokes and reflecting on our times with him. It's been healthy for all of us, but mostly Jim. He's finally able to smile when he thinks about him. Secretly, he's been dreading this first flight without his old friend, but I think he's becoming less traumatized with Hassan's death as time goes on. I also believe losing Hassan was a factor in his talk of giving up exploration and leaving the Marlagans. We have so many new toys this mission. It would be really cool if we are coming to share these with you. Gotta keep this one short. Besides, not much else to tell, and I have to get some sleep. Kimmie, Cam, Beck, Khan, and Jim all send their love, and I love you both very much. Hope you're safe and enjoying your mission.

# Chapter 11

## Brief

Two DAYS into the voyage, the *JohnGlenn* is well beyond the mandatory initial 24-hour manual flight period, so the autopilot has been engaged for several hours. The entire Marlagans crew is assembling in the Briefing Room around the large titanium conference table, which is bifurcated at one end to form a Y shape for presentation purposes, revealing a holographic projected image in full size from the table's built-in projector. This is the first onboard scheduled briefing regarding the current mission's surface excursion. Jim notices a cheery Becca arriving alone in the conference room. He realizes that their paths haven't crossed since the first day aboard the *JohnGlenn*, and she is mingling with the other Marlagans as if she'd been on the team for years. Becca takes the open seat next to Abs, and they give one another a squeeze as she settles in. Jim, who has no poker face whatsoever, is obviously bothered by her cheerful arrival, but no one aside from Abs seems to notice.

Rhoan sits back with his socked feet on the three and a half meter long polished metal table with his fingers interlaced behind his head as Captain Slight stands near the conference haid (chaid) at the table's opening. He opens a presentation which displays an image of each crew member in their appropriate uniforms, the Harvesters and HARVI, the Human Analog Robotic Vehicular Intelligence version 5, on one side and a wide-angle view of Io's southern landscape on the other side.

Jim begins the briefing, "Okay, Marlagans. We've done this a few times now. Most of you know what your assignments are, but every landing zone is different. This will be humanity's first foray this far south of Io, so pay attention. Some of this information will be new because of that and the updates to this mission. We've been given a general lay of the land to study a month ago, but here are some extra details we need to cover before landing. This is the latest map of the entire Illyrikon Regio."

Jim spend several minutes refreshing the crew on the area's terrain and regional features, then he zooms in on the holographic image to reveal the exact landing area. "Using images from our orbiter, this is our most favorable LZ. Take notice of this feature, which appears to be a cave adjacent to our parking lot. All of this appears to be siolens material outside of this feature may indicate that this potential cave could be a siolens den if they are a life form. For the sake of this mission, we will treat this feature as if it is a cave and the life forms as if they do exist. Is that okay?"

Rhoan agrees, "It will give us a clearer picture for sure."

"Good. One theory is that caves protect the life

forms from certain elements of the planet. We really have no idea, and this will be the first time anyone has actually explored the interior of a cave on this moon, so stay sharp at all times."

Rhoan raises a question, "Are we sure we want to be the first to explore a cave on Io, possibly a den, Cap? There could be bears."

Becca's unintended chuckle is accompanied by annoyed looks at Rhoan.

Abs answers, "Hell yeah, we want to be first! Marlagans always lead the way, and we never back down. You know that."

Rhoan replies soberly, "Yeah, I do. That usually means the sinew goes first behind HARVI, which means I will be the first in."

Zin notes, "You gonna make that a big deal and hog all the glory, aren't you?"

Still seemingly sullen, Rhoan answers, "No. Not at all what I'm thinking."

Jim chimes in, "Rhoan, what's wrong?"

"What do you mean?"

"I mean did you have kids on this break or something? You never back down from a challenge like this. What's going on, man?"

"No." He smirks. "I haven't had kids. It's not like I'm scared or anything."

Zin rebuts, "It definitely sounds like you're scared or anything."

Rhoan continues, "HARVI is going first, sis. What's there to fear?"

"Just speaking truth, bro. You sound very concerned right now."

He signals that he's ignoring her and continues, "Cap, my question is what kind of extra precautions are we taking in case these hollows are alive? So far, this mission has sounded far too standard to my liking when it absolutely is not."

"This doesn't sound like you, Rhoan. But if you'll allow me to continue, I'm getting to that."

Rhoan leans back again and waves at Jim. "Go 'head, Cap. Sorry for interrupting."

Slight continues. Using voice commands, he brings up an image of *JohnGlenn*. "Bingo, give me *JohnGlenn*. Zin, you'll be our orbital command as usual. I'm sure you've done your usual great tech mech voodoo to making sure our bots and rover are fit for duty and everything is prepared to remotely send the backups if needed."

He commands the holographic image of Zin to work aboard the *JohnGlenn* in orbit above the holographic moon surface, and her avatar animates moving about the *JohnGlenn* in orbit. The other avatars appear to look over at her from the opposite side of the presentation with various expressions and animations.

Zin, now in a soft cashmere panda onesie with ears, a fluffy tail, and four panda paws, throws her hand up from her Qub (cube-shaped pocket-sized Pyk intelligent computer). "Check."

Jim continues, "Bingo, send down the Harvesters and bring up the Black Swan."

It does exactly as he commands.

Jim further directs the unseen intelligence, "Now board the remaining crew into the Black Swan with Abs as driver."

The Harvesters exit the *JohnGlenn* and head for the

surface. The Black Swan appears in the garage bay, and the avatars of the remaining crew members and HARVI board the Black Swan as commanded.

Moments later, they see the holographic animation of the crew disembarking the Black Swan in the landing zone. Jim continues, digitally highlighting certain areas outside of the cave, "Here is where the modified harvesters (nickname for the AC20s, which are covered hover carts designed to detect and load siolens) will begin to gather this massive field of siolens while we prepare to infiltrate the cave."

Then he turns his attention to Rhoan, "Now, Rhoan, if you'd prefer Abs follow HARVI this time, you can cover the rear. I'm sure Abs won't mind."

Abs agrees, "Doesn't matter to me."

Rhoan says, "Naw. It's not that I'm scared or anything, I just want to know what extra precautions we are taking."

"You know that's twice you've said that now. But let's move on. As you see, HARVI is carrying six Cam Traps. We will muster in wormhole formation at the cave's entrance as 'Harv' lays the traps in strategic locations."

The chaid animates the scene as described by Jim.

Abs raises a question, "Maybe it's my OCD kicking in, but wouldn't it be better if HARVI laid that fourth trap a bit more to the right to form a perfect star?"

"Oh. That's not a bad idea, Abs. I can see that. Zin would you please reprogram that?'

"On it, Cap," she says with confidence while amending the presentation on her Qub as the chaid corrects it in real life simultaneously. Within seconds, she says, "Done." And the perfect star formation is laid as Abs suggested.

Abs likes it. "Yeah, that's better. That image doesn't itch like it did before. Thanks, Zin."

"Yep."

"Great job, Zin." Jim continues, "Now that the traps are down, we slowly infiltrate in Formation Wormhole with Rhoan behind HARVI, followed by me, then Becca, then Abs, then Becca's med box. That's as much as we can animate here since we have no idea what this cave is like beyond this point. We will all have live views from HARVI with the modified Cam lenses for finding siolens. Zin, Rhoan, and Abs will have control of the cameras. Zin, you'll also have eyes through all of the AC20s."

"Check."

Jim covers a range of topics regarding the mission, some basic, some complex, and answers every question as best he can. He is honest in letting them know that they are walking into the unknown...again. Once he has reached the conclusion of their first briefing, he asks one last time, "Any other questions?"

Everyone looks around for a question until Becca raises her hand. "I'm not very familiar with this version of HARVI. What kind of armament does he carry and is he equipped to assist me in case of medical emergencies?"

Zin answers, "HARVI can be remotely controlled to do whatever you need him to do. He has not been programmed as a medical assistant, but if you need me to do something through him, just let me know."

Becca replies, "Cool. How well armed is he?"

Jim responds to that question, "Very. No other

HARVI has ever been armed like this before. He has ionic blasters, laser sightings, SMG, rocket launcher, stars, and my favorite, matter beams."

Rhoan's relief is evident as he pipes up, "What? Why didn't you say that before? Now that's what I'm talking about! HARVI isn't usually that well armed. Why am I just hearing this now?"

Jim smiles. "Protocol. Does that answer your question, Becca?"

"Yes, it does. Thank you."

"Now, Rhoan, they did not want us to know our HARVI was this well armed, so we would not feel this was an invasion. We do not want to use any armament if it can be avoided."

Rhoan smiles. "Not a problem, Cap."

Jim invites others to ask more questions.

Abs probes, "Will there be any other information that we won't be given until we need to know?"

"That is possible. Much of this information, I just got this morning, so we could brief on it today. The WSX may be holding others details until we need to know."

"Understood," Abs accepts that explanation.

"Okay. If there's nothing else, that's all we have. We're done here."

Abs says, "Hold up. Delano's ringing me."

Zin asks, "Delano who?"

Abs answers in his head, "What's up, cuz? Congratulations!"

Jim shouts, "Go public on that, Abs!"

Abs continues, "Hey, Lano, my crew is here and they want to say hi."

Zin says, "Is that who I think it is?"

Abs makes the full size image visible to everyone. And the holographic Delano moves throughout and looks around the room. Captain Slight quickly shuts down the confidential chaid.

Zin shouts, "Holy shrimp! Delano Asbury? How the hell do you know him?"

Delano greets, "Hello, everyone."

Random greetings come from the crew.

Jim says, "That was a great race. How do you do it?"

Delano replies, "So much practice, tons of hard work, and the Lord is with me always. It's as simple as that. But I hear you guys are on another excursion. How do you do that? That's the real question."

Abs says, "You know He's with us too."

Jim answers, "We have a great crew, who puts the welfare of humanity above our own safety."

"Well, that takes a lot more bravery than racing. That, to me, is what heroism is all about. Hey, Bec," Delano says sweetly as his image walks toward her.

Becca, looking lovingly at Delano, answers in her own sweet voice, "Hey, you. When are you going to come see me? You're always promising."

"I know. There's so much training, testing, press, and appearances. Then on top of all that, it always manages to conflict with the Mars launch dates. I've been trying to get my managers to give me the month required to visit Mars, and they did reluctantly promise and have been working with a number of universal travel agencies to give me a month during the next off-season as long as I take my trainer with me. I know Abs is gonna kick my butt when we train together."

"Not true, cuz. You have more gravity than we do, so you're stronger,"

Delano laughs. "Not a factor. Your bionics will destroy me, and you know it. All you have to do is dial it up to eleven. It would be really great to see you all in person."

"Whatever you say. That's so great they're at least acting serious about letting you come this time."

"You mean a lot to this team. If it was just a regular old family visit, it would probably never happen. I know how much—

Abs interrupts, "Wait. Is that the new place?"

"Oh yeah. I just moved in last week. Let me give you the wide view."

Delano widens their environmental view, making them feel as if they're in the room with him now. He proceeds to give them a tour.

At the conclusion of the tour, Delano adds, "Becca, I can't wait to show you around in person when you to come visit me. These surfaces are much more plush than I expected. I'm sure you'll enjoy them as much as I do."

She enthusiastically says, "That would be wonderful. Everything certainly looks plush to the touch."

He continues, "When I come there, be sure to set aside a few days for me. I'd like to see Mars through your eyes."

Jim looks at the two, turning red, and clearly bothered, but keeping his mouth closed.

Becca agrees, "I would love to. It's not like I have anything else going on." Her eyes sneak toward Jim and back to Delano. "I can't wait to see you."

"Same here. I get no time to myself on this planet.

My pyk has gone off three times since we've been talking. Oh wait! It's my driver. I'm supposed to be at a press briefing in ten minutes."

Abs comes back in, "All right, little cuz, we'll let you go make that money. Love you, man. Super proud of you. Let me know if I can ever help in anyway."

Delano answers, "Love you too, big cuz. I'll keep you updated. He's pyking me again. Nice talking to you guys. Talk to you after the next race. Asbury out."

They disconnect.

As they disconnect, Becca turns her head slightly and steals a quick glance at Jim and notices a painful expression of dejection. She is powerless to quell the devilish grin that has taken possession of her face. After spending a few minutes on her pyk, she walks up to Abs, grabs his bicep from behind, and holds on to him as if he is her escort while he speaks with Zin, who is trying to get his advice on recoding HARVI for a new idea she had during the briefing.

Catching the tail end of the conversation, she only hears Zin say, "Oh. That's good. I think that will do exactly what we need. Thanks, Abs."

"Glad I could help," Abs replies.

Very seldom does Abs like to exhibit his genius to anyone due to the unsolicited bullying he did not enjoy throughout his school years, but he freely shares it with his crew to improve their odds for a successful mission. Generally, now that he is an adult, he is learning that most, but not all, people are mature enough to respect and better utilize his intelligence and bionic strengths than mock it because of their own inferiority complexes as they often did when he was younger.

As Zin begins to walk away, Abs, still escorting Becca, catches up to Zin and asks her, "How are you coping with the prospect of live siolens?"

"I just hope there is no life because I know how things work when there's a lot of money involved. If life would slow down the industry that creates wealth, life will suffer. It always does, and knowing that fact alone makes me hope there is no life down there."

Abs nods. "Yeah. I don't disagree."

Becca says, "Whether they're there or not, we won't hurt them, right?"

Zin answers, "I sure hope not."

"I really don't want to be an alien invader if they are there. I am very much hoping those factory workers were mistaken and there's no life on Io."

Zin drops her gaze to the ground. "That is certainly my hope too. We've been through this before on Europa, so things will be fine. Just like there."

Abs adds, "One way or another, it will be all right. We'll make it right on our end anyway."

They all hug and part. Zin and Elf head to her domain, the Garage, while the rest of the crew congregate in the lounge where Rhoan and Jim have started a game of billiards. Popular music videos are playing on the full-size haid in the corner.

Becca declares, "I love this song," and runs over to dance with the life-size holographic image of the performing artist, Si Si.

Rhoan asks, "Dude, why didn't you tell us Asbury was your cousin?"

"I guess it never came up."

Jim remarks snidely, "Well, Becca sure knew him."

Upon hearing Jim's response, Becca looks over while continuing to dance.

"Yeah, that's because Khan and I grew up together, and Becca was part of our family too."

Jim asks, "So, Bec, how long have they been talking with Delano like that?"

Becca, still dancing, yells an answer, "What concern of that is yours? Mind your biz, Cap!"

Rhoan cracks up, "Damn, Cap!"

Jim flushes with embarrassment but doesn't say a word as he takes his next shot at the four ball and misses.

Abs walks over to the bar and mixes a cocktail.

Becca, still dancing, now with her favorite artist, Vonna Robz, to her new number one song, asks, "Abs, would you please make me one of those?"

"Sure thing." He mixes her a drink as well and asks the billiard players, "Who's winning?"

"Rhoan is kicking my butt," Jim admits.

"Too bad there was no wager on this one. I need one of those new upgraded BTR suits," Rhoan adds.

Jim asks, "Rhoan, how do you keep upgrading every time one of those things comes out? I can't even afford that."

"I get by with a little help from my friends. Friends who hire me for odd jobs, that is."

Jim asks, "What kinds of odd jobs do you do? I need some stuff done."

Abs asks, "Jim, you really don't know very much about us outside of work, do you?"

Jim answers, "I like to keep my work and life separate."

His voice tapers off at the end of the statement as

realizes how hypocritical he must seem to Becca and Abs as he says it.

Abs and Becca look at each other as Rhoan lines up his next shot. Jim notices and flushes scarlet again.

After Rhoan shoots, he says, "Well, I think this is an environment where we should know one another as much as we can, so we can know everyone's strengths and weaknesses to better perform on missions."

Jim acknowledges, "That might be right in some cases, Rhoan, but my experience has taught me that can be a mistake sometimes, and your job can consume your entire life."

Becca, starting to perspire from dancing three songs, walks over to the bar where her drink is waiting. "I'm done dancing. Think I'll go check on Zin. Come on, Abs."

Abs gets up. "So long, fellas. Enjoy your game."

They both offer salutations, but Jim watches them with a curious expression.

As they exit, they hear Rhoan saying, "Jim, is there something you're not telling—"

The door closes.

Becca looks at Abs. "Did you hear that bull?"

"Yeah. He apparently is not equipped to handle this situation. He seems to be more aware just how bad he messed up and doesn't know what to do."

"Is it wrong that I just want him to suffer with every breath for as long as he lives?"

"Uh yeah! Especially since you're our doctor. Don't you have a code or something prohibiting you from feeling like that?"

"I have no idea what you're talking about."

When they enter the garage, they notice Zin's panda footies protruding from the driver's side of the Black Swan and her favorite music, movie scores, is playing very loudly throughout the garage.

Abs walks over and turns the classical music down, then hears Zin bump her head.

"Ouch! Shit! That hurt. Who is that?" She extracts herself from the Black Swan. "Oh. Hey, guys. What's up?"

Becca says, "Nothing. Just coming to see if you need any help."

Abs jokes, "Uh. Actually. No. That's not why I'm here."

Zin laughs. "Either way, I'm glad you're here. Let me show you something." She walks over to the HARVI pod and starts typing on HARVI's holographic keyboard. "You see this?" she asks Abs.

"Yes."

"How do I override this line right here so we can use it in manual control while still keeping this line for the other automated functions?"

Abs takes over. "Geez. This coding is so antiquated. This is version 5?"

Zin nods. "This is the latest and greatest in the WSX."

"Wow! It's been a while since I've worked with this. It's like DOS all over again. This is so easy to hack, it's embarrassing."

"You are so wrong for that, Abs," Zin remarks.

Just a few seconds later, Abs finds the solution. "Here we go. See, Zin, just change this here, add this line here, and viola."

Zin shakes her head. "Why do I even try to impress you? It is futile."

Abs looks at her. "Zin, you impress me all the time. I just have a lot of practice overriding code. I hack and upgrade my eye and brainpower all the time."

Becca inquires, "Isn't that dangerous? Don't you worry about messing something up? What if you ruin something and can't get it back?"

Abs laughs. "Been there."

"Really?"

"Yeah. When I was eleven, I tried to integrate a pyk into my eye."

Zin probes further, "You do have a pyk in there."

"I do now. But the first time I tried, I screwed it up so badly, nothing worked. The eye just went scrambled with a barely legible error message. I was so afraid to tell anyone that I walked around like that with one eye for four days before admitting it to my parents."

Both ladies gasp.

"After the factory reset it, I did so much research to learn what I did wrong. Then as I learned more and more, I was able to perfect it myself."

"You are crazy."

"I had no choice since my parents didn't want to pay for the upgrades I wanted and corporate tech couldn't keep up with my pace."

"You could have left it the way it was."

"You know me better than that." He winks.

"True. So what functions do you have now?"

"I'm almost constantly upgrading. Now it has full pyk functionality including the Intelligence, projections, full BTR functions. Though it's not 100 percent functional yet, I can emulate many functions of a BTR suit without a suit, just using nervous system manipulation."

"Wait, are you hacking your nervous system too?"

"Just a little."

"You are insane! Do you realize how dangerous that is?"

"Oh yeah, I do. That's why I've been taking it so slowly, and so far, it only works with my bionics. I'm taking that process very slowly.

"Just buy the suit, Abs, and stop being so reckless."

"I'll take that under advisement, ma'am. But as I was saying, my eye has telescopic and microscopic features and a bunch of other stuff I can't talk about."

"Why? Is it illegal?"

"Not illegal, per se," he continues, "And since it is connected directly to my brain, it behaves like any other part of my body. The same goes for my appendages."

Becca seems stunned. "In all the time I've known you, which is my whole life, you rarely talk about these things. Not sure if I want to hear any more than I should. The less I know about your criminal behavior, the better."

Abs recalls, "When you were a wee lass, you used to bombard me with questions about my oddities."

"I did?" Becca asks. "I don't even remember that. What did you do?"

"I answered every single one of your questions. When you asked, it never bothered me because I knew you were just curious and had no ill-intent."

Zin expresses the opposite, "Well, I would love the chance to dig in there and learn all about your coding. I bet I could learn gobs just from looking at that, even if I have no idea what I'm seeing."

"Zin, it's a shame we don't spend more time together. When we get back to Mars, let's change that. I promise to share some of my private coding with you."

Zin exclaims, "Yes, please! Let's do it."

Becca queries, "What about me?"

"Of course, Beck," Abs says, "I didn't know you did much coding."

"Everyone needs to do some coding these days just to use a haid. I may not be a professional like you two, but we all need to know at least a little bit."

Zin attempts to comfort her, "That is quite true, Becca. So, Abs, are you planning any new upgrades?"

"The next one I'd like to figure out is how to hold conversations on the pyk inaudibly."

Becca asks, "What's that mean?"

Zin inquires, "You mean a thought conversation with someone on the pyk without speaking aloud?"

"Indeed."

Becca asks, "Whoa. Is that possible?"

"I'll let you know. People have always said the little gray men have been doing it for centuries, but my research into that is just beginning, and it looks possible. As of now, I do have the ability to type inaudibly. I'm using an upgraded system similar the antiquated one employed by the great Stephen Hawking, and it's working better than expected so far."

"Dude, you're making me want one of those eyes. And to think, I sometimes pitied you when I first understood the circumstances of your bionics," Becca admits.

"In the days long gone, my disabilities would have been crippling. But tech these days can easily make it an unfair advantage," Abs declares. "Enough of that. Is anyone else hungry?"

They both answer affirmatively. The trio heads up to the galley.

* * * * *

Abs Diary Entry 77A:

Homie and Homette,

Mission is still smoothly sailing along. Flight has been silk. Equipment's doing well and looking good. Lano won his most recent race. He's still on track to break the record. Not sure if you're aware of that where you are. He also has a gorgeous new home and plans to visit us this off-season. So proud of that kid. The crew happened to be ending our first onboard briefing when Delano pyked me. He said he still wasn't able to reach you guys today but sends his love. The juicy part of that conversation was he and Becca doing their usual flirting in front of Jim. I kept stealing glances at Jim. That was pretty priceless and definitely put Becca in a good mood since Jim has no kind of poker face. Still don't think he's done with that drama yet. Zin and I have been doing a lot of coding together the past couple days and decided to create some new lucrative projects when we are settled back home. Should be fun. It will be fun spending more time with her off-mission working on something we both enjoy so passionately. I actually regret that we didn't do it sooner. Glad we're fixing it. All has been pretty uneventful for us, but don't fret. Excitement is never far away from the Marlagans. Just give it a few minutes. Hope your mission is going as well as this has so far. Te quiero muchísimo.

# Chapter 12

# Sabotage

L ATER ABOARD the *Mushroom*, Abs is abruptly awakened in the middle of the night of the sixth day of flight aboard the *John Glenn* by the sound of his internal alarm clock feature in his eye after just four hours of sleep.

"Already? That hardly felt like an hour," he reckons as he tries to escape the fog of slumber that keeps urging him to remain comfortably on his warm embracing pillow. Realizing he only has about twenty minutes to reach to the ship's controls before the general alarm sounds announcing a pilot is needed for the final twenty-four hours before entering Io's orbit, he resists the temptation and rises to the edge of his bed. He takes a moment to collect himself, then beelines for the head.

Using the sonic shower with oral hygiene features, he readies himself in less than ten minutes. On his way to the Control Room, he stops by the galley and grabs his pre-packed piloting snack number four. He reaches his post with three minutes to spare and offers his natural eye for a retina scan on the control board to inhibit the general alarm. He commands Bingo to power up the haid and scrolls through his personal stream recordings list until landing on his favorite future gadgets and technology program.

Shortly after the program begins, Abs steals a gander out the window and notices something is amiss. Jupiter is usually large and in full view at this point in the flight; he's a tad befuddled when he notices that it is not even visible. As the largely ignored tech show continues, Abs checks the HNS (Holographic Navigational System) to verify their position and course. He zooms out for a more expansive view of the solar system and soon discovers the autopilot has veered almost ten parsecs off-course from the projected flight path. Internally, he quickly calculates that the deviation will take approximately two hours to course-correct, which will ultimately cost them an extra day because of the tight windows to enter Io's atmosphere. Fortunately, by regulation, the unusual WSX missions such as this are outfitted with two weeks of additional supplies necessary for the crew to survive in the instance that the mission is extended.

He scrambles to find the culprit, first, by poring piece by piece over every detail of the flight's records to investigate what took place during the autopiloted period. After several frantic minutes of intense digging, Abs discovers the autopilot took evasive actions to avoid an unidentified object three days ago but sounded no alarm. Subsequent to taking those radical actions, it failed to bring the *JohnGlenn* back to the proper flight path. Yet still, that alarm never sounded either. Both incidents should have caused alarms. He examines the alarm system to ensure it is in proper working order. It is.

*Why the hell didn't this thing sound the alarm?* he thinks.

He determines that this is a serious enough situation that he should wake Jim to notify him of the situation.

He pages Jim over the ship's intercom, "Bingo, page Jim."

"Paging Jim."

"Abs, there's no response."

"Bingo, try again."

This time, he hears a groggy grunt, "Wha?"

Unable to conceal his frenzy, Abs exclaims, "Jim! Wake up!"

In the haze of repose, Jim just answers, "Abs?"

"Jim! We have a serious situation."

"What time is it?"

"0010 Z."

"Why are you waking me up so early? What's going on?"

"Autopilot screwed us somehow. We're more than eighteen hours off-course and will miss our atmospheric entry window today. I think this *Mushroom* may be a lemon."

"What? Wait! Okay! Give me a minute. I'll be right there."

Ten minutes later, Jim arrives in the control room in a nonplussed huff wearing pajamas, a robe with socked feet. "How did this happen?"

With holographic displays already prepared to explain the situation, Abs enlightens Jim of the entire scenario from his entrance into the Control Room, through his micro-investigation, and to the present.

Jim mutters, "Why didn't the alarms sound? That doesn't make sense."

"I already wrote this incident report for your approval. I sure hope these alarms were not intentionally disabled. And look." He presses a series of buttons randomly. "We're locked out of manual control too, which makes me suspect it's not just the ship."

Jim ponders aloud, "This doesn't feel…Something must be broken."

"Or sabotaged."

"Why would anyone do that?"

"Not sure," Abs pauses as he contemplates a thought he had when first hearing about their new mission parameters. "This is a somewhat controversial excursion, Jim. Maybe someone who knew or found out about it thought this was a way to sabotage the mission."

"You're being a conspiracy geek again, Abs. And before you ask, no. You cannot do a private investigation."

"I truly hope I'm just geeking out, but this doesn't make sense. You know this makes me want to dig into the cypher to see if anything else has been set to go wrong."

"I can't see the general green-lighting that."

"Why did you mention Arms green-lighting a sabotage? You suspect he's involved in some sort of plot?"

"No. No. Don't put words in my mouth. I can't see him green-lighting a private investigation for a navigational issue."

"So you don't think he could be behind this?"

"Well, I didn't say that. After all, he is the point of this mission's prep team."

"So you do suspect a plot then?

"No. I'm not saying that either."

"Then what are you saying?"

"Abs, I'm just waking up. Give me a minute to wake my brain box up."

"While you do that, just let me verify that there isn't any corrupted coding."

"Abs, we need to follow protocol."

"I knew I should have let your stale ass stay asleep. Just let me take a quick peek. I promise not to change anything without clearance."

Jim grunts as he stands. "Ugh. They'll still know. Let me think about that. We could get in some serious trouble even without changing anything."

"I know that, but this is justifiable because of the ship's behavior so far. This is our first time in the *JohnGlenn*. It could be some type of flaw we need to correct. Don't we at least need to ensure the safety of our mission and crew going forward?"

"We've only missed one day, and it did nav away from the obstacle."

"Not around it, though. Just away from it. If it had gone around it, we'd be back on course and sped up to compensate for lost time. Instead, all the ship did is veer off-course. What if someone expected us to go so far off-course that we wouldn't reach Io at all? We don't even have manual control."

Jim releases another grunt but listens attentively.

"Hear me out. Suppose we had encountered multiple objects on this flight, how far off-course would we be then? Suppose this had happened early in the autopiloted portion of this flight. Where would we be then?"

"I understand your point and already considered that."

"I'm smelling something, Jim. And it is not good."

"I still think we need to follow protocol here, Abs."

"Everyone knows you're a WSX loyal, Jim. And we respect that about you, but what if someone from Maintenance was in on this? This has already put the Marlagans in danger, and we could potentially be in much more peril. We don't know what else might be compromised."

"Even if we have been compromised. Abs, I believe in our system. I know that makes me a company man dorkus, but I trust that the system works especially in situations like this. They will find a solution and whomever, if anyone, is involved if this is some sort of 'conspiracy'," he says with air quotes.

Jim pyks Colonel Djoibjin. She answers with the hoarseness of one o'clock in the morning, "Djoibjin."

"Hi, Colonel Djoibjin. So sorry to wake you. It's Captain Slight."

"Slight? What's going on? Is everyone okay?" she asks, suddenly sounding much more alert but still slightly hoarse because of her maintenance inhaler.

"Yes, ma'am, we are all safe, but somehow our autopilot has us very far off-course, and we're locked out of manual. It will cost us at least one day of exploration if we fix it now."

"How did that happen?"

"We don't know for sure. It seems that the autopilot took evasive action to miss an unknown object a few days ago but neglected to put us back on course. We're checking in with you for clearance to investigate."

"First, the intelligent light following you, now this. Do you think they're related?"

"I was not there, ma'am. I cannot speak to that, but Captain Abernum is shrugging. So it appears we don't know the answer to that question."

"Hmm. Is Captain Abernum willing to do the investigation?"

"Yes, ma'am. He wants to know if he can check and correct the coding if that's the issue."

"Are you back on course now?"

"Not yet, ma'am. Captain Abs…er…Abernum would like to correct the coding to put us back on course."

"I trust him to do both of those things, but let me clear it with the general and get right back to you. We don't want the same issue on the return. Would you mind if we added an additional day to your mission? Per standard order, of course, your craft is stocked with enough surplus in case something like this took place."

Abs signals to Jim, silently shaking his head and motioning across the front of his neck with his right hand, indicating that he does not want to add the extra day.

Jim grunts, then answers slowly, "Uh. No, ma'am. We can add the extra day."

Abs, still playing silent charades, pretends to hang himself, holding an invisible noose.

"Okay. Good. I will get back to you in a few minutes. Djoibjin out. " She disconnects.

Abs, who is now free to speak, expresses his contempt for adding another day, "Grunt!"

"I know. I don't want to add another day either." Jim pauses and looks like he's hesitant to speak but then timidly asks, "Well, since we're on hold here and I finally have you alone, can we discuss the Becca issue?"

"No. We need to get back on course. I can't think about that now, man. Much more important stuff going on right now."

"What? Like waiting for a callback before we can do anything?"

"And the stress that goes into that waiting. Don't forget that."

"Just a quick word. That's all."

"Okay. What do you want to say? Keep it quick. I guess we need to resolve your relational screw ups rather than avoid them…for the mission."

"Thank you, but I thought your cousin was the resolution to my relational screw-ups."

"Who? Delano?"

"Yeah! Duh-Lano."

"Is that what you really what you want to talk about? Moving on."

"No. Seriously. What's going on there? Am I getting played?"

"Are you seriously asking me if you're getting played?"

"Yeah. How long have they been a thing?"

"Not a thing, Jim. Stop trying to deflect blame. Those two have been friends for years, but that's not going to resolve the Marlagans issue and neither is your sudden departure from the team. Your issue is still an issue."

"What do you suggest?"

Abs is growing frustrated that they are still off-course and waiting for clearance to get on-course. "This is bull puck! We need to get this fixed now. I'm going in."

"No. You're not. We're following protocol and waiting for clearance."

"WTF is wrong with you?"

"Here. Sit right here and let's have a conversation that will take your mind off one problem and on to another one."

Abs laughs out of frustration. "No shit. Dude, just have an honest and open conversation between you two. Put it all out there. That's the only way to build trust and salvage a friendship or at least a functional working relationship going forward."

"I know. The looks she keeps giving me are taking their toll, though. I can see the Romeros starting to pick up on the fact that something's there."

"No doubt about that. You two are terrible at hiding your emotions."

"Would you mediate a conversation between us so things don't get out of hand?"

Abs rocks his head and whines, "Jim, I really don't want to be a part of that."

"I'm sorry, Abs, but you need to be there. I don't want things to get hostile."

"What I need to be doing is getting us back on-course. We are bleeding time here."

"I know, man. Just take a breath with me. Inhale. Exhale."

"I'm not having a panic attack. We just need to get back on-course."

"So will you do it?"

"What? What are you talking about?"

"Mediate."

"You're joking, right? You two are a sloppy joe dripping all over the place. It's your mess. Clean it up. What do you expect me to do?"

"Let's just say knowing you are there, I will be much more thoughtful with my words and attitude. I was an idiot. I know it and am willing to admit it."

"That statement doesn't require me to be there to come out of your mouth. Just apologize. That may be enough."

Frustrated, Jim exclaims, "Phillip! Okay. You're forcing me to play hardball here."

Abs asks, "Huh? What does that mean? I can get us back on-course?"

"Not yet. I refuse to speak with Becca about this if you are not there to mediate."

Abs gives him a look as if he's a teacher and a student has just said something completely inappropriate. "Do you realize how stupid this conversation is to me right now? I really don't think you do."

Then after some thought, Jim offers in a more pleasant tone, "Okay. Okay. What's it going to take for you to mediate?"

"Well, well. Now we're talking my language. Let me get us back on-course right now."

"Abs, you know they will see you messing with the systems."

"I really don't give a single kernel of corn in a turd pile right now, Jim. I'm going in."

"Come on, Abs, I'm as concerned as you, but pissing off the upper echelon is not going to help in anyway. We have ample supplies for an extra couple weeks. Just relax."

"I don't want to be out here for an extra couple weeks."

"Neither do I, but we are not even a full day off-course yet. Just relax."

"This is actually funny. Usually I'm the one telling you to relax and take it easy." Abs sits back down and looks at Jim. "What do you want now?"

"Name your price to mediate."

"If you refuse to let me get us back on-course without authority," his voice gets louder, "TO SAVE OUR OWN CREW! Your proposal, though interesting, may take some thinking time. The new BTR Lounger coming out next month."

"I knew you were going to say that as the offer was coming out of my mouth. You're slipping, though. You usually don't need a whole second of thinking time."

Abs laughs. "I'm getting older, Jim. Reflexes are slipping."

The console haid sounds. It's Colonel Djoibjin.

Jim answers, "Slight."

"Captain Slight, General Arms wants you to investigate the coding but report what you've found before making any changes."

"But, Colonel, we feel time is definitely a factor here."

"If time is a factor, the safety of the crew comes first, of course. But if it can be avoided, that is the general's order."

"It cannot be avoided much longer. Captain Abernum may have a coronary if he has to wait any longer. You understand we are still off-course and bleeding time waiting for authorization, ma'am?"

"Thank you for following protocol, Captain. Is Captain Abernum there now?"

Abs plays charades again, motioning all the negative responses he can imagine.

Slight smiles. "Yes ma'am. He's right here. He can hear you. Let me widen your view."

Abs glares at a grinning Jim before Djoibjin comes into her view. Then he smiles pleasantly at her holographic image as she appears. "Hi there, Colonel."

Looking less disheveled than she did during their conversation minutes ago, she turns to face him. "Captain, we are counting on you to uncover whatever is causing this issue and get back to us immediately with details. We will verify the corrections and note them in case other surprises pop up."

"Yes, ma'am. Thank you, ma'am."

"Thank you for your hard work, and please get everyone back safely."

"Yes, ma'am. Will do."

"I look forward to your report."

"Aye, aye, ma'am," they say in unison.

"Djoibjin out," she disconnects.

Jim looks at Abs suspiciously. "Why didn't you want to talk to her?"

Thinking quickly, Abs replies, "I wanted plausible deniability in case she laid some heavy boundaries on my investigation."

His real concern was her getting emotional and saying something that may expose their casual-ish thirteen-month relationship. They agreed to stay undercover until they decided together whether their relationship has become serious enough for publication.

"Oh. Then I guess you'd better get to it."

"Roger that. Are you able to stay here while I investigate or do you need sleep?"

"Sleep is for the ground-bound. Get to it."

Abs connects the console to his internal system and works internally while Jim watches on and monitors the *JohnGlenn*.

It only takes minutes for Abs to say, "Found it. This was an intentional deletion. Someone removed the coding to navigate back on course. I was right. If this had happened early in the flight, who knows where we'd be."

Jim has an audible monologue, "That is what I did not want to hear. This mission is supposed to be secured. If it's about our particular mission, only a few have that information. But then this could be to sabotage Mars Siolens Harvesting Expeditions in total. Who would have that motive? A spy from Big Blue? A person who knows about siolens life forms and doesn't want it public for financial reasons? Becca on a suicide mission?"

Abs shouts, "Don't be absurd!"

"Sorry. That got dark and personal super-fast."

"Jim, just let the colonel know so I can correct it. Let them figure out who is responsible."

"Oh. Yeah. Right." He pyks her again.

"Djoibjin," the colonel answers with surprise in her tone, "is he done already?"

"Only the best make the Marlagans, ma'am."

"Yeah, yeah. What did he find? Is he still there with you?"

"Hello, Colonel," Abs speaks up, "someone has intentionally deleted the commands that would alarm and put us back on course after evasion. We're fortunate the evasive action happened so late in the flight. Had it been early in the flight, we could potentially have ended up in much, much worse shape. Whoever did it knew how to hide the sabotage because they left dummy lines to make it look as if the coding was still there."

"How did you realize they were dummy lines?"

"When I viewed it in three dimensions, it lay above the rest of the coding to be skipped on a cursory review. It was coded in the relatively new Pulse Dimensional language. I didn't think WSX approved use of this language yet."

"It can't be approved. I've never heard of it. Call me crazy, but I can't help but wonder if that orb you described earlier is responsible for this. The WSX doesn't have anything called Pulse Dimensional."

Jim grunts.

"At any rate, this is good luck and good work, Captains. Go ahead and correct that. I will open an investigation immediately. There can only be a very few suspects. I hope to have all the answers surrounding this mystery before your mission's end."

Jim answers, "Thank you, Colonel. Will there be anything else?"

"Other than this incident and the harassing orb object, how is everything going?"

"As planned, ma'am."

"Keep up the great work, Marlagans. For Mars!"

"For Mars!"

They disconnect.

Abs goes to work on repairing the code, then realizes the same issue in another place regarding the orbit coding. "Jim, somebody really wanted this mission to fail."

"Why? What did you find?"

"When I looked through the entire code, whoever did this sabotaged our orbital flight as well. They didn't want us to return at all."

"I'll pyk the Colonel back."

When the colonel hears the latest findings, she is incensed. "Who the fuck is fucking with my missions? This is extremely serious! I'm going to inform Investigations right now. This cannot wait until morning. I'm so glad this was your mission. No other team would have the resources to find this so quickly. Thanks again for being so forward thinking and on top of this incident. Please make all necessary corrections to save this mission. Remain vigilant and look for other issues. Let us know everything you find. In fact, send me everything you have now and anything new you find and correct. As your investigation moves, pyk it to me in real time. I'll open a live private feed on my sixty-fourth channel. This could have huge implications for WSX Mars and beyond."

"Yes, ma'am."

"Anything else?"

"Not at the time, ma'am."

"Thank you. Djoibjin out."

After disconnecting, Abs asks Jim, "Did she say 'missions,' plural missions?"

"She did."

"Wonder what that means." Abs secretly fears that her statement may have something to do with his parents.

"I don't like it. Let's just make sure we get our asses back home."

"Roger that," Abs says. Then he gets back to his investigative work, searching the entire structure of code in Pulse Dimensional. He finds many little niggling sabotages that could have caused this flight to be lost in space forever, even one to disable HNS once about one and a half parsecs off course. Abs shares it all with Djoibjin in real time.

Becca arrives in the control room wiping her eyes and wrapped in a pink and black blanket from home. "Hey, Abs, I couldn't sleep—"

She freezes in her tracks when she sees Jim.

Abs, who is standing closer to the entrance, greets her while still internally investigating, "Hey, Beck. Give me just a minute."

"Oh. What's going on? Why are you both here?"

Jim, whose back is to her while at the controls, offers a soft and peaceful greeting, "Hello, Becca."

She coldly returns the greeting, "Captain Slight."

"Captain Slight, huh?" Jim answers with a hint of dejection.

She asks again, "Why are you both here? Is something wrong?"

"Thanks to Abs, not anymore."

"What happened?"

"Hey, Abs, the Colonel didn't say we couldn't share this with the crew, did she?"

Abs takes a couple seconds before replying in a choppy sentence, "I don't think…she said that…at least…she…didn't emphasize it…if…she did."

"I don't remember that either."

Shocked, Becca implores, "You had to involve the colonel? What the hell is happening??"

"Calm down, Becca. Abs is fixing it right now, but it appears someone has sabotaged our flight."

"What?" Becca inquires with her mouth agape and eyes shifting from Abs to Jim and back again.

"Abs can explain it better when he's done recoding our flight. It seems that someone wanted us to be stranded in space."

"Wait a minute. What are you saying?"

"We are really fortunate not to be completely off-course and without HNS right now."

Abs points upward. "It's as if someone is looking out for us. This could have been really bad. I checked it all, Jim, and forwarded everything to Djoibjin."

Becca interrogates Abs, "So what happened, Abs? The captain says you could give me a better explanation."

After hearing the full scope of the sabotage, Becca is so stunned that she falls in a seat and stares out the window for a while.

Abs steps over to her, kneels down to get eye level with Becca, takes her hand, and asks, "Are you okay, Bec?"

She shifts her focus to him and finally mutters, "So someone really wanted us to be completely lost out here."

"It seems so."

"When we prayed earlier and you said the part about keeping us safe on this mission, do you really think that worked?"

"We could have easily been deep spaced and without HNS right now. That's what someone intended. In fact, according to my calculations, there's only a 2 percent chance that we would not be deep spaced right now. That means something powerful to me."

"Wow. What if we hadn't said that prayer? This is really—" She begins to hyperventilate.

A wide-eyed Jim leaps to his feet and asks, "Is she okay?"

"Calm down, Bec." Abs looks in her eyes and place his hand on her heart (something he's done since she was a child). "Breathe with me. In. Out. In. Out…"

Her breathing becomes more relaxed just as it seems she would pass out in a matter of seconds. The breathing exercise spares her from that embarrassment, especially in front of Jim.

Abs asks, "Are you all right?"

"I think so. Thanks. Should we say another prayer to thank God for saving us?"

Jim finds his seat again.

"Absolutely. Jim, would you like to join us?"

"You go ahead. I'll just listen in."

The console haid sounds.

"Slight."

General Arms replies, "Captain Slight, I just reviewed Captain Abernum's investigative notes. How's the crew?"

"We're fine. Lieutenant Williams is a little shaken, but everyone is fine."

"Are you back on mission now?"

"Yes, sir."

"This is an incredibly serious matter. Keep this to yourselves, but from our early assessments, this may be related to some of the lost orbital launches we've recently lost."

Abs and Jim look at one another with disbelief. Abs whispers to Jim, "They said it was the ROD."

Jim looks back at him with wide eyes and whispers, "That's right."

Arms continues, "We may need Captain Abernum to help us with this investigation. Our investigation may lead to an individual here, but if there's a bigger fish behind all of this, we may need Abernum's help with the complex coding."

Abs says, "I'm no investigator, sir, but am definitely willing to help if I can."

"We knew we could count on you, Captain. We'll do what we can before your return and let you know what we need from you on this one."

"Finding out who tried to kill my Marlagans family? You can absolutely count on me, sir."

"Good. For now, focus on the mission in front of you. We'll handle this until you get back. Great job saving this mission, Marlagans."

"Of course, General."

"Good luck and Godspeed. For Mars!"

"For Mars!"

* * * * *

Abs Diary Entry 79A:

Hi again, Mom and Dad.

As I said earlier, excitement is never far from us. Mission smoothness time is over! It was nice for the few days it lasted, but then, it never really lasts long, does it? Back to the grind. We've had an issue with the ship, but it's under control now. Before that, an orb with obvious intelligence harassed us for a while, almost a full day, before rushing off in a different direction. Those things are really beginning to creep me out. It used to be fascinating; now it's kinda freaking me out, but what a wonderful, strange, and curious universe. Then again after upgrading and reprogramming a few toys for the mission, Zin and I were looking up through the window in one of the upper deck's viewing areas and saw another strange light seeming to follow us, even at these incredible speeds. It wasn't as close as the previous orb, so determining whether it was another orb was difficult. One thing for sure, it was also under intelligent control. It stayed with us only for quite a few minutes that we saw and shot off past us like we were strolling through Itokawa Square. We've already encountered two orbs on this flight so far, and this mission is the first time we've ever seen any orbs. Wonder if it means anything of significance. We reported it but got no serious response. Almost seemed that they weren't surprised. Becca is assimilating very well into the Marlagans. She and Jim have seemed to be making this work better now. They're still ridiculously awkward when in the same room, but at least, they're able to address one another without that same tension and difficulty they had earlier. Hope it stays this way or gets better. Not sure it can get more awkward, well, let me take that back. It could definitely get more awkward.

Jim is asking me to mediate a truce between them. Since I really don't want any part of that, I'm making Jim buy me the new BTR lounger that comes out next month. Bet he won't ask me to do that again. Gotta get to bed. Almost Io time. Hope you're good and your mission is still going well. Still miss you. Love you both.

# Chapter 13

## Trouble with

## HARVI

Hours later, Abs is shaken awake by a pyk from Kimmie. He answers with a somnolent voice, "Hey, Kimmie, what's up? Everything okay?"

She's not in view yet, but Abs hears what sounds like sniveling in the background.

Upon comprehending that she may be in distress, he immediately forces himself away from the magnet of slumber and sits on the edge of the bed. "Kimmie? You there? You okay?"

She remains wordless for a few more moments. As he attempts to ascertain her circumstance, his mind wanders to dark places. He wonders if she has been taken hostage because of the mission, maybe she has been assaulted based on her findings, or even if she has a confession to make because of her part in the sabotage or the mission. When she did speak, it was close to the last thing he expected to hear.

She finally enters frame, unkempt with puffed eyes and looking as if she'd been in tears for quite some time.

"Baby, what's wrong?"

She finally speaks softly through the sniffles, "I almost lost you out there on a mission that I am leading."

"Oh, Kimmie," he says with deep and sincere compassion, "we're all fine. Don't worry."

"I know, but it scared me," her shaking voice pauses, then continues, "It made me realize some things I've been feeling but not saying."

"Hm?"

"Pick up the handheld. Get me out of your head. I want to see your face and be with you."

"Okay. Hold on just a sec." He transfers her to his handheld pyk, which offers more substantial holographic features than his eye.

"That's better. You are so beautiful," she declares as the sobbing begins to choke her words again.

"Thank you?" he says with hesitation, confused by the declaration under the circumstances.

"Abs?"

"Yes, Kimmie?"

"I love you."

"Whoa," he pauses to let it sink in before saying another word.

After what seemed an eternity to Kimmie, he mutters, "That's the first time you ever said anything remotely like that. I thought I was just—"

"Shut up. I know, but let me finish."

"There's more?" he says with a slightly sarcastic tone.

"Yes. We need to have a conversation about us."

"Do you want to have it now?"

"Yes. No. And stop being an asshole."

"What? What did I do?"

"You know what you're doing. Then again. It is you, so probably not," she titters. Her voice is back to full strength with no lingering signs of sobbing.

"You've got a point there. Kimmie, you know you are special to—"

"I said stop talking right now. I know expressing your feelings is not your strongest talent. I just wanted to tell you that and let you know we need to talk when you get back."

"Roger, ma'am." He's still befuddled by the tangents the conversation keeps seeming to take.

She rises then kneels so that they are holographically face to face. "I know you have no idea how anxious I am for you to be here right now, and that is my own fault for not sharing my feelings for you sooner. This is turning out to be the longest two weeks of my life already."

Being the sophomore to relationships that he is, he is not sure how to respond, so he ignorantly changes the subject. "Any word on the investigation yet?"

"What?"

Panicked, he fumbles over his words while facing her but looking all around her, "I'm…uhh. Why?"

Exasperated, she quips, "You are the worst excuse for a romantic ever. No, there are no suspects under arrest in the four hours since you alerted us. That's not the conversation we're having."

"I'm sorry, Kimmie. You know I've only had two serious relationships before. Just consider me awkward putty in your hands. I trust you enough to ask you to teach me how to be in these moments. Please."

"Oh," she moans, "that's so adorable. Okay then. Let's begin with lesson one. When a woman tells you she loves you for the first time, it can be devastating to her when you don't say it back."

"Oh. Sorry. I love you, Kimmie."

Exhausted, she cries, "Ugh. You're hopeless."

"What? What did I do wrong that time?"

"You're an idiot."

"I am your idiot, Kimmie."

"You are my idiot. Aren't you?"

"I'd wager all that I am on it."

"Aww. See, that was sweet. I guess there may be hope for the hopeless after all. Tiger, do me a favor."

"Name it."

"Tell me you will come back to me safely."

"Is that an order, Colonel?"

"You bet your big mag scooter that's an order! And that's coming from the top!" She blushes.

An announcement comes over the comm system, "Abs. We need you in the garage. ASAP."

He answers the call, "On my way. Just let me get dressed."

Kimmie, concerned, asks, "What's going on now?"

"I had to help reprogram some of our equipment," he explains. "It's more than likely another programming issue."

"Pyk me if anything is wrong. I love you."

"Wow. It's just flying out of you now."

"Ugh. You're so frustrating."

Abs laughs. "I'm just messing with you, but I gotta go."

"Let me know if anything serious happens. I mean anything."

"Of course, Colonel that I love."

"Training you is going to be harder than I thought. Kimmie out."

They disconnect, and Abs runs to the garage, where he sees Zin in a giraffe onesie with Becca and Rhoan in uniform along with Elf huddled around the HARVI unit.

He approaches them and asks, "What is this all about?"

"Abs, HARVI activated himself, then shut himself down, and we don't know what that was about."

"Did you check the power supply and the coding?"

"Of course, but I don't see anything wrong. I was hoping you would double-check it to see if I missed anything."

He moves into their midst to access the automaton.

Unable to hide her disappointment of letting the team down, Zin continues with a hint of dejection, "Under normal circumstances, I wouldn't bother you with something like this, but with everything else happening, I just wanted to err on the side of safety."

"That's right. You did right. Let me patch in and see if I can detect anything."

Becca, who is beginning to panic, is pacing with her intertwined fingers on the crown of her head, asks, "What if they have installed a code that would corrupt or hack you when you patch in?"

Abs smiles at her. "That's not possible…"

He suddenly falls to the ground as soon as his connector reaches HARVI's port, appearing unconscious.

The trio panics and drops down to tend to him immediately.

He begins laughing. Becca slaps him hard across the face. Abs, still laughing, screeches in pain. Rhoan stands up laughing. Zin stands up and kicks Abs in the leg. Rhoan can't stop laughing as he helps Abs off the floor.

"That was a good one, Abs."

Becca forcibly rebuts, "No! No, it wasn't! That wasn't funny at all!"

Zin smiles. "It was a little funny."

"Sorry, Bec. I couldn't resist, and I didn't think you'd really fall for it."

"You suck, okay. I'm showing genuine concern, and you do something like that. Ugh!"

"I'm sorry, Bec. Don't worry about me getting hacked. My compartmentalized system is second to none in the universe. Only I can hack me, but it's great that you're thinking that way."

Stifling his laughter, Rhoan displays a rarely seen soft side by approaching Becca to try and put her at ease. "Becca, it's going to be okay. We have been in much worse situations, and we always manage to work our way through it. You're with the best team in the universe. Nothing is going to happen that we can't work through."

Abs glances at the two in bewilderment while reconnecting with HARVI through a physical cable he keeps in his pocket.

"I'm curious," Rhoan asks. "Why do you often use cables to check coding?"

"Less traffic and distractions."

Rhoan nods. "Hm. Guess that makes sense."

Once focused, Abs notices that there are coding

artifacts here he missed earlier because he hadn't thought about looking for Pulse Dimensional language before and all the dummy lines look correct.

"Oh wow. Whoever is behind the sabotage of our mission hacked HARVI too. This will take a few minutes. If HARVI had not randomly activated in front of Zin, HARVI would have failed on mission. In fact, It's looking like he may have even…let me see. This looks like a detonation code. Oh shit! There may be explosives on our ship!"

The crew audibly gasps and looks at one another and scans the room in stunned silence as if Abs just threw a live grenade.

"The sensors didn't pick up anything during the PiL sweep," says Zin.

Abs surmises, "Then maybe we should be suspicious of the PiL Team."

Zin offers, "Or maybe they just weren't thorough enough in their sweeps."

Rhoan suggests, "Or maybe they were given faulty equipment by someone in charge."

Zin finally shakes off her shock and springs into action. She ruffles through her tool kit and reveals her own. "Fortunately, I always keep a detector in my pack."

Becca and Rhoan watch on as they nervously anticipate more news from Abs.

Zin returns to them with her personal sweeper.

Becca asks, "Why do you have a personal sweeper?"

"I guess one might say that I can be a touch paranoid."

Becca acknowledges, "Why would anyone say that about a gal with her own bomb detector?"

Zin laughs. "I have no idea. Anything else, Abs, before I sweep?"

"Uh. Not yet. Go ahead and start with HARVI, then the rest of this area."

"Check. Come on, Elf," she replies as she powers up the device and begins sweeping the garage for explosives.

Becca struggles to keep her internal panic internal, but fails. Her breathing becomes labored again. The only words she has been thinking in her head manage to sneak their way through her vocal cords and then her lips, "Oh god! What are we going to do?"

"Becca, breathe," Abs, still plugged in and searching for answers, slowly continues, "Have…faith, Bec. An important…part…of…prayer is…believing…that your… prayer is heard…It matters…to God."

After a few breathing exercises, her breathing has normalized. Becca takes a seat on the bench along the wall with Rhoan and is rocking back and forth but doesn't speak.

Zin reports, "The garage is clean. I'll keep going through the adjacent rooms."

"Great, Zin. I have overwritten the detonation code, but be diligent. Check the airlock. Explosives placed there could be most devastating. Really any place can be. Just check everything. We don't fully know what we're up against yet."

Zin replies, "Check."

Becca finally speaks up, "But that's good, right? The bomb is disarmed, right? That's game over for them, right?"

Abs answers cautiously, "Could be, but we just want to make sure there isn't anything else set against us. Until now, we've been playing defense. Now we need to go on the offense and get ahead of whoever this is."

"Okay, can I help?"

"Yes, Bec, you could let Jim know what's going on down here. Are you up to it?"

She turns to Rhoan. "Would you please inform the Captain, Rhoan?"

He flashes her a compassionate gaze and nods. "Sure. I'll tell him."

Rhoan pages Jim, "Cap, we're working a bomb situation down here."

Jim shouts, "What?"

"Don't worry. It's under control."

"Shit. Don't call me with something like that! Get your ass up here and tell me what the hell is going on!"

"Be right there, Cap."

Rhoan optimistically declares, "I'll be back soon."

Zin yells from the Briefing Room, "I've got something!"

Abs, finishing up the recoding, hollers back, "Let me tidy up here. Be right there!"

"It doesn't look like it's armed!"

A few nail-biting moments that seem like an eternity in a bombing situation pass as Abs recodes HARVI. Becca begins pacing nervously again, embracing herself, and murmuring internal reassurances.

Abs unplugs and grabs Becca's hand.

She resists. "I'm okay right here where we know the bomb isn't."

Abs gives her a stern look. "That's not how we operate, Bec."

"But I—"

"We are a team. All hands, Bec. Let's go."

She takes his hand. "Be happy I trust you…with my life even…I guess."

He continues looking at her. "Actually, you should be happy I trust you with my life."

She understands the implications of that statement, so she puts on her brave face, grasps his hand firmly, and follows him.

When Abs looks at the explosives in the cabinet, he realizes it is dormant. "Replacing the detonation code with a dummy code definitely has taken this one out, but it may be linked to another. Keep sweeping, Zin. Be sure to double-check the airlock. Just to make sure."

"Check. Come on, Elf."

"I'll dismantle this one while you do that. This placement is pretty clever. This is probably the second most vulnerable point on the whole ship to breach the hull's protective barriers."

"Dismantle?" Becca asks. "This is not a red or blue wire thing, is it?"

"No. This isn't so antiquated. I have to completely dismantle it."

"You can do that?"

"Almost done as a matter of fact."

"Rhoan said this is nothing like what happened on Europa."

"Oh. Yes. Europa. He's right. That was a whole different monster. And I'm done with this one."

"You've dismantled it already?"

"Yep."

"You sure?"

"Yep."

"That's kinda comforting. So what happened on Europa?"

They exit the room to catch up with Zin and Elf.

Zin shouts, "Abs! Abs! Got something in the airlock!"

"Goodness! On our way!"

Becca relents, "This is so much. I'm feeling fear, Abs."

"Swallow it. Let's move."

"What good am I doing right now?"

"Learn. Watch how I dismantle these things in case something happens to me."

They reach the object.

Abs notes, "This one is dormant as well. Glad you double-checked, Zin. Imagine the massive havoc this could have caused had it gone off. Someone was very serious about stopping us. We need to check everywhere twice."

Zin shakes her head, "This is crazy. Not sure how I missed that the first time."

"Probably a roving signal. That could have caused the PiL to miss it too. Now that they're dormant the signal can't rove anymore."

"Clever. I'll continue my sweep. Twice."

"Thanks, Zin. Call if you find anymore."

"Check."

Becca asks, "How are you so blasé about all of this? We should just turn back to Mars while we still can."

"Come on, Bec. Pull it together. Watch how I dismantle this one."

"I can't even see straight. There's no way I'm learning that right now."

"Sit right here, Bec," he says calmly, knowing how

soothing tones works to calm her more than anything else.

She sits beside him cautiously as she says, "I have never in my wildest dreams imagined I'd ever be this close to explosives. We're explorers. Not this."

"Bec, what's the first thing I taught you about exploration?"

"Expect the unexpected."

"Did you expect this?"

"No."

"That means you need to broaden your concept of the unexpected."

"Are you done already?"

"Yes. Did you follow it that time?"

"No, Abs. I didn't follow it."

"Well. At least you sat near it without panicking. See? Progress."

"Interesting. That's true. Very interesting."

Zin yells, "No more down here. I'm heading up!"

"Thanks, Zin!"

"Let's go up with her."

"Europa?"

"The same way you can't focus on disassembling these explosives, I can't focus on that right now. Let's talk about that when everything calms down. That's a long story."

They head up to the Control Room.

"Hey, Jim, did Zin check in here yet?"

He answers, "Not yet. Why didn't she come here first? Where are you, Zin?"

He hears, "I'm in the galley!"

"Check the Control Room next!"

"Check! Galley is clean!"

Jim asks, "How is everyone holding up?" With the intention of ascertaining how Becca's managing her nervous condition during the intensity of the situations the mission has faced so far.

"We're good, Cap," Rhoan answers. "Right, Becca?"

Still holding Abs's hand, she nods reluctantly and answers, "Yeah. We're good."

Zin begins to scan the Control Room.

Jim says, "I don't remember the giraffe, Zin. Is that one new?"

"Yes, sir. I finished it a week before we left the surface."

He replies, "That's really cute, but the lion is still my favorite."

"Oh, I didn't know that. Then I'll greet you with the lion after you return from the surface."

"Yes! That would be fantastic!"

"Control Room is clean."

"Great job, Zin. Keep going," Abs responds.

"On it. I just need access to everyone's room."

"I'll remotely unlock them now," Jim orders Bingo to use the master key to unlock all the rooms on the ship.

Rhoan requests, "Let me pick up a little before you go in my room."

Zin nods. "Please do. The less I see of your weird and disgusting private business, the better."

Jim inquires, "Have you forwarded the detonation information to MOS4, Abs?"

"Not just yet, Jim."

"Why not?"

Abs asks, "Guys, can we have a moment alone?"

Rhoan, befuddled, demands, "Dude! We're Marlagans too. No mission secrets. You know we don't roll like that."

"Well. I do. But…" Abs pauses, "okay, you're right, Rhoan. Jim, I can't escape the thought that this may be an inside job."

Jim wonders aloud, "Inside? Like who? Not one of the Marlagans?"

"No. Not one of us. But consider this. So few people know what our true mission is. If someone is opposed to truly discovering Io life forms, who knows what they'd do to stop us from finding out that they exist?"

"That would be stupid, though. If we don't succeed, they'll just send another team. This feels more personal against our team to me."

"I've thought about that, of course, but everyone loves us."

"Not everyone."

"Well. Not everyone. But consider this, stopping this mission may be enough of a delay for someone or some organization to benefit from keeping potential life form information secret at least long enough for one more major transaction."

"Do you suspect the colonel?"

"No. Not her. Probably no one we know, but maybe someone who is watching updates from our mission, whether by hack or privilege."

Jim grunts.

Abs continues, "If there are some other explosives onboard, I'd like to hold off on reporting that we found the explosives until we know we have dismantled them all in case someone has a remote detonator."

"I see where your thinking is." Jim begins to scroll through his mental contact list.

"It just feels smart to eliminate as many potential remote threats before disseminating more information."

Jim, still in deep thought, grunts. "Ugh. Yeah. I get it. That is smart. I am coming up zero on my list of suspects."

"Thanks, Grunt. I haven't even had time to think of suspects, yet. Right now, getting through this safely is all I can focus on."

"Work fast. We have about twelve more hours until orbit. I'm going to need a break soon."

Rhoan jumps at the chance to prove himself competent after a major Europa flight blunder on a previous mission and offers, "I can give you a break, Jim. At least up to minus four (four hours before destination). We don't want Abs to stop what he's doing. Just let me pick up some stuff in my room real quick."

"Sounds good to me," Jim accepts.

Excited for the chance to prove himself, Rhoan runs to his room and picks up certain personal BTR equipment. He picks up several clumps of dirty clothing to toss them into the laundry chute and grabs a quick snack, then runs back to the Control Room.

Rhoan is back within ten minutes, and Jim briefs Rhoan on all matters of the flight.

As they are wrapping up, Zin reenters the Control Room.

"All clear. Whoever is responsible for this may not have had much time to plant the explosives. They could have recoded HARVI and synced him to the explosives before he was placed on the ship. Maybe just some kid testing his skills and wasn't too serious about hurting our mission."

Abs answers, "Oh. They were very serious. If we weren't so protected, without doubt, we should be DS'd by now."

"You're not going to start that God stuff again, are you?"

Becca inserts herself, "Rhoan, you cannot deny what we've experienced here!"

"That's just fortunate happenstance. Luck does happen, you know."

She rebuts, "I'll just say that I have never prayed before this mission, and from what I've seen, the effects are undeniable."

"I just don't believe in fairies, myths, and ancient stories like that. Technology saved us. Abs's technology. All of that can be explained by tech and safeguards."

Abs remains silent when Becca looks to him for backup.

After realizing Abs won't engage, Becca says, "Rhoan, you say you don't believe in those things, but yet you believe in luck? I guess you're entitled to believe what you believe, but so am I."

"True. I'd never dispute that."

Zin wonders, "Rhoan, why are you sitting there?"

"I'm giving the Caps a break."

Her immediate concern evident for all to see, Zin asks, "What? Why? Do you want me to sit up here with you?"

"No, you've got to get the surface equipment staged. I got this."

"Just don't let—"

He cuts her off, "That will not happen again. I learned my lesson. Relax. It'll be fine."

She looks at Abs. "Abs?"

"He's fine. Besides, what choice do we have? We have to secure the integrity of our equipment and get some rest before orbit."

Rhoan makes his annoyance known. "Thanks a lot, Cap."

Zin capitulates slightly, "Yeah. I guess. Is the Armory equipment staged, Rhoan?"

"That only took an hour. I did that before I came to the Garage while you were prepping the Swan."

"You sure you don't want me to sit with you just for an hour or so?"

"Sis, blow! Be gone."

"All right. Elf and I'll get back to it."

"Thanks, Zin," says Abs.

"Check. I'm going to sweep one more time. I'll let you know if anything else pops up. I'll be back in a little while to see if you need anything too, brother."

"I'll call if I need anything."

"Oh. Okay then," Zin replies with nervousness as she looks back at him sitting at the main console.

A more relaxed Abs advises, "Thank you, all. You'll find me in the Galley buttoning up for a little while, then trying to finish my nap. Is your AC8 [MedCart] all set, Bec?"

"Yes, it's all set. It's very advanced. Hopefully we won't need it, but I'm excited to try some of the new features."

Rhoan agrees, "Yeah, I'm hoping the same thing, Doc."

Zin heads out. "Me too."

Abs looks over at Rhoan, who is studying the HNS. "You're good, right?"

"As good as it gets, Cap."

"Thanks, Rhoan."

He and Becca exit for the Galley.

In the Galley, Abs asks Becca, "Are you hungry at all?"

"Surprisingly starving."

"Me too. Let's grab some grub before I button up."

While preparing a couple SRMs (Space-Ready Meals), Becca breeches the subject again, "Are you going to tell me about Europa now?"

Abs turns from the food processor to face Becca and recalls, "Oh yeah, Europa," then he turns back to the meals and continues, "So we were in flight and Rhoan took over flight duties. Keeping this short. Later when I took over, we were so far off course because Rhoan misread the instruments. His miscalculation cost us two days, but that wasn't our biggest issue. We were testing a new, still classified by the way, excavation/subterranean vehicle on the frozen surface. Things were going according to plan. Once we were all set on the surface for putting the new equipment through its paces, we started burrowing. We burrowed for about two hours when it started making a very unsettling noise and began vibrating violently. Then it just stopped. Nothing had ever stopped like that before. Just stopped cold in the ice. We looked at one another because we were aware that the surface had closed in behind us. So I told Rhoan to try the reverse gear. There was a clunk then a hiss, and we lost power, as well as the forward and reverse gears.

We were stuck two kilos deep on Europa, smelling burning circuitry, and the surface was closed in above us. We couldn't get out to investigate the issue. It was tight quarters, so movement throughout the vehicle was difficult at best. Fortunately, the salt84 insulation protected us from freezing to death. We were stuck for three hours completely encapsulated in ice."

Sitting on the edge of her seat, Becca says, "Oh hemlock! I would hope you brought extra pants."

Abs laughs. "It was intense. But Zin worked out the problem remotely from orbit, and when that thing cranked up, we celebrated like we all just lost our virginity in an orgy of supermodels."

"Disgusting."

"Haha! It is, but we just dug ourselves out and went straight back into orbit."

"So you didn't finish the mission?"

"Being that the mission was to learn how well the simulations proved themselves in practical application, we succeeded in showing that there was more work to be done on the Deep Diva…at least that's what we called her after that."

"That sounds so terrifying."

"I told you when you asked to join that we are usually assigned the toughest challenges because we're the best."

"You did. I see now that I underestimated the weight of that statement."

"Any regrets?"

"I'm still alive, so not yet. That may change after if we don't survive. Ask me then."

"Ha! Now you're getting it."

"I've been pretty anxious, and I'd even go as far to

say I was terrified at one point today, but I believe this is what I need. It'll make bad boyfriends feel like Mars dust in my boot. Just shake it off and move on. When we survive this, I don't think anything else will seem like a big deal ever again."

"Now you're really getting it. One word of caution, though. It is addictive. Some people begin to feel invincible. So don't get careless or cocky."

"Yeah. Captain Slight made that abundantly clear on MOS4 at the weirdest times."

"He sure did. Also remember we succeed by problem-solving—"

"I know. I know. We succeed by solving the problem, not whining about it."

"Bingo!"

"Yes, Abs?" Bingo answers.

"Disregard, Bingo."

"Okay, Abs."

Abs shakes his head. "That's the third time. I keep forgetting that thing was installed throughout this ship. I need to reprogram Bingo's wake-up call for my voice."

Jim pyks Marsha once he's settled down in his quarters.

"Jim?" she answers with bewilderment since his routine has always been not to contact her during missions.

"Hi, Marsha," he says in a somber tone.

"What's wrong?"

"Nothing really," he lies.

"Why are you lying? You said you'd never call as long as things were going smoothly. The last time you called was from Europa."

"I know. There are some things that happened, but we fixed them. I guess I just needed to let you know I love you."

"Is everyone okay? What do you mean some things happened?"

"Of course you know I can't go into detail. We're all okay, though. There's a chance we will be delayed a day or two getting back. How are you and Drena?"

"UTC or Mars day?"

"Mission, so UTC. Are you two okay?"

"Uh sure. Yeah, we're fine. Is everything back to normal?"

He grunts. "Mhm. As far as we can tell. We're still on guard."

"Looks like you're in bed."

"Yeah, I had to pilot for an extended period, but let's not talk mission right now. I just want you both to know I love you."

"We love you too. Looking forward to seeing you again."

"Me too. Remember that trip to Disney Motherland in UCA?"

"Of course, how could I ever forget? That was such a wonderful time. It's so crazy how crowded everything was."

"And the smells. My goodness."

"I know. We forget how fortunate we are sometimes to be on Mars."

"We do, but there is nothing on Mars as fun as that day was…even with the smells."

"Remember how upset Drena was when she outgrew her authentic Disney pajamas and t-shirts?"

"Totally bonkers."

Speaking to someone out of view, Marsha says with botheration, "Okay. Okay. I'll be right there," then she turns her attention back to Jim, "Jim, honey, I have to give a briefing. Are you sure everything is okay?"

"Yes. We're all fine. Please just remember what I said."

"You love us?"

"Remember that."

"We love you too, Jim. Just be careful out there and stop making me worry."

"I will. See you in a little while."

"With details. But then again, I probably don't want to know."

"You probably don't."

"Wish I hadn't heard that. Slight out."

They disconnect.

* * * * *

Abs Diary Entry 78A:

Hi, Mom and Dad,

Today has been very troubling. Just remember to ask me about today. Use the code words, HARVI and sabotage. That will remind me of today. We had some touch and go moments, but if you're reading this, it's likely that you know it's all been sorted out. Fortunately, Becca's anxiety is beginning to improve. Today could have easily sparked another of her mega panic attacks and almost did. I was hoping traveling with the Marlagans would help her condition, and it seems to be working. As the day progressed and the situation escalated, she seemed to handle each obstacle better and better. She eventually started fixing the problems rather than adding to them. Just know that for now, we're all safe and staying very diligent to arrive alive. I'm happy you'll be reading this after we are together safely. If you saw this now, you might be freaking out. I heard from Nikki again today. She still wants to get back together. How many times can a dude turn a girl down? Maybe my messaging is too soft. Bec says she's just trying to wear me down. Then I remembered that was the same technique she used to get me to date her in the first place. Can't fault her for trying. If she wasn't so flaky, demanding, and possessive, she'd be great. Oh well, hope she moves on soon; she's beautiful enough to attract anyone she wants. I'm really tired. Just wanted to say a few words before dozing off. Gotta get some sleep before go time. Hoping to see you in a few hours. Love you both.

# Chapter 14

## Medic!

THERE IS a hurried buzz of last minute scampering throughout the *JohnGlenn* as the crew rushes to complete orbital preparations. They complete their tasks with more than three minutes to spare. Now comes the moment that they were meant to miss. With their destination well in sight, each Marlagan is strapped into their respective position in the Control Room as *JohnGlenn* begins approaching Io orbit. As Jim pilots the ship, the entire crew sans Becca is laser focused on the HNS. Becca is so in awe at the spectacle of Jupiter that she can hear or think of nothing else. She is completely captivated and amazed by the visible gasses being emitted, the glorious ballet of unfathomable storms, the lively party of brilliant and muted colors, the enormity and organization of it all in symphonic harmony and anarchical chaos at the same time. Her eyes well up as she recognizes the smallness of man in this moment.

Unwittingly, her mouth has been open so long that it has become a desert inside her helmet.

Bingo gives corrective measures, "Turn right three degrees. Pitch forward two degrees."

Jim replies in kind as they reach hit a turbulent pocket produced by Jupiter's overbearing activity.

Jim strains at the controls as colorful gas streams decorate the ship's many windows. "She's fighting."

Abs checks on him. "You got it, Jim?"

Bingo instructs, "Pull back one degree…"

"Yeah, I got it. I'm getting the sense this region doesn't want us here!"

Zin reminds, "No one's been down here before. This might be the norm. Anything I can do?"

"No. We're fine. This would be a cinch in the *Neil*. Guess the *Mushroom* isn't used to this. Either that or I'm not accustomed to the *Shroom* yet."

"Maintain course for orbit."

Jim struggles against Jupiter's intrusions to maintain the course for a perfect orbital approach around its tiny satellite. Seconds later, the moderately turbulent ride suddenly becomes more bearable, and the *JohnGlenn* smoothly transitions into an orbit of the Jupiter moon, Io.

"Well done, Jim. Well done indeed."

Sweating inside his suit, Jim replies, "Thanks, Abs. I'm not sure I enjoyed that."

"Well, you did it."

"No thanks to the *Shroom*."

Becca manages to mutter a sound, "Whoa."

Rhoan remarks, "Amen to that. I don't think I could ever come here and not be astonished by the sheer glory that is Jupiter."

Finally able to form words through her amazement, a wide-eyed Becca agrees, "It's just astounding. It's overwhelming. I never imagined it would be like this. So colossal. To actually lay eyes on it in person is something that cannot be described, taught or even relayed through holograms. It's surreal…and…" she searches for a word to describe the experience more clearly but lands on, "unexpectedly emotional."

Bingo exclaims, "You are now in artificial Io orbit at four hundred kilometers above the moon's surface. The time is 1542 Zulu. Welcome to Io, Marlagans!"

Becca begins to cheer, but cuts her glee short when she sees and hears everyone else unbuckling and seeming busy and focused. "Wait. Am I supposed to be doing something right now?"

Abs looks at her. "Time to get your excursion gear and prepare for departure. Remember when we said since we are entering orbit later, we will head down to the surface very shortly thereafter?"

"Yes."

"Well, shortly thereafter is thirty minutes from now."

"Oh crap. Okay."

She bolts out the door with everyone else.

Nearly fifteen minutes later, the crew is assembled in the Garage with gear, equipment carts, and HARVI. Rhoan performs final inspections and disburses arms.

Zin makes one final plea before they board the surface vehicle, "Please, please, please make sure your sulfur detectors are activated. Decon can do a lot, but somehow that sulfur got through last time, and I do not want to put up with that odor in my Garage again."

They all check and verify its activation for her.

As the Surface Team boards the Black Swan, Abs reminds Zin, "I just verified our steady orbit. Please keep an eye on the HNS to catch anything out of the ordinary as it happens."

"I will, but you reset the alarm parameters, right?"

"I did, but I'm human. Humans miss things."

"You are not human and you don't miss things."

"As much as I wish that were true, it's not. So please—"

"Check. Got it. Got it. I'll keep a careful eye on it and let you know immediately if anything strange happens. Would you please say a few words for the Marlagans before you drop, Abs?"

"Of course. Heavenly Father, you have been so faithful in getting us this far against all odds. We can't thank you enough for your grace, love, and mercy. We also thank you for your continued protection and favor. Thank you for loving us enough to care about us puny humans even though we are unworthy. Please continue to bless this mission, each excursion, and guide our steps to its completion and help us discover whatever there is to find on the surface and bring us all back home safely. We love you. We need you. We're nothing without you. Thank you, Lord. Amen."

Jim extends his appreciation, "Thanks, Rev."

"Wait," Becca challenges, "I thought you were all atheists."

Zin admits, "We basically are, but it doesn't hurt to get everything and everyone on our side. Ever since we started working together, Abs has prayed for us, and we made it home safely every time even though the odds were never in our favor. So it's our ritual now. Might be something to it. Might just give us a bit more luck. Who knows?"

Abs speaks up, "I know, and if you're being honest with yourselves, you know too."

"All right, Rev. Now is not the time for preaching. It's time for action. You ready?"

He smiles and gives her a thumbs up before sealing the Black Swan. Zin closes the airlock portion of the Garage and awaits the thirty-second countdown. Then she spaces the equipment and her crew.

Rhoan looks back. "That's funny. It does look exactly like a mushroom. My sister's in a fungus. She's covered in fungi."

Zin replies over comms, "I heard that, Rhoan. Grow up."

Becca observes. "Is that a volcano erupting in the distance?"

Jim answers, "Yes. That happens very frequently here. Io's landscapes shifts and morphs very rapidly due to Jupiter's crazy power over it. We have to be extremely careful how we step. We had an experience early in Io exploration when we planned a mission in a specific area before launch to the MOS, and by the time we were ready to deploy to the surface, that entire region was very different, almost completely wiped out."

"Do we have a way of predicting those changes while we're on the surface?"

"We do. We now have satellites that monitor Io's meteorological activity and Jupiter's pull and gravitational effects."

"How much warning will we get?"

"About a day, but volcanoes won't stop our excursion.

Only major shifts in the surface's vitality will cause a cancellation. Trust your gear and the big brains that monitor the surface. All of our equipment and gear are insulated to protect against the ravages of all radiation, weather elements from volcanoes to liquid nitrogen and beyond. We and everything with us are safe."

Autopilot flies the Black Swan and trailing equipment down through the thin atmosphere, which is easily breeched by the excursion equipment. The ride down is incredibly fast. They reach speeds up to six hundred fifty knots and experience occasional moderate turbulence.

At one kilometer from the surface, Abs takes over manual control. "That is our landing zone right there. Good shot, Zin."

"Thanks, Cap! Don't forget Elf."

"Geez. Okay. Thanks, Elf."

Becca teases with a giggle. "You just thanked a robot, Abs."

"Yeah. I did. It's better than the back and forth with Zin had I not."Jim says, "Looking good, Abs. Right on target."

Abs announces, "Thirty meters, twenty knots. Hover initiated."

The jolt of the initial braking power sharply jostles all four heads in the rover and Becca let's out an audible "Oomph."

The Black Swan hovers to a smooth textbook landing. The accompanying equipment follows suit and gently lands on the programmed marks.

"So far, the surface looks pretty close to the planned expedition layout," Jim mutters.

Abs commands, "Prepare for disembarkation."

The bustling sounds of unlatching, spacesuits rustling, equipment movement, and chatter fill the vehicle. All comms checks are successful between the ground crew and Zin in orbit.

"Go, Marlagans! For Mars!"

They all repeat, "For Mars!"

Ten minutes later, the crew is ready to disembark.

Jim asks, "By the numbers, Abernum?"

"Check."

"Slight?"

"Check."

"Williams?"

"Check."

"R. Romero?"

"Check."

"Z. Romero?"

"Check."

"That's all points go. Abs, release the seal."

"Aye, Cap."

*Ca-thunk. Boop.* Hissing noise seems to go on for fifty seconds before the whir of the doors folding upward.

"Marlagans, test your footing before you commit. This is a new region for all of us," Slight advises.

As they gingerly exit, Rhoan advises, "How is your side, Becca? This side is not solid."

"This side is good," she answers, standing by the door. "Climb on over. Need any help?"

"I've got it. Thanks." A couple seconds later, he says, "Wait. I do need a hand. My pack is caught on something."

Abs, who hasn't fully exited, climbs back into the Black Swan to loosen Rhoan's snagged pack.

"Thanks, Abs."

"No problem. Good thing you didn't pull yourself free. You comm pack was snagged."

"Not a rookie, Abs. That lesson was learned long ago."

The team forms in front of the Black Swan for Jim's next orders.

"Welcome to Io, Marlagans. Against the odds, we have come further than someone wanted us to today. Stay vigilant. Expect the unexpected. Look for everything here to try and kill you and your crew mates. If you die here on Io, know that you died a member of the most elite team in the universe paving the way for future exploration and furthering humanity's foothold into the unknown. But more than anything else, you died for duty and…for Mars!"

They all repeat, "For Mars!"

"With that said, we are Marlagans, so just shake off any death you may catch out here and keep it moving. Assignments. Abs, activate the Harvesters."

"Check."

Zin disputes the generic term over the comms, "AC20s!"

"Here we go," Rhoan squawks.

Jim continues, "Becca, ready your MedCart and equip yourself."

"Roger."

"Rhoan, activate and arm HARVI."

"Check."

"I'll secure the Black Swan and prep the traps for deployment."

The Harvesters hover and extend their multi-tooled arms with shovels, pickers, and various suction hoses. The ultraviolet lights begin to sweep for raw siolens, which luminesce a neon pink to the naked eye when hit with ultraviolet light. Immediately, they confirm the sight of more siolens than anyone has ever seen littered all over this region. Beyond the ultraviolet lighting of the AC20s, the usually clear material appears bright blue and veiny through the visors of the Cam-Mets.

Slight remarks, "This is going to be a massive haul. The Harvesters will need to make several trips, Zin."

Abs agrees, "Indeed. This will be an incredible load. Never would have predicted this much. Hope the *Mushroom* can handle it."

Zin acknowledges, "AC20s. Ahem."

Jim corrects himself, "AC20s. Sorry, mom."

"That's better. Fill 'er up! We have plenty of storage."

As HARVI activates, Zin reports, "I have all eyes on you now and recording. That is definitely more material than we've ever seen. Our vacation planners were spot on about this region."

"They sure were. They will have to send a few more missions to get all this loot," Rhoan adds.

"Medical is ready, Captain."

"Thank you, Lieutenant."

"Arms and HARVI all set, Cap."

Thanks, Rhoan. How about the ACs, Abs?"

"One of them is being stubborn. Give me a second to troubleshoot."

"Standing by."

Abs continues searching through the coding for a problem. Rhoan walks up to it and sees that it looks stuck in an unfamiliar gooey substance. He kicks it free and actuates the Harvester.

Rhoan brags, "There you go, Abs. Troubleshooting—whoa. Look at this. What's this stuff?"

The crew walks over to observe. Recognizing this is not a substance they've ever seen on Io, Abs retrieves a specimen container from Jim's pack.

"This is very strange. It sort of reminds me of the stuff those siolens workers found. I wonder what it's comprised of and what its purpose is," he says as he prepares the equipment to scoop it up.

"Yeah, it does look a little like that, but different. Just be careful handling that, Abs. You never know, it may be alive."

"Okay," Abs says softly while nervously approaching the substance.

Jim nervously advises, "Easy now, Abs. Careful. You—"

Abs snaps, "Yeah, Jim! Goodness! I got it."

"Sorry, man. Just trying to help. Don't put that stuff back in my pack."

Abs holds up the collected specimen and illuminates it with his helmet light to see through it. "Sorry, Jim. Didn't mean to snap at you. That was a pretty tense moment made more tense by the commentary."

"Guess that was me working through my own tension."

"No big. I dig."

"Please don't start that again, Abs," Zin pleads.

Observing Abs holding up the container for an extended period, Becca asks, "What are you looking at?"

"I'm trying to use my microscope to see what's in it."

"See anything?"

"There is something in here, but we are going to need the lab to do a more detailed analysis."

"Just make sure it's safe before we take it back to the ship."

Still scrutinizing the container, he says, "I don't see any movement in it. This stuff is unlike anything we have come across before. I don't think anyone has ever seen a red like this in nature anywhere. Not even on the red planet. There isn't much of it here. This is the only patch of it as far as I can see. Zin, can HARVI see any in the distance?"

"No, he's been looking and nothing in sight."

"Thanks."

Abs places the specimen in one of the specimen compartments in Harvester 4.

After seeing the container is secured, Jim looks around and orders, "Okay, Marlagans, let's form up in wormhole and prepare to move out."

The Marlagans form up behind HARVI in wormhole formation, two abreast staggered, Rhoan followed by Jim, then Becca, then Abs, and finally the MedCart. The Harvesters continue the furious work of mining for siolens.

"Zin, send in the clown."

"You got it, Cap."

Zin activates and sends in the mapping drone, which makes a preliminary sweep of the cave's interior to map a route and investigate and highlight any hidden perils. Minutes later, the drone emerges from the cave.

Zin announces, "Nothing in there as far as the drone could see. Sent the map to HARVI and the crew."

Jim orders, "Thanks, Zin. Remember, Marlagans, we are only going in to observe. If you see anything unusual, alert the team, but don't touch anything unless absolutely necessary for safety or security. Understand? Can I get a 'yes, sir'?"

"Yes, sir!"

"Let's do this. Zin, send HARVI into the cave on point. Activate the radar and scope."

"Check. Here we go."

"How's the rearview, Abs?" Jim asks.

"All clear."

Abs is linked into and controlling HARVI's separate rear facing camera system, which is 2.2m above the surface in periscoping configuration. Zin and Rhoan share the same access and management of his front facing camera. She also shares the feed and control of the rear-facing camera system with Abs.

Jim commands, "Marlagans! Into the void."

They follow HARVI's lead.

As they reach the jagged mouth of the cave, Rhoan says, "No bathroom breaks once we cross the threshold, Becca."

"Hey. What's that supposed to mean?"

"You know how females always...'

Jim cuts him short, "Stop talking, Rhoan. Time to focus. Eyes open. Keep sharp, everyone."

As they enter the cave, Zin notes, "Wow. Unit 1 is already on its way back to the *Mushroom*."

Jim states, "This is the strangest interior. Are you recording this, Zin?"

"Of course."

"I'll record my observations now. The interior of the cave is reminiscent of an earthly cavern with stalagmite-like structures near the walls. There are numerous stalactite structures hanging all over even from the walls. They almost look like a network of roads or paths on which something can travel back and forth. The color is mostly a yellowish-orange with lines of grayish-green and some black specks. It seems frozen solid at the entrance, but less so as we look deeper inside."

Zin announces, "There is another patch of the red substance in the distance."

"Which direction?"

"West northwest about two decs."

"Eyes open, Marlagans."

Zin warns, "Stop."

"Why? What do you see?"

"I think something moved inside that patch of substance."

Rhoan replies, "Shit. Here we go. HARVI's hot."

Jim asks, "Anyone else see it?"

"No."

"No, sir."

"Is it still there, Zin?"

"Not sure. It was only a flutter. We're not detecting wind on any sensors. Do you feel wind?"

"No sign of wind."

Metallic whirring and clicking noises emanate from HARVI.

Zin answers, "Careful. HARVI's finger is on the

trigger. I don't see anything now. Shall we proceed, Cap?"

Captain Slight, who has been grunting quietly off and on since entering the cave, directs, "Proceed. Quarter speed and let us know if there is any more movement."

"Check."

Slowly, the formation journeys deeper into the strange cave.

Zin calls, "Becca."

"Yes? Go ahead?"

"You are spiking. Practice your breathing."

"Wouldn't your anxiety be spiking too?"

"Breathe in."

Becca breathes in.

"Breathe out."

She breathes out.

After a couple minutes, Zin advises, "You're back in the green."

"Thanks, Zin. Sorry about that."

"Check."

Jim holds up his gloved fist. The formation halts. Zin stops HARVI.

Abs asks, "What's up, Cap?"

"Movement."

"Where?"

"On the wall ahead."

Abs says, "It's probably just siolens sliding down the wall. Zin, do you observe movement on the wall too?"

"Affirmative."

"It could be siolens forming and falling to the ground. Jim, you should ready the traps."

Jim states, "I'm already on it."

Zin notes, "That would make more sense if the ground near the walls was covered in siolens, but it's not. I mean, there is some but not a bunch. You know what I'm saying?"

"Yeah, but we have been traveling uphill, so it could all be dumping out to flat ground, which may be why there's so much outside the cave."

"Possible. I didn't see the movement that time, Jim. Do you see it anymore?"

"Negative."

"Ready to proceed at your command. We're only a few meters from the red patch where Zin saw the fluttering."

"In sight. Proceed at quarter speed. Eyes open."

"Proceeding," Zin acknowledges as HARVI begins to move forward.

They try to quiet their steps to avoid detection, but from what? There shouldn't be anything to hear them on this whole planet.

Upon reaching the red patch spotted earlier, Abs pulls another specimen container from Jim's pack. "Zin, did Unit 4 return with the specimen yet?"

"It's on its way up now. Why? Do you want me to do anything special with it?"

"No. Standard procedure is fine. I just wonder how this interior specimen compares to the exterior specimen."

Jim turns to look at the specimen Abs is studying, then screams, "OWWW! SHIT!" He collapses to the ground, grabs his knee, and rolls back and forth on the ground.

"What? Did you hurt your knee?" Becca asks as they run to his rescue.

"No! Something stabbed me in the ankle!"

The suit only flexes enough for him to grab for his knee, but he is unable to reach the area of pain.

Rhoan and HARVI take defensive positions prepared for battle but see and detect nothing. Rhoan is wielding his new pistol in his right hand and an ionized sword in his left. HARVI has gone into Sentry 2-SFW (squat/full weapons) Mode. In this mode, he can swivel much more quickly, has a much stronger balancing arrangement, and weapons systems are facing all four quadrants.

Abs and Becca tend to Jim and immediately notice a tear in his suit and his flesh. Thankfully, the suit compartmentalizes the damaged area to maintain breathable and safe environment to the rest of Jim's suit. Still, Jim's breathing becomes erratic and pronounced due to the intense pain.

"Jim, you have to lie flat and let your knee go, so I can take a look," Becca says calmly.

"Hurry. It really hurts!"

Becca goes straight to her duty of injecting an injury solution into the medical line on his HAS4/LGS7 suit so it can quickly reseal the tear, disinfect and protect the wound, stop the bleeding, and ease the pain.

Abs positions himself to calm and reassure Jim as Becca works feverishly on his wound.

Jim quickly begins to feel relief. "That's already feeling better. Thank you, Becca."

She asks, "Did you step on or kick something?"

"I don't think so. It just seemed to happen...out

of nowhere. If it was something I stepped on, I surely didn't see it. You were right behind me. Did you see it?"

"I didn't see anything, and it didn't look like you stepped on or into anything."

Rhoan is still running a thorough security sweep of the immediate area, looking for something to shoot. He sees nothing. No one does. Not even HARVI. Nor Zin.

Abs calls, "Zin, these new visors aren't picking up anything. Would you please send an AC20 in here to light up the area for us?"

"Check. Unit 3 is headed your way in one minute. I just have to override it. Standby."

"Standing by."

"Maybe HARVI saw something."

"HARVI wasn't looking that low in rearview. There's a feature to reinstall rear ground cameras."

Zin remarks, "That is a bummer. The one time we need it, it's been removed for those new sensors. Figures."

HARVI and Rhoan expand the search perimeter but still find nothing.

Abs asks, "How're you holding up, Jim?"

Jim grunts through labored breathing. "Ugh. I'm okay. The…pain has not gone completely but is easing."

"Bec, will he be able to walk?"

"I doubt it. His ankle is in a very bad way. We will have to go back into orbit to get that wound under control. We should go with him. I don't trust the MedCart to get him there on its own."

"Understood. Zin, you copy that?"

"Copy. Let me know when, and I'll prep for the Black Swan."

"Thanks, Zin."

Rhoan rejoins the team in befuddlement. "I didn't see anything at all. This is crazy. It had to attack from hiding somewhere."

"It? Attack? Come on, Rhoan. Jim had to step on something."

Becca positions the MedCart next to Jim and activates Gurney Mode.

Becca asks, "Guys, we need a little more room for the scoop and transport."

Abs and Rhoan take a few step back to make room. HARVI is still in Sentry 2-SFW Mode as Unit 3 arrives. Rhoan argues, "Show me, Abs. What did he step on?"

"All of these jutting elements in here. It could have been a number of things."

"Where's the blood on any of those things?"

"Where's the blood from an attack?"

Bec steps in with authority booming. "Guys! Let's work that out later. Now we have to get the captain to surgery."

"Unit 3 is right behind you, Abs."

"Right. Sorry. Thanks, Zin. Would you please collect any siolens you see in here as it sweeps the area?"

"Check."

As Jim is secured for transport, Unit 3 continues its scan but comes up empty.

"Abs, there's nothing here," Zin apprises.

"Thanks, Zin. That's so strange. Anything in the traps?"

"Nothing."

"Let's leave them in place. We have to get out of here and take care of that wound. We'll come back tomorrow, check the traps, and figure this out."

They hurriedly gather up and head back to the Black Swan in the same formation with the exception of Jim riding on the MedCart's gurney in front of Becca. Upon exiting the cave, Rhoan spots a fresh patch of the unusual red substance.

"Hey, Abs, there's a new patch of red. That wasn't there when we entered the cave."

"That's right, Rhoan. There is definitely something going on here. Let's not touch that patch and see if it's still here tomorrow. I'll mark the location on our HUD."

Becca says, "Jim, your heart rate is increasing. Talk to me. How are you doing?"

"I'm okay, but it feels like the pain is moving further up my leg and getting worse. Almost like something is moving inside the wound."

Rhoan notes, "That might be the reason we can't find it. It's in his leg."

Zin says, "Rhoan, why would you say that?"

"Why not? Could be true."

Abs informs, "Becca, we need to contain the leg at all times in case Rhoan's right."

"Let me figure that out after we're secure."

Jim grunts and moans as they lift him into the rear of the vehicle.

As they secure Jim into the rear ambulatory area of the Black Swan, Becca straps in next to him. "That does not sound good. We'll get a thorough look as soon as we reach the *Mushroom*."

Jim, still on comms, says, "Becca?"

"Yeah, Cap?"

"I'm sorry."

Becca is too focused on her patient to realize what he means. "What? About what?"

"You know what I mean."

When she looks at him for clarification, she realizes he is about to out them. "Save it, Captain. Let's talk about that later. Right now, you need to focus on your breathing so you don't go into shock."

He grunts. "Ahh. Okay. The pain is starting to climb again."

Becca asks, "How much longer, Abs?"

Jim passes out.

"Hurry, Abs. He just lost consciousness."

"We're all set. Everyone secure?"

Everyone affirms that they are ready.

The Black Swan hovers, moves into a clearing then blasts into orbit.

*  *  *  *  *

Abs Diary Entry 78B:

Good evening, Mom and Dad. Guess I don't have to tell you how emotionally difficult it was to reach Io orbit and not see you or get any details about meeting up with you. I guess it is evident to me now that I put too much faith in my hope of seeing you on this mission. Set myself up. I'm trying to hide my disappointment from the crew, but my snappy disposition might be giving it away. Our arrival at Io is thanks to Rhoan and Jim, and I guess me too. Someone is pretty serious in their efforts to kill us. Hope we are able to stay ahead of them and get to the bottom of who is sabotaging our mission. We did manage to get into orbit and are about to land on the surface. I have to keep this brief because we head down in mere minutes. I guess there is still hope. Maybe you're down there. Sorry this is so short, but I will...gotta go. Love you.

# Chapter 15

## Leg Goo

**Z**IN RUSHES over to assist as the rest of the Marlagans speedily evacuate the Black Swan and rush an unconscious Jim up to the lift on the side of the Garage on the way to MedBay. Repeated attempts to wake Jim still fail. At the lift, they begin to lose their minds during the intensely frustrating moments of waiting for the elevator to reach the lower deck. They'd never noticed its insanely slow thousand-year-old tortoise pace before. The lift is so slow that the crew has time to strip out of the encumbering outer shells of their suits before it reaches them. Of course, the pile of clothing and equipment adjacent to Zin's work area frustrates her, but she manages to ignore it for Jim's sake. After what feels like a lifetime, but was actually less than two minutes, the doors to the lift finally open and the freshly lightened and unencumbered team makes haste.

While heading upward in the lift, Abs notes, "This is a horrible design, having the MedBay upstairs since most injuries will likely happen on an excursion. This move makes no sense. On the *Neil*, he would have been in surgery already. Everyone with an ear is definitely going to hear about this."

Becca asks, "Abs, as soon as we get Jim on the table, would you please set up the IV?"

"Of course."

"Thank you. That will save precious time."

Abs huffs, "Time the lift has stolen from us anyway."

Once finally on the upper level, the team whisks Jim to the operating table. Becca immediately grabs the surgical kit and begins to remove sections from the right leg of Jim's suit to expose the wound. Jim pops awake and begins to squirm violently as the discomfort continues to travel slowly up his lower leg. His movement causes the bed to clamp his arm down so the program can begin the IV. Abs employs Rhoan to hold the captain's hand steady because the clamping alone is unsuccessful at holding his arm still enough.

"There. The IV is started. Thanks, Rhoan."

"No problem," Rhoan replies as he releases Jim's hand.

They all gasp at the sight of his bluish-red discoloration of the otherwise surgically clean wound, which goes completely through his ankle, removing an entire section ankle bone. Fortunately, the automated medical pressure applied through his suit to slow the bleeding has kept his blood loss to a minimum and his bleeding on the surgical table is very light. As she continues to remove sections of the suit, they are bewildered to see that his bruising extends from his ankle all the way to his knee.

"I'll need everyone to stand back as I scan his leg," Becca instructs.

The others comply. They retreat slightly to give the scanner space as instructed but keep their eyes on the medical haid projection above the table, which displays a direct real-time feed of the scanner's imaging alongside Becca's live feed of the procedure.

Zin reacts to the severity of the wound, "Eww! That looks just awful. What could have done that?"

Becca reports, "I don't see anything inside the wound, Jim. So that's a good thing."

Jim, who's now a little more relaxed from the medication added through his IV, remarks, "It sure feels like there's something in there."

Becca informs Jim, "I'm going to put you out now so I can fix you. While you're out, I will take a more detailed look into why it feels that way. Okay?"

"Okay. Thank you, Becca. Just tell me what you found later."

As she injects the anesthetic into his IV, she offers, "You guys are welcome to stay and watch, but, Abs, I need you to assist."

Abs queries, "You know I'm just a maladroit surgeon."

"Trust me. I know. I will never ask you to do that again."

"Good. In that case, I'll help however I can. What do you want me to do?"

"Be his anesthesiologist for now and keep a steady eye on his breathing and assist as I call for it."

"As long as you're not asking me to '-ectomy' anything, you got it."

"There should be no '-ectomy-ing' anything today,"

she releases a hint chuckle, which could just be nerves, then jests, "That comes during your next surgery."

After catching a closer glimpse of the incision and blood, Rhoan cries, "I'm out. Not interested in seeing this. Just let me know how it goes."

Zin remarks, "You big baby. It always baffles me how you could be this ultimate trained killer, but are such a big punk at the sight of blood or gross and painful stuff."

As he walks away, Rhoan replies, "I am an enigma, sis. I break 'em and leave the dirty work like this to the professionals. Just let me know when the Cap is better."

Zin turns her attention back to the operation. "He will be all right, Becca. Won't he?"

"Of course. It's a simple but just a little bit weird type of injury. I'm going to have to print some replacement bone to fix his ankle and part of his tibia."

Zin asks, "That is just a little bit weird, though, right?"

"Just a little bit. I'm more concerned about the bruising and his feeling that something is moving up his leg. There's nothing we can see there, but I'll keep investigating his claim."

"Okay, I'll take your word for it. Reach me in the Garage if you need anything or have any news. Your suits all piled up on the floor of my palace is eating at me. I'll have Rhoan help me put those away and peek back in shortly."

Abs acknowledges, "Thanks, Zin. Let us know if anything unusual is happening in the store room with the siolens."

"Wilco, Cap."

"How's his breathing?" Becca asks, wrist-deep in Slight's leg.

"Breathing's still normal."

"Good. Hand me the BRF."

"I'm not a surgeon, Becca. What the hell is a Barf?"

"Oh. The bone reduction forceps. On the right."

"This?"

"Yes. See now you're a surgeon," she says as she receives the implement.

"Be honest with me. What's so weird about this injury?"

"Besides the pristine hole through his ankle, you know the red stuff you sampled?"

"Yes?"

"It seems that same color is fused to his bone beyond where it broke, like it is spreading up his leg. That could be what he was feeling."

"What does that mean?"

"I'm not sure. I've been trying to remove it, but it's fused itself to the bone, so reducing it a millimeter or so should remove it."

"I just hope it's not alive…and deadly."

Suddenly frightened, Becca exclaims, "Why would you say that? Get Rhoan back in here just in case."

"You got it." Abs pages for Rhoan. "Bingo, page Rhoan."

Becca asks, "How do you think this happened? I've never seen or heard of anything like this."

"I have no idea. I don't believe he was standing near the puddle we saw when this happened. Maybe there was some red goo we missed on the stalagmite where he was injured."

Rhoan arrives in a hurried state. "I've got my battle gear like you asked. What's up?"

Abs answers, "We don't know what this stuff is or if it's alive. We need your eyes on the scene in case this stuff springs to life and begins attacking us."

"What? Okay. Okay. I got it. Let's go. I'm ready."

Becca replies, "Thank you, Rhoan. Okay. I'm starting now. Stay sharp."

Abs asks, "Rhoan, did you see any of this red substance near the Cap? We're trying to figure out how this could have happened."

"I didn't see anything that could have done this. You know I would have destroyed it had I seen it."

Becca says, "How could all of us…We definitely missed something down there. Regardless, we don't want to leave a foreign substance in him, especially one we don't know or understand."

"Is it coming off?"

"No. Surprisingly, it's acting like it has intelligence of some kind. It may be burrowing deeper into the bone or it is already deep into the bone. It's hard to tell."

"So what do we do?"

"I don't want to take away so much bone that he has an asymmetrical gait."

"Just how asymmetrical are we talking?"

"About 5 millimeters."

"Oh. That could be significant."

"What should I do? Should I print additional bone?"

"Why are you asking me? You're the professional here."

"I know, but you know him better than I do. Which

do you think he'd prefer? This is something I would usually ask a family member."

"Okay. In that case, I think he would prefer a noticeable limp over some unknown and possibly intelligent substance fusing itself to his body parts. Can't you just print and fuse new bone material in its place?"

"I can, but the more printed bone we use, the longer it takes for the bond between real and print to become as strong and stable as regular bone. The smaller, the easier on the patient. But I think, he might prefer that over leaving unknown goo in his body."

"Knowing Jim on a mission, he would rather limp a little now if he can use the leg rather than wait longer for it to heal."

"It won't heal before the mission's end either way."

"In that case, he'd prefer no limp. I know that's what I would prefer."

"I would too. Hand me the circular."

"I know what the circular is. Here you go."

As the motor whirs and the blade begins to rotate at speeds fast enough to become just a blur, she says, "Last chance to change your mind."

Abs replies, "Go for it. Let him be pissed at me if he wants to be. This is what I would prefer given those options especially if he's unable to return to normal duty on this mission either way."

As she makes contact with the bone, Abs notes, "His breathing is picking up."

In a sweaty huff, Becca replies, "Give him a hit of bag B."

"How much?"

"Twenty CCs for now. Let's see how that works"

"Okay…Done."

A couple seconds later, Becca reports, "So is the amputation. That's got it all from what I can see."

"Good job. Well done."

"Thanks, Abs."

"Could we bag up pieces of that fused bone for my lab and for more intense observation back on MOS4?"

"Absolutely. Rhoan, would you please glove up, bag these fragments, and place them in the frost?"

"I don't want to touch that."

Abs orders, "Not a request, Sergeant Romero!"

Rhoan stands stunned at the notion of Abs's order before accepting that this is happening.

"I did not sign up for this mess," Rhoan huffs as he pulls gloves from one of the containers on the wall.

A double ding comes from the bone printer at the perfectly opportune moment for Becca to retrieve the printed material.

Abs asks, "How did they come out?"

"These came out perfectly. The DNA match is a 100 percent. Time to reassemble the Captain."

Rhoan, still squeamish and angry, remarks "These things are still warm and dripping with blood. Is that a pulse? Oh my god!"

"Goodness, Rhoan! That's probably just your pulse. Calm down and just put it in the frost."

"They should invent thicker gloves so we can't feel things like that."

"Rhoan, they're just bone fragments. Wait until it's a penis to spazz."

Becca and Abs laugh as Rhoan finally places the bag in the frost.

"I'm not coming anywhere near this room if there's a penis injury. That's a guarantee."

*Crunch*!

"Ooh!" Abs contracts his head back from the surgical site before turning back and looking again.

"Okay, Doc. I'd appreciate it if you would keep disgusting sounds like that to a minimum."

"I'll try for your sake, Rhoan. But I can promise nothing."

"Figures. Just let me know when the threat is over so I can go work on getting my sanity back please."

"You bet."

After nearly an hour of frantically paced surgery, Becca proclaims, "I think that'll do it. Let's close him up and we're done."

Rhoan begs, "Great. Can I leave now…please."

"Yes, I don't think we're under any more threat. Thank you, Rhoan."

"Wish we had a suggestion box in here. I've got a doozy."

They chuckle as Rhoan turns to leave.

Before Rhoan exits, Abs informs, "Please let Zin know we're finishing up in here. The cast is almost done."

Rhoan snips, "Aye, Captain Abernum. Right away, sir. Anything else, sir?"

"Um. No. Not right now. You and your attitude are dismissed, though."

"Very good, sir." Rhoan leaves.

As she nears completion of the cast's robotic programming, Becca states, "Abs, I'd like to join you in the lab when you study this substance if that's okay."

"Absolutely. I was actually hoping you would. A

medical observer would make a huge difference especially when I examine the effect on the bone."

Moments later, Becca declares, "His robotics fit perfectly. Just need to reboot it with the new programming."

"Any special programming for extra ankle performance?"

"Nothing special. Just the ability to stand without weight and pressure for now. Movement comes later."

"Well at least he can stand."

"Only for a short duration at first. Eventually, he will heal well enough to use that leg just like before. For now, the cast is programmed for two weeks before it will begin to allow him to flex the ankle at all."

"Becca, you were amazing under pressure today."

"Not really. I should have been a little more assertive and confident. Instead, I added pressure to your plate on how to proceed."

"Not really. You were just getting other opinions. Nothing wrong with that."

"There. All done here. Let's move him over to the cold room so he can wake up." Then looking frustrated with herself, she mutters, "I should have just made that call myself."

"Becca." Abs puts his hand on her shoulder and looks her in the eye. "You did a hell of a job. I'm proud of you."

"Thanks, Abs."

Now that Jim is resting in recovery, Abs asks Becca, "Do you want to be there when he wakes up?"

"Preferably, no. I definitely don't want to be the first person he sees."

"Understood. Let me just store this sample in the lab and rush right back here."

"You got it, but hurry. He won't be out long."

Abs grabs the bone and substance samples and heads to the lab a few dozen steps away.

While Abs is in the lab, Jim begins to stir.

Becca, who is beginning to feel uncomfortable, murmurs to herself, "Come on, Abs. Hurry."

She continues cleaning up the equipment from the surgery.

Abs reappears seconds before Jim opens his eyes. Abs asks, "What'd I miss?"

Becca meets Abs at the entrance. "He's awake, but he hasn't seen me yet. He's all yours."

"Check, Bec. Thanks. And good job."

She waves as she heads to her quarters.

Jim looks around and aridly mumbles, "Wha…?"

"Hey, Cap!" Abs says in a soft slow tone, almost baby-talking to him.

"Hey, Abs," Jim mumbles groggily, "how did it go?"

"It went well."

Rhoan enters more upbeat and less angry. "How are you feeling, Cap?"

"I'm sleepy. Leg feels really weird. I need to get some of that anesthesia for my room. That stuff is the best."

"We don't need those kinds of problems, Jim," Abs jokes.

Jim nods off again.

Rhoan leans in and ask Abs, "How is he doing?"

"Back so soon. Still mad at me?"

"I'm always mad at you."

"I know, because you love me so much."

"How is he?"

"He just fell back asleep, but he's good. As you know, everything went as well as it could. Jim's not likely to have a limp, but since we had to print bone, his recovery may be longer than we want."

Becca peeks in. "Make sure he stays awake!"

"Oh!" Abs tries to rouse him, "Jim! Wake up, Cap!"

Jim grunts, "Hm."

"Wake up, Grunt," Abs says, "we need you to lead us on the next mission."

"Mission?" Jim sits up and is almost instantly alert. "What's the mission?"

"How is your leg feeling?"

"Oh yeah." He looks down and rubs his lightweight robotic cast. "It feels weird, but at least, you were able to save the leg. Where's Becca?"

"She is cleaning herself up. Yeah, we saved the leg but had to replace some of your bone with prints to get that mystery goo out of you."

Jim sits in silent contemplation.

Rhoan says, "Cap, do you need any ice?" He hands him a cup of ice chips.

Jim takes in a couple ice chips from the cups and drops his head back to the pillow.

Zin enters the recovery area. "Hey, Jim. Glad to see you're up. How are you feeling?"

"Hey, Zin. I'm doing all right. Sleepy."

"Right, Becca said you would be. That's from the pain meds."

"Why'd she give me pain meds? She should have just wrapped it with a LocBan."

LocBan is the brand name of the company that

invented and manufactures smart bandages and medical wraps that contain and release local anesthetic according to setting.

Abs answers, "Don't tell me you're one of those patients. You know we couldn't leave that on as long as the cast has to stay on. And the cast will eventually help you walk."

"Right. Right. No. I'm not second-guessing. Where is Becca?"

"You just asked that, Cap. She's cleaning up."

"I did?"

"Don't worry about that. It's the drugs."

Becca enters the room. "How are you doing, Captain Slight?"

"Hi, Becca. How are you doing?"

"I'm fine. I wasn't the one injured. How are you feeling?"

"Groggy but not bad. My leg feels funny. How did things go? Abs told me I have DyNA bone."

Becca's reluctance to engage with Jim is evident to the rest of the crew, but she does so with as much professionalism as she can muster. "That's true. The procedure was a success. We were able to save the foot. However, we did need to trim the portion of the bone infected with the unknown substance and replace it with prints. That funny feeling is the fusion occurring between the prints and the natural bone. You may notice slight unsteadiness the first couple times you attempt to stand, which you should not attempt for at least twenty-four hours. Keep your leg elevated today. We left a cane and a crutch near your bed. Use whichever you find most helpful as you recover, but start with the crutch today and tomorrow. Captain Abernum and Sergeant Romero will hover you to your cabin for rest when you're ready. Any questions?"

"O…kay," Jim replies slowly. "Thank you." He takes note of her crisp tone and chooses not to say anything further although there is much more he'd like to say.

"Very well," she says coldly, then nods and leaves again.

Rhoan asks, "What was that?"

Jim answers, "Don't ask." He takes a sip of the little ice water formed beneath the ice chips then asks, "Abs, you up to moving me to my cabin?"

Rhoan answers, "We all are, Cap."

Abs looks toward the exit. "How about you two move Jim, and I'll go study the substance to see what we're up against?"

"Sure, Cap. No problem. Let's go, Other Cap," Rhoan orders.

* * * * *

Abs Diary Entry 78C:

Hello, Parental Units.

Big happenings today. Yes, this is the same day. We rushed to the surface to get exposure and scout a bit. There's something strange down there. We have evidence of microbes, and something attacked Jim. Completely destroyed his ankle. He needed serious surgery, so we cut our excursion short. Becca was a rock star. I played his anesthesiologist and her assistant. We fixed him up. She was truly amazing. All her anxiety disappeared when we needed her most. She was in the zone, so focused, and right on it! Even with such great medical care, he won't be joining us for our excursion tomorrow. There's a chance he might the day after, wearing his robotic cast. We did not see you on the surface. I'm holding on to one final ounce of hope that we just didn't travel far enough to reach you. As you can probably tell, I keep creating new narratives for myself each time we cross a new barrier to potentially seeing you. My last hope is that you are in the area and stranded or abandoned by your equipment. Despite the facts that no one has mentioned your team to us, we don't have room for another crew, and there is no indication of another crew in the area, my ridiculous optimism is waning right now. If we don't see you tomorrow, I'll just hope to hear that you're home soon. Jim is resting now. Bec and I are heading to the ship's lab soon. Love you both.

# Chapter 16

## Lab Work

AFTER A quick respite in his cabin, Abs knocks on Becca's cabin door. No answers. He knocks again. Even knowing that sound cannot penetrate the barrier between himself and the other side of the door, he calls, "Hey, Becca, you okay? I'm about to study the substance."

Still no answer. He knocks one more time, and she startles him when she taps him on the shoulder from behind.

"Whoa, ninja woman. I'm going to study the—"

She grins. "I heard you as I was leaving the restroom. Let's go."

En route to the lab, they pass the Romero siblings transporting Jim to his cabin. Jim looks as if he has fallen back asleep. The sibs wave as they pass but seem focused on giving their passenger a smooth journey. Zin has improvised a leg elevator for Jim's injured appendage from a blanket in the MedBay.

Becca whispers, "Anything to report?"

"Not yet. All's well, but we are struggling to keep him awake."

"He can sleep now. He's fine."

"Great. Didn't want to keep fighting that fight," Zin says, opening Jim's cabin door. They disappear beyond the threshold.

Becca turns to Abs. "Can I just thank you?"

"For what?"

"Today. Being here and seeing what I'm seeing. Performing such an unusual surgery successfully. This experience already has been far more than I could picture, and I am loving it so much more than I expected. Just thank you."

Abs smiles. "I am surprised to hear that. I have been expecting you to tell me how much you hate me for bringing you here after the attempts on our lives we've encountered so far. You seemed so terrified."

"Oh, for sure, I was and still am. Maybe you weren't listening. I only thanked you for today. The rest of that garbage is not what I'm grateful for. So there may be more freaking out during this trip. Do not think this conversation means I won't spazz or wish I was still back home in my bed anymore. But if we die out here, I want you to know that life has a slightly different meaning to me than it did a few days ago."

"Wow. In that case, you're welcome…for today."

Abs presents his eyes and right index finger. The Lab door slides open. The dark sterile room slowly brightens incrementally until the lighting reaches its preset configuration. The Lab and MedBay share the same brilliant white-covered walls, but everything else is bare titanium for the sake of weight.

Once in the lab, Abs and Becca don hazmat suits to be safe. Abs walks over to the lab's frost and pulls the container labeled "Slight leg." He also grabs another container labeled "Surface Goo 1." The Slight container, placed in the lab by Zin, holds goo-infused bone fragments from Jim's surgical procedure. The other was the first sample Abs collected during their excursion on the surface. Abs holds the encased samples up to the light so he and Becca could see how they look in the light and observes, "How very, very strange. This red color is blowing my mind. If I indulged in acid, I'd think I was high right now."

"It is trippy."

Referring to the container without bone, Abs notes, "I thought it might look less strange under the lab lighting. It reminds me of the chameleon paint colors but more alive."

Becca agrees, "That's a better description than I can come up with. It's funny, though. Since the Io atmosphere down there is a little unnatural to us, I sort of expected that color to look different in here, but this stuff looks just as weird in the lab on that bone as it did in that puddle."

Abs notes, "Dang. Maybe those guys in processing actually did see something."

"This stuff does look eerily similar to the sample the colonel showed us in the briefing."

"I wonder how this stuff looks on Io without those new visors offsetting the atmospheric conditions that are harmful to our eyes. How would it look down there if we could view it with our naked eyes?"

Becca shrugs.

"Anyway, let's see what is in this stuff."

He carefully shaves a slice of bone and places the sliver on a slide and returns the rest of the container to refrigeration. He also places a drop of the gooey liquid from the surface sample on another slide.

While Abs prepares the samples, Becca asks, "Can't you just use your microscopic eye to investigate it?"

"Remember I tried that on the surface."

"I do."

He continues mocking her with a slow sarcastic tone, "And remember after that, I said I can't wait to look at this in the lab?"

Flashing him an irritated side eye, she barks, "Okay, smarty-fart. I get it."

Abs laughs. "My eye wasn't detailed enough. Besides, there are two other disadvantages of me doing that right now."

"And they are?"

"Aside from this microscope being far more powerful than my eye, one, the atmospheric distortions and not being able viewing it directly would probably produce misleading indicators…and two, it's easier to share the image with you and send a copy to MOS4."

"Fair enough."

They walk over to the microscope and secure the first sample, the one without bone. Abs projects the holographic image above the telescope and shouts, "What the hell!"

"What?"

"There's movement! Look!"

Becca observes, "Holy shit! Are we calling that life?"

"That's not my call to make, but I feel like I'm in Jurassic Park. I want to say life always finds a way."

Abs adjusts the microscope and observes the image in multiple configurations. Unable to understand what they're seeing, Abs asks Becca, "What in the universe is this? Have you seen this before?"

"Never even heard of anything like that."

"I'm searching the image, nothing is coming up on Bingo so far. I don't see anything remotely like this."

"Have you tried the chemical sensor yet?"

"Not yet. This second image search is taking a while. Let's do that while we wait." The second search ends and Abs notifies, "Nope. No matches. I'll do one final deeper image search while we set up the sensor." He shakes his head. "What is this stuff?"

"The sensor will tell us."

Moments later, the chemical sensor reads: Unknown

Becca doesn't understand. "Unknown? Like nothing in this is known to our science. Not even hydrogen. Nothing."

"How can there not even be one familiar element in that soup?"

"Did we just discover new life on Io?"

"It sure is looking that way. Nope. Nothing on the Bingo search engine. Let's try Hero."

"Hey, I just noticed your Bingo didn't answer that time. What did you change your wakeup call to?"

He shouts, "Ay. Yo, Bingo!"

A pleasant female voice answers from overhead.

"Yes, Abs," Bingo answers.

Becca notes, "And you changed him to female."

"I guess I prefer the pleasant voice of a female ordering me around rather than some dude barking orders at me."

Becca nods with an expression of understanding.

The pleasant voice repeats, "Yes, Abs. Did you call?"

"Bingo, where is Zin?" Abs asks.

"Zin is in Captain Slight's cabin."

"Thank you, Bingo."

"My pleasure, Abs."

"That wake-up call is hilariously twentieth century."

"Yeah, I got it from some vintage show called *Fresh Prince of Bel-Air.* I'm looking forward to saying it in front of Zin."

"That's too funny. You two have a funny relationship, but she really loves you."

"She does? How do you know?"

"Girl chat."

"I won't ask then. What's your wakeup call for Bingo?"

"B-I-N-G-O."

"Yes, Becca," the standard male Bingo answers.

"Where am I?"

"Becca, you are in the Lab."

"Thank you, Bingo."

"You're welcome, Becca."

"That's cute, I've always liked that one. Zin's is even funnier. She says, 'Hello, Husband!'"

"No way. That's hilarious!"

"Those are definitely words she will never use for anything else. Unless she does marry that blue-haired mug, Michael."

"She likes him?"

"It looked that way in the Docking Bay during PiL."

Becca agrees, "It kinda did."

"He's quite unique. I guess that might be the only

kind of guy who would interest her after she's only been into females all her life."

"Maybe. Or he may be talking to her about reconfiguring."

"That would make more sense. That wasn't part of your girl chat?"

"Abs, I'm starting to grow uncomfortable with this conversation."

"Why? Do you have a problem with genects (gender-elects/gender-corrects)?"

No. It's not that. I'm just thinking this is how rumors start, so instead of having a conversation of speculation, I'll ask her if it's something she is willing to discuss. If she is into him, that's huge news to us, especially considering all we know about her."

"Couldn't agree more, Bec. Wait. I just had a thought."

"What's that?"

"If this substance contains or is life, does it mean that the red stuff attacked Jim?"

"There's a thought."

"Think about it. Considering we didn't see anything else attack him, we should eliminate it as a suspect before discounting that possibility. Definitely warrants more research."

"But it's so tiny."

"Consider the oceanic microbe blooms on Mom."

"Touché."

"This is mostly speculation again at this point, but you see in this image how it looks to bind to itself?"

He again points to the holographic projection of the

live microscopic image on the microscope's haid viewer atop the microscope.

"Yes, I do. You don't think it changes properties, do you?"

"Not sure. I want to run another sample through the sieve and see if there's any difference."

"Want me to do it?"

"Sure. I'd appreciate that."

"No problem."

About a minute later, she hands him a slide with the sifted sample. "There's no visible difference."

"Thanks, Bec. Let's see if the microscope agrees."

Abs places the slide under the viewer, makes adjustments, and involuntarily releases an audible sigh.

"Well?"

"I don't see anything different. You?"

"No. Not really."

"We absolutely have to go back down there to investigate this substance more closely. The traps were still empty when Zin came up to see Jim."

"Would you be upset if I admitted this is actually getting a tad scary?" she expresses revelatory angst.

"A tad? We don't even set our alarm clocks for a tad scary. Consider the possible implications. This is buttloads of scary! And exactly what Marlagans live for. This is why this team exists. Moments like these are what we live for."

"You warned me about the perils long before I chose to join the Marlagans, so I can't say I didn't know."

"To be honest, that was me trying to talk you out of it without actually talking you out of it."

"You did not warn me about Jim, however."

"Why would I? I never saw that coming, and you did all of that behind my back. Had you come to me beforehand—"

"I know. As it was happening, I kept thinking I should ask you about him. But at the same time, I wanted to feel like my own grownup person, who didn't need my big brother looking out for me. And I worried you might talk me out of it. Of course, in hindsight, it was stupid, I know."

Abs listens attentively.

"It was also me wanting to feel like a big boot and make my own mistakes."

"Do you feel like a big boot who has learned anything from it?"

"Stop being sarcastic. Of course I learned my lesson."

"That wasn't sarcasm. I really want to know if you learned anything you plan to use going forward."

"Okay, Dad! As I was saying 'I wanted to make my own mistakes,' I heard how stupid that sounded coming out of my mouth. Now I know how stupid and painful choosing to intentionally make my own mistakes feels."

Abs smiles and nods. "But those hard lessons often stick with us the best. Human nature is such a flawed thing."

"Here's the lesson I've learned about dating. Get the full blood work-up along with full background and credit checks and reference interviews before giving my heart away again."

"That may be a little much."

"Not considering how I feel right now."

"I'm sorry, Bec."

"From now on, I'm also seeking advice from people

who have already made the stupid mistakes to lessen my chances of ever feeling like this again. You are the one who always told me to seek advice from people who are where I want to be and warnings from people who are where I don't want to be."

"Can't argue with myself on that. Exactly how do you feel at this point? Is it getting better?"

Her arms fall, and she melts into a puddle. "Abs, I feel so betrayed and used. I'm totally heartbroken. I really believed him. I believed in him. I believed in us," she chokes back tears but her breaking voice betrays her, "and allowed myself to fall completely in love with him."

She begins to sob but is unable to wipe her tears because of the suit.

Abs steps closer and attempts to embrace her, but the suit hampers the warmth of his intention. She emotes unintelligibly through a flood of tears as he continues his attempts to comfort her, "I'm so sorry you're going through this, Bec. Just remember you don't have to deal with this on your own. You know so many of us love you in very real ways."

After taking time to gather herself, she whimpers, "I know. Thanks, Abs. I'm really lucky to have you looking after me."

"Of course. We're family. That's what we do."

They pull away from the closeness. Abs offers her the leave to scrub and clean herself up.

She indicates that she is okay. "When are we going back down to the surface?"

"After breakfast tomorrow."

"What time is breakfast?"

"05Z"

"Geez. Why so early?"

"Why not? We need answers, and since we're a man down and got cut short today, plan on a long excursion tomorrow."

"Guess we'd better get some rest."

"It has been a tad of a day," he teases. "Are you still thankful for it?"

"Har-har, Mr. Tad of a Day. It's been a hell of a day. Absolutely incredible, that is until you brought up that Jim stuff again. But yes. Absolutely thankful."

"What? You brought up the Jim stuff."

"Let's not get caught up in the blame game here. Fact is you brought it up and now we're moving on."

"Why do I put up with you?"

"Because I'm the best sister a guy could ever have."

He throws an arm around her. "You're hard headed, but still pretty great."

Becca blushes.

Abs states, "We need to share this information with the rest of the crew. Let's clean up and head to Jim's cabin."

* * * * *

Abs Diary Entry 78D:

Hey, Folks Far from Home.

Becca just thanked me for today. Did not expect that. Jim's recovering. We're discovering, as usual, if I may brag on our team a bit. I bet whatever you're doing is going to make everything we've ever done feel ever so small. Do you remember that day in school when Gene Bushnell stole my Turbo Turtle and I was the one who got into trouble breaking his ribs? Well, I just got a message from him. It was actually an apology. He said he saw the WSX-M piece on the Marlagans a while back, and his conscience kept eating at him, so he wanted to make sure we were okay. What a strange and random thing to happen during this mission. He has a family now and wants to use this as a teachable moment for his kids. He says his apology is sincere and is inviting me to dinner. I actually think he just wants to show his kids that he knows me. But then, is that my own arrogance thinking that way. I'm torn whether I'm wrong for feeling like I'm this big deal that people would actually take time to create a scenario to prove they know me or if he is genuinely apologizing to be an old example to his children. This is when I miss you more than usual. Dad might say it doesn't matter what his intentions are as long as you're doing the right thing because it could be a good lesson for his children. And Mom might say not to let that bully turd use you like that. But then, I know both of you would say to just pray about it and God will show you what to do. Guess that's how I'll handle this too. It's funny how when we become adults we still hear those lessons from our childhood. Thanks for the thousand or so lessons you've taught me all throughout my life. I still miss you and would rather have you here with me, though.

# Chapter 17

## Drama

AFTER FINISHING up the lab work and securing the lab, Abs and Becca join the balance of the Marlagans, who are still assembled in Jim's cabin.

Upon entering and seeing Jim awake and speaking with the Romeros, Abs asks, "How are you feeling, Jim?"

"I'm good, man." He grunts as he sits up taller in his bed at the sight of Becca. "Never better. Ready for action."

Abs chuckles, "That's good. Glad to hear you haven't lost your acerbic sense of spirit, Grunt."

"What's the point in life if you don't live?"

"Well said. Becca and I just finished a preliminary study of the red goo."

The entire cabin turns in interest.

Jim coaxes for more. "And?"

"There appear to be signs of very unfamiliar living microbes in it."

Stunned, Jim asks, "Are you saying we found life?"

"I'm saying it looks that way. But—"

"We found life! We'll be in history books." Rhoan and Zin cheer and high-five each other.

Abs insists, "I said it looks that way!"

Jim asks, "Does this mean the red goo attacked me?"

"We can't make that determination yet. More intense study and observation is definitely needed."

"So what's the hold-up? Study it."

"Someone more studied in the field than me has to do that."

"Stop being modest and get us some answers."

"I'm just not equipped to do that here."

"Dangit! Did we at least catch anything?"

"I just checked, and the traps are still empty."

Rhoan asks, "When do we go back down?"

"I'm looking at 06Z."

"It's 21Z now. Guess we need to get prepped and rested," Rhoan suggests.

Abs turns to Jim. "You should sit this one out, my friend."

"I won't fight you on that. I would only slow you down and create too much liability on the surface, so I'll help Zin assist from orbit."

"So you'll slow me down instead?" Zin quips.

Abs is just relieved Jim didn't put up much of a fight.

Jim takes slight offense, "What?"

"I'm kidding. It'll be fun," she kids in a sarcastic tone and makes an agonizing grimace.

"Hardy-har-har, Zin. I see what I'll have to put up with in orbit, Abs, so be sure to count me in on the following surface excursion."

"You got it, buddy."

"Did you forward all of today's data to MOS?"

"Jim, I haven't. But before you go all company man on me, allow me to explain why."

Jim grunts and crosses his arms. "I'm listening."

"Why did you close me out before I even started?"

"What? I said I'm listening."

Zin interjects, "Your body language, Cap."

"What?" Jim looks down and notices his posture. "Oh."

Zin nods. "You see?"

He opens himself back up and asks, "Better?"

"It's an attempt at least. Listen. I know we can trust the colonel, but that same confidence doesn't extend to her peers and superiors right now. It seems safer to hold this information until we return safely. I will send normal updates without these huge revelations just to protect the Marlagans."

"Will you share information about my injury?"

"I'm considering not telling them."

"I think we should, but it's up to you to paint the scenario that caused the injury. I don't like it but will trust your judgment on this simply because the Marlagans are not out of danger yet. Besides, I'm in no shape to do much to protect the team myself nor will these drugs allow me to fight you on this right now."

"Is everyone okay with my strategy to keep us safe? We don't know who to trust right now." Abs peruses the team.

They all nod and agree.

Zin jests, "Guess I'll trust your judgment, Abs. This time." She smiles. "Just joking. I know you're always looking out for us, and I really do appreciate it."

"We're family," Abs says, "and times like these especially, we need to look out for one another."

Jim seems to get a little emotional. "Aww, bring it in, Marlagans."

The team does a group hug around Jim's bed.

Though part of the group hug, Becca takes her place as far from Jim as she can and remains silent.

After the group hug, Abs asks, "Exactly what are you taking, Jim."

"I'm not sure, but it has me feeling all weepy and emotionally expressive. Not that I don't love my team, but this is beyond my control."

"Okay, Marlagans. Big day, early day, and possibly super long day tomorrow, so let's get prepped and rested."

As they begin to peel out of Jim's cabin, Jim asks, "Abs, Becca, can I talk to my surgeons in private for a moment?"

Abs throws his head back in exasperation, suspecting he really is not interested in discussing the medical procedure at all. Becca hesitantly agrees to turn around. Zin and Rhoan look back but exit the cabin and close the door.

"Are you ordering me to be here, Captain Slight?" Becca asks.

Jim, looking hurt, says, "Of course not. There is something I think you need to know."

Abs takes a few steps closer to her and rubs her back. "It's okay. Just hear him out."

She turns to Abs and softens. Before Jim says a single word, Becca already appears to be fighting back emotions.

"Thank you, Abs. Becca, I know you don't want to

hear this, but I have to say it whether you believe me or not."

Looking up through the window in the ceiling, Becca rejoinders, "I'm listening, Captain."

"Becca, what happened between us—"

"What happened between us? What happened between us? You make it sound like some little elementary school girl crush that happened twenty years ago. This is still very real and painfully happening to me right now, Jim."

Jim acknowledges, "You're right. I'm sorry. What I want to say is that I am so sorry for hurting you. That was definitely not my intention."

"This is not starting off well, Captain!"

She crosses her arms and taps her foot nervously as she continues to focus at the vastness of Jupiter outside the ceiling window to keep tears from escaping.

"Becca, you may think that this was some sort of fling for me. It truly was not."

She still focuses upward, but ragged breathing betrays her attempts to mask her hidden sobs.

"I am fighting my own feelings for you to try and do the right thing here."

"What feelings for me?"

"I fell in love with you and had every intention of ending my Union with Marsha. But things changed when I saw her on MOS4. I felt anguishing guilt, surprising compassion, and some feelings for her I hadn't felt in so long. That's when I was knocked over by how terribly conflicted I truly felt. It is not at all something I unexpected."

She glances at him for a sincerity check, and the tears

breech the dam and careen down in buckets. She quickly takes her gaze back from Jim to the ceiling window and turns her head. Hoping to keep the remaining welled tears from further spilling onto her face. Abs grabs her hand, causing her to turn to him and betray her efforts of hiding her emotions as the streams rush past her cheeks and onto the breast of her uniform blouse. Abs pulls a portable pack of facial tissue from his breast pocket and passes it to her.

Jim continues, "I'm so very sorry, Becca. The last thing I ever wanted to do was hurt you. Please believe me."

Becca remains silent as she continues sniffing and wiping her face.

Jim begs, "Please say something."

She considers remaining defiantly silent, but in a tone rife with sobs asks, "Will that be all, sir?"

Jim replies, "I don't want it to be."

"May I be excused, Captain?"

He drops his head in disappointment. "Yes, Becca. You can go if you'd like."

She grabs Abs's hand and exits. After closing Jim's door, she asks if she can join Abs in his cabin for a brief moment.

They step across the corridor to Abs's cabin and enter his quarters, and she falls to pieces.

"How can I do this?" She sobs uncontrollably.

Abs just holds Becca and allows her time to feel everything exploding out of her before saying a word.

"Bec, this is obviously very difficult for you. You need to process this pain in a healthy way. The unfortunate thing is we don't have the luxury of time for you and

Jim to have a massive conflict that could jeopardize our safety or our mission."

She pulls another tissue from the pack he gave her earlier to desiccate the flood overtaking her face.

"Do you understand what I'm saying?"

She nods several times. "I know. I know. It won't be a problem. After hearing Jim's words, I feel less used than I did before. I'm realizing now that our relationship was not as lopsided as I feared it was."

"It doesn't seem that it was lopsided at all."

"I'm still not ready to forgive him. It still hurts too much."

"That's understandable, Bec. But remember withholding forgiveness tends to hurt the forgiver more than the forgiven."

"Yes, I know."

"I hope his confession did help get you a little closer to moving on."

"He's still a big fat juicy turd with nuts, corn bits and an extreme amount of sulfur in it, but I may be able to sleep more than 3 hours tonight. That would be improvement over the episodes of uhtceare I've been having since we arrived at MOS4."

"Good. Mars needs you focused and at full capacity to get us through this mission."

She straightens her disposition and wipes her drying eyes. "Yes. Right. You're completely right. I need that reminder from time to time."

"Do you think you and Jim could work alone, just the two of you, if it was necessary without there being a bunch of drama or disruption to the mission?"

"Yes. I will if needed. I didn't kill him when I had him under the knife."

"That's true, but a little disturbing that you would even say that."

"You know. I think I should go back in there and show him that."

"Show him what exactly? Have you forgiven him?"

"Hell no! Well, let me take that back. I'm closer to forgiving him now than I have been."

"That's a step in the right direction. If you do intend to have a conversation with him about a professional working relationship between you, just don't make him feel forgiven if he isn't forgiven. I'm just saying you don't have to put it all out there if you still have to figure out how to forgive him, just bear in mind, though, that God forgives us as we forgive others."

"What does that mean?"

"Have you never heard the Lord's Prayer?"

"What's that?"

"There's so much to teach you, young one. But suffice it to say that we all fall short of perfection in this life, but in the eternity that follows this tiny slice of eternity as human beings, we will be judged, assessed, and rewarded by how we live this time out. He sent His own son, Jesus, as our sacrificial lamb so we didn't have to earn His forgiveness. You know what? I'm getting too deep now."

"I want to hear what you were going to say. I always thought Jesus came with more rules of what not to do."

"No. He certainly did not. He came to tell us we could never follow all the rules for which the Pharisees, or religious rulers at that time, were holding us to account.

He came to show us how we should live, give us the new rule, and die for all of our sins."

"There's that word."

"What word?"

"Sin. That's why there are hardly any churches anywhere today."

"Jesus allowed himself to fall into the hands of his murderers, so we don't have to worry and feel guilty about our imperfections. But he only asked one thing of us."

"What's that?"

"Love."

"Love?"

"Love."

"Like make a bunch of babies?"

"If that's your thing, but no. There's a whole discussion we could have around the different types of love we're called to give, but let's start with the basics. He tells us to love God above all else and love one another as we love ourselves. That covers all we need to know. I'd add that if we learned how to love ourselves as we should, the loving others would be natural."

"That is true. Most people don't love themselves like they should these days."

"That really is nothing new and is usually rooted in the fact that they don't love God above all else."

"Now it's my turn to say 'hmm.' I know that's your thing, but that may have just blown my mind." Becca contemplates further. "So most of the hate throughout history could be attributed to people not following that one rule, huh?"

"Indeed. I believe that's absolutely the case."

"That could explain why you never seem bothered or terribly upset about anything?"

"Indeed, but I do get upset. It just doesn't last long or overtake me, but trust me, some things can vex me."

"I've never seen it."

"Because God always takes care of things that bother me or he takes care of me so they don't bother me, and I always try to use difficulties as lessons to be a better version of myself for God."

"That actually makes so much sense in some of the lifelong observations I've made about you."

"Creepy that you're observing me."

"Ha. Ha." She lightly punches him in the deltoid.

"Just be patient with yourself. It could take a while for you to get feeling to the place where you can appreciate the lesson from this. A year from now, I will ask you what you learned from the Jim and Becca saga, and you will be able to tell me how it made you better at whatever you may have learned."

"You really think so?"

"Let me ask you this. What have you learned from your thing with Dorn?"

"Ha! That's not fair."

"Did you learn from it?"

"I learned that it is impossible for me to make an unhappy person a happy person when they themselves aren't interested in being happy the way you want them to experience happiness."

"Will you ever do that again?"

"Hey. I never thought of it quite that way. There may actually be something to this thing you're into. But what if we don't pray or believe in God, wouldn't these things happen anyway?"

"Possibly, but for me, my relationship with God keeps me aware of how much He really does take care of us and constantly on mission for Him and my fellow humans."

"What does that mean?"

"This conversation we're having right now is part of my mission."

"But I see all the old streams of people with megaphones and telling other people how to live and especially giving up all your money to follow some kind of corrupt leader. That's what I thought was the mission of the church."

"Money and corruption?"

"And control over people."

"That does exist and has since humans began making themselves God. Those people were and still are very wrong. What I'm doing right now is what we're supposed to be doing. I'm telling you this stuff because I love you."

She grabs him and buries her head in his torso and weeps. He holds her, wondering what part of his statement caused this reaction from her. He asks, "Are you okay?"

She nods against his chest and lets out a muffled "Mm hmm."

He gives her time to collect herself.

She finally speaks after wiping her face on Abs's shirt. "Sorry about that. I can't understand why people only talk about religion like they do with such negative fervor."

"That's because atheism is the new majority world

religion, and they want to justify themselves as much as any other religion.”

“But it’s wrong, right?”

“Well, humans are nothing more than humans, and wrong is what we do best. On a more personal level, I do have one question that I’ve been wanting to ask but not sure how you would take it.”

“You know you can ask me anything.”

“I wonder if you tend toward older men—”

“You don’t need to finish that sentence. I know what you’re going to say because I wonder the same thing.”

“It’s definitely worth pondering and figuring out.”

“Ever since I was old enough to like boys, I’ve always been attracted to those older than me.”

“I know.”

“I have asked if that had anything to do with not ever knowing my father all the time. Boys my age have never been my thing. Does that mean I am trying to know how it feels to have a father figure? I’m not totally sure, but I think it may have a lot to do with it on a subconscious level.”

“If you’re happy because of who the person is, that is fine, but if you’re trying to compensate for something you feel is missing, that’s not okay. Khan and I have been trying to help fill that void for you.”

“Want to hear something insane?” she asks with a glow in her eyes.

“What’s that?”

“I used to have the biggest crush on you.”

“What? That’s even creepier.”

“I know it is now. I was just about six when it began, and you always treated me like I was a person, not just a pipsqueak, not a pain-in-the-butt kid. That always meant so much to me. Maybe it's your fault I like older men."

"Hmm. That is interesting."

"See. There's your hmm. Why are you hmm-ing?"

"You're shifting the blame. Very interesting."

"No, I'm not. Think about it. The two people closest to me were you and Khan. That was where I was most comfortable. The boys my age growing up were childish and gross. I guess that may be the answer right there."

"You know, that's how it's supposed to be. Older people are duty-bound to look after and protect the young ones. That shouldn't be something that causes a love affair or crush."

"I was just a child. Children develop crushes, but I don't still have a crush. That would be gross. Like I said, it just became my comfort zone."

"I guess that does make sense."

"Yes—"

Over the intercom, they hear an excited Zin, "Hey, Marlagans! Get down here! A Cam Trap inside the cave caught something!"

* * * * *

Abs Diary Entry 78E:

Mr. and Mrs. Abernum,

Something exciting is happening! Just want you to know that. No time to talk. Wish you were here.

# Chapter 18

## RTB?

UPON HEARING Zin's declaration overhead, Abs and Becca look at one another and dart to the Garage, where they meet with Zin and Rhoan. Zin has Jim on the haid in the Garage.

She zips right to it. "Look. It's trap number two near the entrance. The motion camera feed was unable to capture the trapping. Somehow." She cues up the footage. "Watch. There's nothing there. We see the trap shut, but the camera doesn't pick up anything."

"Hmm," Abs wonders, "could it really be that fast? So fast we can't even see it?"

Zin says, "It's all so mysterious. They could travel at light speed. We have no way of knowing until we study whatever is in that trap."

Rhoan asks, "How would we catch something traveling at that speed?"

Abs continues, "The green light indicates there's

something inside the trap. Apparently, the Cam Traps are how you catch something that fast."

Rhoan adds, "But then again, it could just be a malfunction."

Abs nods. "True."

Jim notes, "There's only one way to find out what's really happening down there."

Abs still contemplates aloud, "Oh wow! I just had a wildly ridiculous thought."

"What?"

"What if they are capable of invisible camouflage?"

Jim wonders, "Yes, that's a ridiculous thought. It's more likely that they are just invisible period."

"That's even more ridiculous."

Zin advises, "If that's the case, we are in trouble because we don't have gear that detects invisibility. But we can sense weight and visible movement."

Rhoan recommends, "It's more likely that the trap is malfunctioning. Maybe we should try the ultraviolet feature on our visors."

Jim agrees, "It's worth a try, but I see no reason to believe UV detects invisibility."

"Have we ever used it to look for invisibility? No!"

"Besides, the infrared visor didn't ever detect anything unusual moving on Io before."

"What do we have to lose? Let's just try it."

Jim finally relents, "What the hell. Zin, is there a way to use the UV filter on this footage?"

"Not with this equipment, but I could send UVCCs (ultraviolet-capable cameras) down there tonight or you could take them with you tomorrow."

"Go ahead and set them up on the surface tonight, so

we have a better idea of what we're facing before sending anyone else down there."

"Check. Just let me know where you want them."

"Inside that cave for sure."

Abs states, "Let's hope they give us some answers before we go back down."

Rhoan cosigns, "It would be really nice to know what we're up against before we head back down there. We may be walking into a trap."

Becca speaks up, "Abs, before we go back down there, you should share the lab footage of the weird red substance."

"Yes!" Zin exclaims.

Abs agrees, "For sure. Let me pull it up."

"That would definitely help in our quest to understand what's happening down there," Jim suggests. "The more we know, the better."

"It's crazy. Wait until you see it. The organisms were so strange, and they were precisely organized," Becca blurts out.

Jim cries, "Show us!"

"Okay, but I'm still not sure it would wise to share it with MOS4 yet," Abs says as he pulls up the findings. "There appears to be an intelligence to their movement. Check out the footage we captured." He shoots a holographic projection of the footage from his eye.

"Whoa! Look at that! That's scary," Zin says. "This could mean the liquid could form unlimited solid sizes and shapes then return to liquid state before anyone could detect it. Is this circulatory, skeletal, nervous, or muscular system? Is this the entirety of their forms? Is this something different than the potentially invisible creatures? I have so many questions."

"We need to keep an eye on the samples we've collected," Jim cautions. "They could be dangerous on their own."

"For sure," Abs agrees, "We should double-check to make sure all the sample containers are still intact."

Becca adds, "We know the containers in the Lab are intact. Are there any down here?"

Zin answers, "None down here. I took them all to the Lab frost."

"I would like to take one of those UV cameras up to the lab just to double-check. UV signatures is one test we didn't do."

Zin reaches in the cabinet below the haid. "Here you go," she says as she hands a tiny UV device to Abs.

"Thanks. I'll be right back. Rhoan, give me a hand and bring your gear just in case."

"On it. Give me sec to run to the Armory."

Moments later, Rhoan returns from the Armory fully armed and geared up.

Abs reminds him, "Just remember we don't want any gunfire inside the craft. I know the hull of the *Neil* could contain ballistic blasts, but we don't want to find out the hard way that the *Mushroom*'s hull isn't as durable."

"I know that, Cap."

"Then why do you have that Tookuk?"

"It's just a fashion statement."

"Don't use it. You are only authorized to use stunners and ionizers on the ship."

"I've got those too. Stop worrying, Cap, and let's go!"

Zin sighs. "I've got a bad feeling about this."

Becca asks, "About what they'll find?"

"No, about my stupid-ass brother."

"I heard that. I've got a bad feeling about your stupid-ass face."

"Grow up, Rhoan."

"Tell your face."

"Ugh."

"Protect and serve, sis!" He disappears as they slowly ascend on the lift.

Abs dons the UV device, scanning the areas leading to the Lab. "Nothing out of the ordinary yet."

"Just point me to the action if something pops up."

"Okay, I'm going to unlock the Lab. Be ready."

"Always."

Abs opens the door swiftly, scans the room, and sees nothing to Rhoan's disappointment.

"I'm not even sure these things can be detected with UV. There could be invisible creatures all around us right now, and we wouldn't even know it."

"That's not funny, Cap."

"Not trying to be. At least there are no puddles of red goo anywhere. Let's check the frost again."

"Go."

"The containers are still intact, so nothing there. Wait. There's one missing."

"What do you mean?"

"Jim collected four samples. The second container from the cave is missing."

"Seriously?"

Abs calls, "Zin, do you remember how many samples you brought up to the Lab?"

She replies over the intercom, "There were three. Why?"

"We brought back four samples."

"Uhh."

"We'll be right down."

Jim chimes in, "What's going on Abs? Is there a broken container?"

"Not sure yet, Jim. Rhoan and I are going to check Harvester 3. Everyone stay where you are."

"Is the UV camera working?"

"It works. It's powered on fine. We just have no way of knowing for sure if the UV filter is not detecting any invisible creatures or if there just aren't any."

Rhoan growls, "Dude!"

"What?"

Rhoan admits, "Nothing. This is getting intense."

Zin queries, "Rhoan, don't tell me you're turning mouse again."

"Why would you think that? I just said this is intense. The anticipation is building. That's all I meant. Trust me, I'm always ready. Let something pop off, I'm all up in it."

Abs refocuses the siblings. "Not now, Romeros. Stay focused, Rhoan."

"Check."

"Check."

As they pass Zin and Becca in the Garage for the Storage Room, Abs focuses on the UV image. "Still nothing."

Rhoan opens the door to storage, does a skimming sweep, and clears Abs to enter.

Abs does a cursory scan and still sees nothing. "This UV isn't picking up anything. Let's find Harvester 3."

Annoyed, Zin corrects him again, "AC20, Unit 3."

Abs pokes. "Jumping Jehosaphat, Zin! Do you want to really want to act like a stick in the mud at a time like this?"

"Stop it. Whatever. Just find it."

Becca laughs, "Good one, Abs."

"Here it is. The specimen door is open, and the specimen is missing."

"Are you being serious or still playing around?"

"Playtime is over. That container is not here."

"Is it completely missing or busted?"

"Completely missing."

Donning her own UVCC, Zin concludes, "Oh no. That is not good. Apparently, UV is useless for this application."

"I'm hopeful that it was left on the surface or misplaced somewhere."

"At least there's no evidence that it broke free. There aren't any goo puddles anywhere that I've seen. Be sure to check around your cabins."

"What?"

"Oh. Hell no!"

Jim shakes his holographic head. "Abs, why would you say that?"

"Trying to keep us safe and make sure people check their surroundings."

Becca says, "Sounds like there's about to be a slumber party in your cabin, Abs."

"Second," Zin agrees.

Abs calls, "Okay, everybody calm down. You're all

talking. For now, let's all meet in Jim's quarters to figure something out."

Jim asks, "Yes, please. I feel estranged and totally useless up here."

On the way the Jim's quarters, Becca asks, "What is happening? Is this my real life?"

"Not sure yet and yes. Let's get to Jim and figure it all out as a team."

Abs knocks on Jim's door.

"Come on in," Jim answers. "Hey, team. What's going on?"

Abs asks, "Jim, are you sure you collected that fourth sample?"

"Of course. Well," his confidence begins to wane, "Come to think of it, that was right before I was attacked. I remember opening the specimen door. Did I have time to put it in the collector? It's kinda fuzzy. Maybe. Now I'm not sure. Becca, can I please get up now?"

Becca informs, "This is the WSX, Captain. We only have the B-rated robotic casts. You have to wait the full twenty-four hours before putting weight that leg, then you can use it as normal. Where's your pain level?"

"There is no pain."

"Good. That means it's working…"

Rhoan breaks in, "Glad you're feeling better, Cap, but we've got a pressing issue here. What are we going to do about this invisible creature on our ship?"

Abs answers, "Dial it back, Romes. We don't know that for sure. It could still be on the surface."

"I may not have collected the sample. It was right before the attack on my leg. I remember collecting it but may have dropped it. I wish I could remember."

Abs asks, "Did anyone else handle or remember what happened to that sample? Maybe someone saw it on the ground after Jim's injury?"

The crew looks around, hoping someone will speak up, but no one does.

Rhoan asserts, "If it was there, I would have seen it on the ground while HARVI and I were guarding the scene."

Becca offers, "We were all so busy caring for Jim. It could have rolled behind us out of your view."

Jim orders, "To be on the safe side, let's just stay alert and mindful that we may have an unwelcome guest, who is most likely quite small. Treat it like a mutated alien rat that we can't see or know much about."

Becca lets out an unintended yelp and frantically surveys the floor of the room.

Rhoan offers, "Don't worry, Becca. I'll keep you safe."

Everybody looks up at Rhoan in surprise as if to say, "Where did that come from?"

Zin slowly says, "O-o-kay…"

"Abs, when was the last report sent to MOS4?"

"Yesterday, Jim."

"What?"

"I have a concern, Jim."

"No one in here but Marlagans. Spill it, man!"

"My concern is we know this has to be some sort of inside job."

Jim stops him. "We do NOT know that. This tampering could be totally unrelated to our mission. This could just be some sort of terror tactic by the Lynx."

"Jim, think about it. Why this particular crew on this particular mission?"

"Do you think those launches to the MOSs from the surface had the same mission or were those accidents or were they victims of the Lynx? You don't know, do you? None of us do! Until you have definitive proof, send the reports! Is that understood?"

But, Jim, I don't—"

"Captain Abernum!"

"Yes, sir. I'll send them now. Just remember this was your order."

Jim adds, "I understand your concern, Abs. But if something happens to us out here, someone needs to have all the information possible to investigate this thing. If we die out here and that information dies with us, then we get no justice, and worse, if they find we've been withholding information, there's even more peril waiting for us when we get back."

"I said I get it, Jim! Let's move on. The information has been sent."

Jim yawns. "As I was saying before, just be on high alert."

"You okay, Cap."

"I guess that drug is still active. Suddenly, I'm getting very sleepy."

Becca advises, "Your adrenaline is lowering, so the drug's effects are becoming more apparent."

Jim nods. "I guess so. It's hitting hard."

"Do you have more for us or should we just let you sleep?"

Yawning again, Jim says, "I'm about to get real useless. You can go."

Becca says, "Jim, may I speak with you for a moment?"

"Sure. I'll see the rest of you later."

Abs looks back as he exits. Becca nods at him as if to say, "It's okay."

Just then, Abs receives a pyk from Djoibjin. "Colonel Djoibjin is pyking me."

"Get back in here."

"Abernum," he answers.

"What the hell is going on out there? Why am I getting this so late?"

"I'll explain that later," Abs says.

Jim orders, "Put her on public, so we all can speak with her."

"I'm taking you public."

Once Djoibjin has sight of the room and crew, she asks, "Captain Slight, how are you feeling?"

"Very sleepy, but I'm fine, ma'am. I'll be able to walk on it tomorrow."

"Why am I getting these reports so late? They're supposed to be real time."

"Our mistake. In all the chaos, it just got lost in the shuffle. It won't happen again."

"And what a lot of chaos it has been. I'm looking at this potentially organic material in the reddish substance. Very fascinating. And it also seems you may have an invisible creature onboard."

"That's only one hypothesis, ma'am."

"Captain Abernum, you said you would share all information with me in real time."

Jim answers, "Ma'am, the captain has the best intentions. He is concerned that this is an inside job and sending that data may cause us to experience more system malfunctions or dire circumstances when or if this information falls into the wrong hands."

"Interesting. We share the same concern. Don't worry, Captain. I am very cognizant of that possibility or, should I say, that likelihood. So few people know of the purpose of this mission, so I have diverted slightly from the usual dissemination protocols in this case."

Abs, relieved, says, "Thank you, ma'am. I'll feel much more confident sending in real time now." He smiles at Jim.

Jim shakes his head and smiles back, whispering, "You'd better be glad you're my best friend."

Abs tries to hide his surprise at Jim's declaration of their friendship, but Jim notices.

"Okay, thank you, ma'am," Jim says.

"And one more thing," the colonel states, "according to this, there were two explosive units disarmed by the good captain."

Jim answers, "That is correct, ma'am."

"With all of this going on, RTB (return to base) is granted at your discretion. But please bring back the triggered trap if you're up for it."

Jim boasts with a chuckle, "Ma'am, you know that is not how the Marlagans roll. We will get the job done, even at our own peril."

"Yes, I do know this. But be smart enough to return safely. Is there anything else I should know?"

"No, ma'am. We will keep the information coming in real time henceforth."

"Thank you. And, Marlagans?"

They all answer in chorus, "Yes, ma'am?"

"Very good work. Come back safely."

"Aye, aye, ma'am!"

"Djoibjin out."

"See, Abs, they're not as dumb as you think they are."

"I got it, Jim!"

"You all can go now. Becca, you wanted to talk?"

"Oh yeah. It's not important," she expresses as her earlier bravery has slipped away while she watches the rest of the crew exit. "It can wait. Let's just do it another time when you're not so tired."

His cabin door closes behind the other Marlagans.

"I'm fine. Let's talk."

"I had the courage earlier, but now I'm not so sure."

"Then I'll start. I'm so so—"

"I don't want to hear another apology, Jim." She finally allows herself to look at him and lets her anger and true feelings slip. "God, I loved you, Jim!"

"I still love you, Becca. I just—"

"That's not what I meant to say. I'm sorry. Damn. Apologies are turning my stomach lately. I came to talk about forgiveness."

Jim smiles. "Okay."

She focuses on a spot on the floor. "I don't forgive you yet, Jim."

His smile fades. "Ouch."

"But I want you to know I'm working on it. Abs asked me if I could work alongside you with no one else around and not be distracted from important tasks. I believe I can do that now."

"That's good," he says softly.

"I don't want to be patronized or reminded of what we were. If I want anything, it's to learn from how stupid I was for letting this whole thing happen."

"Aw, Becca…"

"No. Just don't say anything. I know you said you were sorry and that I wasn't just a side piece to you. I'm willing to consider that there may be truth in that, and I'm working on forgiveness. Not necessarily for you but for myself and for my own sanity."

Jim looks at her with a serious expression, nodding, but remaining silent.

"That's all I wanted to say."

"Do you want to remain with the Marlagans after this mission?"

"I think so, but I'm still trying to figure that out. It all depends on the progress of my forgiveness. If this thing between us hadn't happened, it would be an easy yes even with all the insanely scary crap going on. No question. But since it did, I have to work on some things within myself before I can give a definite answer to that."

"I understand. Just so you know, Lieutenant, I would be honored to keep you as part of our team. If we could move beyond my solecism, I think you are the perfect medical officer we need."

"To me, this was more than just solecism. It was and still is…" she pauses as if holding back or searching for the right word, "I have been devastated by this, Jim. Don't belittle it."

"I'm sorry. You're right."

"Another apology. Hm. That's all, sir. I'll leave now."

"Thank you, Becca. I mean it."

She exits without a response and knocks on Abs's door. He doesn't answer. She checks the Lab.

Abs opens the door. "Hey. That was quick. How did it go?"

"He asked me to stay with the Marlagans."

"And you said…"

"I want to but just need to work on my personal issues first."

"What personal issues? You have personal issues?" Abs jests.

"Not funny."

"Did you tell him what those issues were?"

"Sort of."

"What did you say?"

She goes on to tell the entirety of conversation. "And then I made to clear to him that I need to get to a place of forgiveness for myself, not for him."

"Ooh. That's good. Go ahead, Lieutenant. Put those chrome bars on tight!"

She dips her head and smiles. "Thanks, big brother. I don't know how I'd survive this without you."

"Girl, you're strong. You would have worked it all out. No doubt."

"Maybe. What are you doing in here?"

"I'm checking the slide that was left at room temperature again just to see if the temperature had any effect."

"Did it?"

"Look. This red stuff cannot survive at this temperature. Nothing is moving. Since it was found in the icy cave, it must prefer lower temps."

"But it remained liquid in negative one hundred degrees Celsius."

"It's remarkable, for sure."

So it remained alive and in liquid form from minus one hundred to four point five degrees, but everything died around," she looks at the thermometer, "twenty-three degrees."

"Very interesting, right?"

"Can we assume it can't survive in temperatures comfortable for humans?"

"Only with this slide sample. I am going to put a container in this sealed incubator overnight and see if the entire sample dies or if this was a one-off."

"This stuff has to be too valuable to just kill. It's rare, even on Io."

"That thought crossed my mind, but the more we know about it, the better for everyone, not just the rich."

"That is true. What if it gets out and tries to kill us in our sleep?"

"This incubator is bulletproof. Look how thick this polycarbonate is. Feel how heavy it is. If it could break out of this, we're in worse danger than we think we are now. Besides, all the refrigerated containers are still perfectly intact. If they haven't broken out of the containers and the frost yet, I think we're safe."

"Those sure sound like famous last words."

"Yes, Becca. Yes they do. Thanks for pointing that out." Abs secures a container in the custom incubator. "I'll check on it very early in the morning before we deploy to the surface."

"All right. I'm exhausted physically and emotionally. Thanks for everything, Abs. I'll see you in the morning."

"Love you, sis."

They hug, and Becca leaves as Abs finishes setting up the experiment before leaving for bed himself.

Abs Diary Entry 78F:

Mom and Dad,

This day has been insane! Right now it's all classified, and even though there's a micro-chance that my diary is being monitored, I'll only talk personal level stuff. I don't remember if I told you this before, but it is worth repeating. Kimmie said she loves me. This thing between us is more serious than I thought. One weird spin is that we were attracted to one another because neither of us was ready for a serious relationship. I just knew I wouldn't have to worry about her falling in love, so I kept myself emotionally distant. Now, I'm not sure what to do. I have strong, very strong feelings for her but was able to suppress them until now. I don't want to lose her because she's so amazing. But am I ready for a Union? Oh goodness. Just the thought of it makes me dizzy. I know it would make Mom very happy, especially since you two get on so well. I feel myself getting used to the idea of a life partnership. One thing that has always been important to me was to stay United for life once it happened, and I'm not sure I'm able to do that right now. After all, I'm only twenty-eight years old. Is that too young? Haha! Not according to my mother, it isn't. Kimmie's not asking for a lifetime, but hearing "I love you" shook my universe quite a lot and opened a floodgate of my own emotions. And believe me, I was not smooth in my response. I put quite a shame on our entire family name and history in my handling of that moment. Sorry for shaming you in such a massive way. Gotta sleep. Love you both so much.

# Chapter 19

## Trust

ABS IS awakened half an hour before his alarm is set to sound by a pyk from Kimmie.

"Would you mind telling me what the hell that was?"

Still half asleep, Abs asks, "What? Wait what's going on?"

"I've been bashing my head against the wall all night. Now I have uhtceare and can't sleep."

"Why? What's wrong?"

"Why didn't you trust me with enough to send that data to me in real time like you promised?"

"Oh. Hey, Kimmie."

"Don't 'hey Kimmie' me. Please explain to me why I'm feeling that you don't trust me right now."

"Oh no. That's not true. I do trust you. I really do. We have just been so busy, I didn't get a chance to speak with you alone until last night. I was leaving Jim's cabin to call you right when you called. Honestly. We had just wrapped a conversation about sending you the updates when you called."

"Right!" she snarks sarcastically. "What a coincidence. We must be so in tuned to one another."

"That sounds sarcastic. You don't believe me?"

"Would you believe me in this situation?"

"Absolutely. I trust you with my life."

"Then why did it feel like you were holding out on sharing this information with me?"

"I didn't get a chance to talk to you before I sent it. Things were crazy here as you can see."

"Hmm. Well, it really hurts to feel that you didn't trust me."

"Never think that. I was actually trusting you more than I was trusting Jim in this situation."

"How can you say that?"

"Listen. I was planning to pyk you as soon as my conversation with the crew had ended to let you know that I hadn't sent the information in real time so you could have your guard up to look out for us, but you pyked me right as we were wrapping up that conversation. Jim had no idea I was withholding information until I was able to speak with you. I understand how it must look since you pyked first, the optics don't favor me here. It never occurred to me to even ponder for the tiniest of moments that you could think that I don't trust you."

"I wish I had pyked you back immediately instead of waiting until now. It would have saved me a great deal of emotional anguish…and my soap dish. I need to buy a new soap dish."

"Why a soap dish?"

"Don't ask."

"I'm sorry, Kimmie. I wish you would have pyked me right back too. I had no idea you were troubled by our conversation."

"After the way Jun betrayed me, trust is something that doesn't come easily."

"I understand that. I'm sorry things here got so hectic that I couldn't reach out before you called. Trust me when I say that I was sincerely less than five minutes from pyking."

"Okay. Okay. Maybe I was reliving some issues from my past and transferred that hurt to you. I'm sorry for doing that."

"You don't have to apologize for that. I completely understand."

"Well, I'm apologizing for all the names I called you that you'll never know." She slyly giggles.

Abs chuckles. "I'm content that I will never know."

"Don't lose hope. We're still pretty young, and depending on how things go, you may yet have many opportunities to hear them."

"Lucky me."

The badinage between them goes on for a while until Kimmie brings the focus back to the investigation. She says, "I studied the slides of the red goo organisms last night between my fits. That is tremendous."

Excited by her enthusiasm for his findings, Abs offers, "I doubt I will be going back to sleep. If you want, I'll don my gear and go to the Lab to see the results of my overnight study."

"What do you mean?"

"I left a full container of the substance at room

temperature to see if the whole batch would die or if that was a fluke."

"I have about an hour before I have to be anywhere, and it's not like I can sleep either. Let's do it."

"I'll be ready in just a few seconds."

"Maybe you should let me help."

"Help what? The experiment?"

"No, the getting dressed."

"Oh. It's done. I'm dressed already."

"Maybe next time."

"However you can make that work from there, I'm with it."

"I'll figure something out."

"Well, for now, let's head on over to the Lab."

"This should be interesting. You know, this could change so much."

"I do. Speaking of that, have you guys come up with any suspects or indictments yet?"

"We have POIs but no indictments yet. If whoever is responsible for all of this had succeeded, this could have been so disastrous in so many ways. Least of all, losing you. You're such an important team to the WSX, and losing you…" She sighs. "Well, I'm worried about you."

"There's a surprise. Queen Tuff Stuff is worried about me. That is not something—"

"Oh. Just shut it. I should have kept that to myself."

"Aye, ma'am."

"Smart ass."

Before he picks up the specimen, he softly mutters, "Your smart ass."

"What?"

"Okay. Here it is." He shifts their attention to the

specimen in an effort to cut off any opportunity for her to dig further into him. "Let's see what we have."

"Does it look safe?"

"The intact container is a good indication that we may be safe. We were concerned about something escaping the container, which is why we placed it in the bullpen (bulletproof incubator). So that is encouraging and a big relief unless, of course, it's just playing dormant, waiting for the container to open to attack."

"Sure hope that isn't the case. Make sure you're using the gloves inside the incubator and not using your bare hands."

"Of course, and I'm wearing a hazmat suit. We always try to wear that when dealing with unknown substances."

"Well, that's protocol. You're supposed to do that. You always do that, right?"

"Yes, it looks completely intact."

"Right?" She repeats louder, looking for his confirmation.

"What's that?"

"Never mind. I probably don't want to know. Just wear the hazmat suit like you're supposed to."

"I am. I'm going to throw you to the window to put you in third person so you can see better and I can use my pyk's microscope preliminarily."

"Good. There you are. I do miss you."

"I miss you too, Kimmie," Abs says slightly annoyed that this conversational tangent feels distracting at such an edgy moment. "Now, let's see what we have here."

He examines the container as best he can through his personal microscope while the container is still in the bullpen, but is unable to see much. "It is too far away. I have to reach in and pull it to the glass."

"Please be careful," she says through the lump in her throat as she watches from over his shoulder.

"It looks dormant, for sure. I'm confident that it's safe enough to remove the container from the bullpen."

"First, I think you should wear the protective apron."

"Apron? That's a manly protective shield, not an apron. Who says apron?"

"What? You're hilarious. Please put on your apron, sweetheart, and bake my pie," she teases in her best Cagney voice.

"Ha. Ha. Very cute. I'll don the shield," he rebuts in a superhero voice.

"Thank you."

After affixing the thick black metal/rubber shield to the hazmat suit, Abs asks, "Happy now?"

"I'd rather you be here safely with me, but under the circumstances, wearing the doily apron you got for Mother's Day does help."

He shakes his head. "Who's silly now?"

"Still you."

"We need to focus now."

"Okay. I'm just chatty because I'm nervous. Let's continue."

"Here we go. Nothing jumped out or moved. I'll project the microscope for you. Becca is going to be upset that she wasn't here for this."

"She probably will be, but let's proceed."

"They're not moving. The microbes' hue seems to have faded in intensity as well. It's like they've become ashen like humans."

"You mean decomposition?"

"Exactly. They appear to be decomposing. It seems that they break apart or lose connection when they die. I wonder what the cause and process of death was here. It appears they cannot survive at room temperature, and the highest known temperature in which they can survive is four degrees Celsius."

"This could just be another state of survival in the higher temperature climate. Don't assume they're dead. Like you said, it could be a dormant state or playing possum."

"That could be. Good thinking. I just wish we knew more about this stuff. We need answers."

"Let me just double-check the refrigerated sample to make sure the goo hasn't just expired."

"First secure the other sample. The refrigerated sample could wake up or reanimate the warm sample. We have no idea what's possible here."

"It's already going in. Isn't this exciting?" he chirps.

"No. My heart is beating so hard, it's about to break my rib cage."

Minutes later, Abs verifies the cooled sample still show signs of life. "So it was to be the warmer climate that affected the other sample."

"So there's your answer."

Abs sits the cooled sample outside of the bullpen and watches to see if the samples seem to have any impact on the other. What he notices is that the cooled goo becoming less active. "Now I don't know if the cooled goo is slowing its activity because of the warm sample or if it's just reacting to the warmer temps. The warm sample still appears inactive. We need more thorough studies. We need answers."

"We will get to the bottom of it. Our priority is for you to get back here safely. Bring us some samples back to study, including the possibly dead ones."

As Abs places the cooled sample back in the frost, he pleads, "Please be careful with this information, Kimmie."

"That's beginning to feel like a lack of trust again."

"No. It's not that at all. I just want you to be careful for your own safety. All we know is that someone we may trust has to be behind this and that person is probably desperate to keep their involvement and this information secret. Who knows where this investigation will lead?"

"Yes, sir. I'll be careful."

Surprised by her submission, Abs reacts slowly, "Thank you. I'll put the rest of this warm specimen back in the frost, too, to see if it is just dormant or dead. There's a possibility it could reanimate."

"You should put the slide in there too."

"Actually, I just remembered I put the other slide in there last night. Let's take a look."

He puts the cool slide under the microscope. "Still dead. I'm still going to put the container back for a larger test group."

"Thank you."

"Thank you. You know, we haven't had the opportunity to talk as much as I would like. What have you been up to lately?"

"Honestly?"

"Yes, be honest."

"Investigating and worrying."

"You know my views on worrying."

"You wanted me to be honest. That was me being honest. I don't want to lose you. This mission is making me very nervous and has me deeply concerned for your safety."

"You're not going to lose me. We'll be back on schedule with monumental new research. This is going to be a massive new field of study and a massive inconvenience for whomever is trying to stop us, I'm sure."

"Apparently." A loud tone is heard in the background. "Oh dear. That's my alarm. I guess I'd better get ready to tackle the day that awaits."

"Yeah. Me too. Gonna grab some grub, a shower, gear up, and hit the surface."

"Abs?"

"Kimmie?"

"I so love the way you say my name."

He smiles at her virtual presence and walks up close.

They reach their hands to one another, and Djoibjin emotes, "This trip is making me realize just how much you mean to me."

"If I'm being honest, I have felt this for a while now. It didn't take extreme peril to make me realize it. I have just been trying to fight it because I thought it wasn't what you wanted."

"Really?"

"Really."

"Let's BTR tonight."

Abs chuckles with joy. "Aye. Aye, ma'am! Yes!" He does a happy dance, then abruptly stops mid-step and says meekly, "But please be gentle."

She shakes her head. "You are the silliest man I know."

"But I'm your silly man."

"I guess you're right about that…fortunately. Tiger, I have to go."

"Already. You just got here."

"It does feel that way. I miss you and love you a great deal."

"I love you too, Kimmie, and can't wait to be with you again. But for now, we have our BTR date tonight." He blows her a kiss.

She pretends to catch it in her right hand and puts that hand to her lips, then pretends to be refreshed by that gesture. "Ahh."

"Who's silly now?"

"Still you."

"Have a great day and catch our saboteurs."

"I will. You stay safe and come back to me."

"I will."

"Djoibjin out, love."

They disconnect.

On the way back to his quarters, he sees Becca walking away from his door.

"Hey, Bec, what's up?"

"Don't tell me you went to the Lab without me," she says with disappointment seeing Abs in his hazmat suit.

"Don't be upset. I did. But that's because the colonel woke me up early and made me look at the specimen with her there."

"What's up with you and Colonel Djoibjin anyway?"

"What do you mean?"

"There's something going on between you two. I'm

not entirely sure what it is yet, but the truth will come out."

"Why would you say that? She just wanted to see it for herself. I told her you'd be upset that I didn't wait for you."

"Don't forget. I know you. I've seen you in a lot of situations and even helped you through some. Something's happening, and you will tell me eventually."

"Speaking of the lab…the microbes did not survive the night."

"Interesting. What about the slide we put back in the frost?"

"Dead, but not as dead…maybe. But I put the container back in the frost to see if the larger test sample will behave any differently than yesterday's slide sample."

"Stellar!"

"I thought so too."

"So most likely, if anything has broken free on the ship, it would not have lived past last night, right?"

"That is how it appears."

"That's a relief."

"Looks like you're almost ready to deploy. I still have to get ready myself."

"You have time."

"Yeah. Let me get to it. See you in a little bit."

"All right, see you in a bit. Guess I'll grab breakfast."

"Sounds good. I should be in there soon."

Becca heads to the Galley for breakfast and sees Zin. Zin greets her, "Hey, Becca. How are you feeling today?"

"Pretty good actually. Thanks for asking. How about yourself?" she asks as she finds a suitable breakfast, a preserved egg and ham English muffin, in the cupboard.

She pops it in the restore for a perfectly cooked and toasted breakfast sandwich.

"I'm fine, but there's a question that's been plaguing me for a few days, and I want us to have an open and honest friendship."

"Oh. What's that?"

"You and Jim? What's that? And if you say 'Jim who?' that will speak volumes."

"Jim who?" Becca laughs.

"Seriously," Zin says concerned, "that's not okay. You know he's United."

"I'm just kidding. Well, kinda. Can I trust you with this?"

"Absolutely, but I will be honest with you about my feelings."

"I can live with that, but please don't let this go beyond the Marlagans."

"Nothing ever does."

"Jim and I met for training some time ago. Somehow, we got into a conversation about whether he was going to renew his Union. He was in a rough place at the time, so we became friends and got dangerously close to doing something wrong, but he has decided to renew his Union with Marsha, so we are moving on, and now it is a nonissue."

"Thank you for sharing that with me, Becca."

"It actually felt good to tell you that. It's like a release valve was just opened. But please don't let Jim know I told you. I think he wants to behave as if nothing happened even though we both feel a slight loss."

"Becca, can I tell you something in confidence?"

"Sure."

"My brother doesn't even know this, but I have to tell someone or I will explode. And if we die on this mission—"

"Don't say that."

"But seriously, I don't want to die without telling someone my truth. It's killing me inside, and I have to get it out."

"What is it?"

Zin says, "I'd prefer we go to my cabin where no one can hear this."

They take their breakfast to Zin's cabin. Becca realizes she hasn't had a chance to see the inside of Zin's cabin as they approach. Upon entering, Becca is immediately awestricken by the amount of mechanical parts, tech bits, and animal art strewn and posted throughout the cabin.

Once they and their breakfasts are situated on Zin's bunk, she starts to break down.

Becca puts her arm around her. "Zin, whatever it is, I'm sure everyone will support you through anything troubling you."

"Not my family," she says through sobs.

"Well, I will, and I know the Marlagans will."

"I really feel like you will. That's why you're the first person who will hear this. But I hope you're not the last. You're like Abs in a lot of ways, so I feel I can trust you enough to tell you that I think I'm a person in woman flesh."

"I don't understand what that means."

"Let me ask you this, are you comfortable in your female skin?"

"Yeah. Most of the time. There are still times when being a woman is difficult, but—"

"That's not what I mean. Have you ever felt you're not a woman, but you're supposed to be?"

"I think so, but tell me exactly what you mean."

"To simplify it, I don't think I'm supposed to be one thing. Sometimes I feel like a boy, sometimes I feel like a girl. Sometimes I feel like something else entirely."

"In what sense do you mean? Sexually?"

"Not necessarily. There are times I just feel like a boy, but not really. And sometimes I feel like a girl but not really. Why can't I just be Zin without claiming to be anything else?"

"You can be Zin. What you're describing sounds like gender x."

"Maybe. Because I've never been settled as just a girl, but I don't want to be a boy."

"That sounds exactly like gender x. That's no big deal. Why have you been holding that in?"

"The problem is my mother's family believes strongly that it's a birth defect and that," she uses air quotes, "people afflicted with this disease are cursed. So I always tried to force myself to play a role for them that has been killing me inside since I was a kid."

"Oh, Zin. That's not right. I'm so sorry. Are they old-time religious or something?"

"No, they aren't, but my mom's grandparents were and they passed down a lot of that hateful and destructive judgment to my mom."

"What about your stepdad?"

"My mother is the head of our family. Dad just lets her make the rules."

"That could be a partnership that might eventually accept your situation."

"It's not. My mother's word is the rule of the land, and my grandparents have corrupted her too deeply."

"That's not right. I'm so sorry you have had to bottle this up for so long."

"It hasn't been fun."

"Well, what do you want to do about it?"

"I'm not totally sure. Right now I just feel like telling someone. That's why I told you."

"Then I'm happy you did. Have you talked to Abs?"

"You're the first."

"Zin, I'm honored, but you really should not have kept this inside. I'll help any way I can, and I can just about guarantee Abs may be able to help in some way."

"I was planning to talk with him before this trip ended, but he's been so busy and preoccupied with everything going on."

"True. On top of everything else, he's been spending so much time putting me back together."

"He's really good at that.

"I know."

"I wish I'd grown up with a brother like him."

"It was really helpful. He and Khan have gotten me through so much stuff when I couldn't talk to anyone else. They're absolutely my best friends."

"You are a fortunate one. Count your blessings."

"I take it Rhoan isn't a person you could call on for support."

"With some stuff, he's a great confidant. But not this. I'm afraid my family has polluted his mind with their intolerance."

"Well, he's been a Marlagan for a long time. He may have been influenced differently by now. Have you ever talked to him about the hateful rhetoric before?"

"We have discussed it, and he's better than he used to be, but my family isn't, and he still has a certain loyalty to them that keeps me too cautious to share this with him."

"It makes me sad to know that you've been carrying this with you for so long."

"I had to be—"

An interruption from Abs comes over the intercom, "Marlagans, we deploy in twenty minutes."

"Well, maybe we can both have a conference with him after this deployment to the surface," Becca suggests.

"I'd like that very much."

They stand, and Zin hugs Becca.

"Then we'll do it."

"Becca?"

"Yes?"

"Thank you."

"Of course."

They hug again, and each goes to prepare for the excursion.

* * * * *

Abs Diary Entry 79A:

Howdy, y'all!

That's me pretending everything is fine. I need your strength and encouragement right now. I've been praying. God's doing his part, but this is harder without you two being here, for sure. I'm trying to keep the crew encouraged and trying to keep Kimmie from panicking. But I'm unable to show how scary all of this is for me. We could easily have been dead three times over by now. God is keeping us safe, but someone is giving him a lot of work to do in that department, and it's not all us this time. I'm sorry for putting all of that on here, but I'm just being transparent with this journal right now because I can't be this transparent with the crew until we're all safe. And then I probably still can't until I retire from these excursions. I know you have shared similar feelings with me in the past, and that has helped me to be okay when I feel this way. For some reason, this is more frightening than usual. Does that mean Kimmie has given me something to lose, because I really do want to get back to her safely and live out a future with her? I'm blabbing. Thanks for listening. I have to grab some breakfast and get to the surface. Love y'all.

# Chapter 20

## Zin

MINUTES BEFORE the crew is scheduled to depart for the second excursion to the surface, Jim shows up in the Garage in full excursion gear. Fortunately, Abs is the only crew member down there and ready to deploy.

"Hey, Jim. What are you doing up?"

"Becca said the bots and bionics will have me back to normal today. Let's go."

"She said in twenty-four hours, and that was if we did not use printed bone. You'd better get your butt in bed before she gets down here."

"Abs, I am not going to let this keep me from doing my job. I'm supposed to be the leader, and this is too important for me to miss."

"This is too important for you to slow us down by hobbling around and maybe even re-injuring yourself unnecessarily."

"I won't re-injure anything."

"Captain Slight! Get your ass in that chair and stop standing on that leg."

"Abs, I have to—"

"I will carry your big butt with your busted leg up to your bed and order Rhoan to guard your door if I have to."

"Be serious!" Jim waves off Abs's threat. "You need Rhoan on the surface."

"And you would be the cause of us leaving him here in orbit because of your childish stubbornness."

Zin enters the room in her adorable gold tabby kitten onesie. "What's this noise about? Cap, what are you doing down here? And why are you in excursion gear?"

Abs answers, "He thinks he can order us to take him with us."

"Cap, get upstairs. We'll keep the feed and comms open for you."

"But—"

Zin interrupts, "Nope!"

"But what if—"

"Nope."

"But suppose—"

"Nope. Upstairs now."

Becca and Rhoan enter the Garage.

Becca asks, "Captain Slight, what the hell are you doing?"

"You said I would be back to normal activity today."

"You heard what you wanted, didn't you? I said twenty-four hours and you would miss today's excursion. And that was without printed bone. We had to print bone. Tomorrow, you may…it said MAY…be ready. I'll reevaluate your condition in the morning. But if you keep walking on it, it will take longer for the cast and bots to do their jobs."

Jim stews and pouts quietly.

Abs suggests, "Can he sit here in the Garage with his leg up and help manage the team from here?"

Becca answers, "If we brought a hover lounger from MedBay, then he could stay here for the duration of the excursion."

Zin objects, "Uh. Nope. I don't do assistants except for Elf."

"Think of me more as your backup. Not as an assistant who will slow you down or mess up your chi."

"But I don't—"

"Please, Zin. I promise to be good and stay out of your way."

Abs interjects, "Zin, you know he'll go crazy in that cabin while we're down there. Just until we get back."

"Ugh! Fine. Just stay out of my way and you can stay."

"Yes! Thanks, Zin. Can't believe I'm thanking you for letting me do my job."

"Just make sure you're not in my way."

"Promise. Abs is right. I just can't sit in bed while an excursion is underway."

"Fine. Just find your own workspace that doesn't interfere with mine."

"You got it."

Minutes later, Rhoan returns with the lounger and situates the Captain next to the haid in the Lounge.

"Comfy, Cap?" Abs asks.

"I am. Thank you. Thank you, Becca. Thank you, Rhoan, for the lounger. Thank you, Zin, for putting up with me being useful."

All respond in turn.

"Let's prep the equipment for excursion," Abs orders.

Abs and Zin prep the comms and coding for the mission while Rhoan grabs gear from the Armory. Becca runs to get necessities for Captain Slight to stay comfortable during the excursion. Then Abs, Rhoan, and Becca prep for departure after Zin stages the Harvesters and HARVI in the airlock.

"We're ten minutes late!" Abs exclaims.

The crew scurries and take another five minutes to run final checks and form ready at the Black Swan. This time, they all fit in the front three slightly staggered bucket seats.

"Zin, Cap, we'll see you shortly," Abs states as they enter the airlock along with their cast of automatons.

Zin counts down, "Three, two, one, launch!"

They safely enter the atmosphere and gently land with one less crew member than they had one day earlier.

Still seated in the Black Swan, they find another huge haul of siolens where they cleared them the previous day. Abs notes, "Something is producing more siolens here. We never saw this much production this quickly anywhere else on Io."

Becca asks, "What does that means?"

"I hope it doesn't mean we're surrounded by invisible creatures right now," Rhoan answers.

"I'm going UV," Abs advises.

"Do you see anything?" Becca asks nervously.

"Nothing so far. Remain in the vehicle for a few minutes and study for movement," Abs commands.

After several minutes of looking around, they notice

nothing different from yesterday as the Harvesters continue their work.

Rhoan notifies, "I don't see any of those red puddles today."

"You're right, Romes. I wonder what that means," Abs acknowledges. "I'm going to hover around a bit before we get out, just to get a better lay of today's environment."

"Sounds good, Cap," Rhoan says.

"That's smart, Abs," Jim says over the open line. "I sure wish I was down there with you."

"I don't see anything on the vehicle's sensors or cameras. We've traveled five klicks from the LZ."

Jim notes, "Look over there in the distance, about two o'clock and three klicks."

"Looking," Abs says, "what do you see, Jim?"

"It looks like either lava flow or something else moving like liquid. It doesn't appear to be lava, though. But the UV could be distorting the color."

"I doubt it. The blue light does that, but then again, how could we be sure of anything out here?"

"True." Then Jim asks, "Zin, are you okay over there?"

Zin answers, "I thought I heard something in the Storage Room. I'll check it out."

"Be careful," Jim warns.

"Jim, that's not lava. It's a massive formation of siolens glistening in a strange light. Where's this light coming from?"

"Zin?"

"What's going on?"

Comms go silent from the *JohnGlenn*.

Abs calls, "Jim?"

Still nothing from the *Mushroom*.

"Zin? Jim?"

Still no response. Then suddenly there's a commotion over the comms.

"What's going on, guys? Is everything all right up there?"

Aboard the *JohnGlenn*, Jim hovers into the Garage to see what was behind the ruckus he just heard. He looks across the area near the storage facility and finds Zin has fallen to the floor motionless in a small pool of blood. He shouts, "Zin!"

No response. No movement that he can see.

He hovers closer. She appears to be completely unconscious and bleeding from her injured torso. Jim hovers even closer to her. At her side, he notices the ripped torso of her kitty onesie moving in a very unusual manner. He repeatedly yells her name and carefully reaches down to rouse Zin and investigate the strange motion in her bloody torso and feels movement from something small and slimy partially covered in Zin's blood. He fears her organs are separating from her body in some strange way, then he feels an extreme pain in his hand, which begins to bleed. Then he realizes there's something he cannot see attacking Zin. He dislodges one of his crutches from the side of the lounger and begins swinging it wildly at the air just above Zin until he hits something he still can't fully see or make out, but the remnants of Zin's blood help keep it from being completely invisible. Jim watches the red spots appear like a tiny path on the garage floor and uses it to aim his swings as Zin's blood sheds off the creature quickly. He pants and feels himself becoming weak from the chase and wild frightening movements. After connecting one of his hardest swings, he hears a thump on the bulkhead and sees a small blood spatter where the creature must have impacted. He follows the very faint blood trail that has become less dotted and more like the dits and dahs of Morse code. Jim realizes the dragged lines of blood must indicate that the creature is injured, so he chases the bloody artwork and the sound of skittering. Despite the increasing exhaustion and pain in his right hand, he swings like a madman and scores several more hits. He continues to follow the slowing and fading trail of Zin's blood, tailing the creature to keep tabs on its position and lands numerous additional hits. Then he notices a new trail of the strange red goo beginning to form. The trail moves slower and slower with each pummeling. Then Jim makes one final aimed connection and hears a thump into the airlock followed by a red goo splat on the bulkhead. He zips over as quickly as the lounger will allow and closes the invisible assailant in the airlock. He surveys the room for more activity to ensure there are no other creatures lurking about, and he sees nothing else. After he's satisfied that he and Zin are alone, he peers through the clear airlock door and sees the weird red color slowly growing throughout the airlock but sees no other signs of life.

With the airlock safely closed and his growing confidence that the encounter has ended, Jim finally becomes aware of the ongoing and frantic calls from the surface.

"JIM! Zin! What's going on?"

"Abs," Jim finally answers breathing heavily, "we…
there was…Zin…blood is…" Jim passes out.
"Jim? Jim? JIM? What is going on? JIM!"

To be continued…

# Glossary

Blarks—a harmless brownish-red crawling insect native to Mars.

BTR—(Better than Reality) a proprietary brand of virtual reality systems and suits that claim to feel better than an experience in reality.

Haid—holographic artificial intelligence device.

Hope1–5—Earth's orbital communities.

MAEMA—Martial Arts Earth Mars Award.

Matternet—dark matter–powered extranet, which is 3×103,000 times faster and more powerful than the Internet of the twenty-second century.

MMG—Magnetically Manipulated Gravity.

No Hope—Earth's orbital penitentiary.

PiF—pre-flight matters.

PuF—post-flight matters.

Qub—cube-shaped computer-like device.

ROD—(Reduction-Obstruction Device) prototype
device used to sweep orbital launch railings.

Salt84—a clear, airy, lightweight, soundproof, and
radiation-proof substance made of siolens and
Altonium84 used for various applications.

SDSP—(Station de Super Processeur) a series of
successful French satellite-like devices which
are positioned throughout the space between
Jupiter and Venus to help spread the Matternet
throughout the universe.

TiCordel—a clear, stronger than steel, and lighter than
glass material invented by a WSX engineer

TRM—(The Relief Movement) the worldwide effort
to reverse humanity's damage and the Earth's
environment.

UAC—United American Continent.

UCA—United Continent of Afrika.

UCoN—(United Consortium of Nations) a collection
of earth nations bound together in the effort
to clean and rescue Earth's environment.

UCT—(Universal Coordinated Time) the time used by humans throughout the entire universe to ensure everyone has a common time zone. Also known as Greenwich Mean Time (GMT) or zulu time.

Uhtceare—an Old English word referring to the anxiety experienced just before dawn. When you wake up too early and can't fall back to sleep, tired, or not, usually worrying about something.

Um—Union mate, spouse, life partner.

WSX—World Space Exploration.